MAN C

Born in Brighton in 1932, Roland Curram attended Brighton College and the Royal Academy of Dramatic Art. As an actor he has a wealth of theatre, film and television experience, including: *Darling, Some Mother's Do 'Ave 'em, Big Jim and The Figaro Club, The Crezz* and *Eldorado*. West End appearances include *Little Murders, Grand Manœuvres, Enter a Free Man, Design for Living, Noises Off* and *Ross*. *Man on the Beach* is his first novel.

ROLAND CURRAM

MAN ON THE BEACH

Richard with much love.

Roland Curram

Copyright © 2004 Roland Curram

The moral right of the author has been asserted.

Apart from any fair dealing for the purposes of research or private study, or criticism or review, as permitted under the Copyright, Designs and Patents Act 1988, this publication may only be reproduced, stored or transmitted, in any form or by any means, with the prior permission in writing of the publishers, or in the case of reprographic reproduction in accordance with the terms of licences issued by the Copyright Licensing Agency. Enquiries concerning reproduction outside those terms should be sent to the publishers.

Matador
9 De Montfort Mews
Leicester LE1 7FW, UK
Tel: (+44) 116 255 9311 / 9312
Email: books@troubador.co.uk
Web: www.troubador.co.uk/matador

ISBN 1 904744 41 9

Cover illustration: from a painting by John Miller

Typeset in 10pt Stempel Garamond by Troubador Publishing Ltd, Leicester, UK
Printed by The Cromwell Press, Trowbridge, Wilts, UK

Matador is an imprint of Troubador Publishing

To Paul, with love.

Contents

	Characters		ix
	Prologue Rosie's Secret		
		Pavilion Theatre. Bournemouth. 1972	1
1	Man on the Beach	Maspalomas. March 2000	5
2	Nemesis		8
3	Peroxide Angel		13
4	Confidences		17
5	The Old Vicarage	Cornwall. April 2000	32
6	Assignation	London	43
7	Happy Memories		46
8	Pop!		56
9	Family Secret		64
10	In The Dock		81
11	The Stanhope		85
12	Appraisal		91
13	The Tomb of the Black Prince		94
14	Finding Out Whores		100
15	Liz's Secret		104
16	At Her Majesty's Pleasure.		115
17	On Examing Art		122
18	Rosie's Tea Shop		129
19	On Rule 43		142
20	Reunion		148
21	After Dinner Mince		162
22	Correspondents and Conspiritors		174
23	The Defective Intention		185

24	Leaving the Cell		194
25	The Lost Summer Season		200
26	Going For It		214
27	Put To The Test		221
28	Redemption	Palm Springs. January 2001	237
29	Heart to Heart		242
30	Going Straight		259
31	A Private View		264
	Acknowledgements		279

Characters

ROSIE	a chorus girl
LIZ	her sister, a Welsh schoolmistress
MICHAEL STANHOPE	an Art Dealer
KIANY	a Malaysian dancer
IOAN WILLIAMS	a male model
JONATHAN COURT SMYTH	a schoolboy
Col. COURT SMYTH	his father
MARGARET COURT SMYTH	Jonathan's mother
Col. GEOFFREY WHITE	Jonathan's Godfather
POLLY	Ioan's landlady
NICHOLA	Michael's ex wife
DAVID WILLIAMS	Rosie's husband
WILFRED ABERY	a worldy artist
JULIE 'RED' WILLIAMS	Rosie's step-daughter
JOYCE HOWARD	Michael's co-director
SIMON BARCLAY	Curator of Nylwen Art Gallery
JOSEPH FUDGE	a Cornish farmer
LENNIE	an embezzler
RAT FACE	a thief
OSSIE	a black prisoner
THE S.O.	a senior prison officer
TERRY BOYCE	a murderer
RAFAEL AUGUSTIN	a retired Spanish professor
Mr BLAKELEY	a Harley Street surgeon
GRAN	Red's grandmother

Prologue

Rosie's Secret

The Pavilion Theatre. Bournemouth. Summer, 1972

Dressed as a tube of toothpaste, holding a giant pink toothbrush in one hand and a telephone in the other, Rosie should have had qualms, she had none.

'The thing is, I'm overdue.' She waited for her sister's reaction. Silence. Flicking a stray blonde curl out of her cornflower blue eyes her cap fell off. 'Hold on, I just dropped me hat.'

Opposite the phone booth, the stage door keeper sat in his cubicle eyeing her as she bent down. Her succulent butt wrapped in taut white plastic was as good as anything in his 'Tit Bits' and live.

'Sorry. I'm back' she said, awkwardly trying to re-attach her cap.

'Don't tell me!' wailed Liz, back home in Pontypridd, 'Don't tell me! Oh cariad!' Her pronounced Welsh lilt did nothing to diminish the drama. 'You've only been gone two months.'

'Two months gone. Quite! I thought last month was just a miss. But nothing's happened again this time.'

'You told me you were on The Pill.' Then there was a sigh. 'So, when did you last see David?'

'Before rehearsals. It's his.' Rosie hoped she sounded confident, but the phone went silent again. 'Well, it has to be, doesn't it?'

'That rather depends.' Then in her grown up way Liz said, 'Have you seen a doctor?'

'No.'

'I'll come down.'

'Now, hold on, Liz! I'm going to have it. I'm not having one of those abortion things. The only thing is... well, David hasn't actually asked to marry me yet.'

'Oh, he'll marry you. He's been dotty about you ever since you left Coed Y Lan Comprehensive, we all know that. He's only sulking. This all, is just a blip.'

'It's no blip Liz. I'm having it.'

'I meant his disapproval of you working in theatre. He'll come round, you'll see. I told him how grand you were in the show. I think he'll probably visit later, come to your last night.'

'That's no good, Liz, that's not for two months. I gotta see him before that.'

'Mmn,' muttered Liz, 'I do see.'

'So, um...' Rosie bit her lip.

'Rosie, you've not got mixed up with someone else, have you?'

Writhing, Rosie met the stage door keeper's eye. It winked. Her smile faltered. Absently she waved the toothbrush at him. 'What if I have?'

'Oh no, Rosie!' admonished Liz, in familiar schoolmistressy tones.

'Well, serves him right!'

'Oh no!'

Dying to tell, Rosie said, 'He's lovely. He's a student working with the stage crew.' Suddenly her voice rose an octave, 'Well, you met him!'

'I did?'

'At the first night party. Mickey! The tall one. Big curly hair.'

'Not the one with the Afro do?'

'Yes. He's got a motorbike too.'

'Oh no!'

'What do you mean, oh no? He's gorgeous!'

'He was English!'

'I was hardly thinking geography, Liz!'

'Whatever's happening to you? I thought there was something going on between the pair of you. Surely to God, you're not going to throw over a dependable Welshman like David, for a one night stand with an English stagehand?'

'He wasn't a one night stand! We've been out heaps. Anyway, dependable blooming David wasn't so dependable, was he? He wasn't even here! I jolly well needed some fun.'

'It seems you had it!' said Liz.

'Well, it's his own fault. Getting all huffy about me working in show business. He's collected me from enough dance classes! How can he pretend to be surprised me wanting to be a dancer? I was so off him.' Rosie glimpsed her pursed lips in the phone booth mirror. She pouted to rearrange them more prettily. 'Anyway, I've had a think. You always said what a good mum I'd make. And of course I do love him really. So what I wanted to ask was, could you drive him down here Saturday... for the weekend like? Would you do that... Cariad?' Her wheedling endearment was the last remnant of the Welsh Liz had taught her.

'You mean, so you can sleep with him?' Cynicism was creeping into Liz's voice.

'You could hint like, if he did visit, I might marry him.'

'I think that would sound rather better coming from you, dear.'

'But he respects you, Liz. You talk to him.'

'If he marries you, he'll make you give up theatre.'

'Well, we'll see about that. I'll fix up the tickets and a separate room for you. Now keep your trap shut, and not a word to Mam.'

'I'm hardly likely to blab to Mam, she'd have a blue fit! Rosie, now listen to me. Your whole future is at stake here, and a child's future. And what about this English boy? Think it through now.

You must realise what you're doing?'

'I do. Bless you, cariad. Love you. Must dash. Bye!'

'Darling, now listen...' But Liz was disconnected.

Rosie stepped out of the phone booth, flashing shapely legs in fishnet tights and white high heels, on her way to the stage she waved her toothbrush at the door man, saying, 'You're wicked you are.'

'Takes one to know one!' the old boy grinned.

Rosie pushed open the Pass Door, and with perfect timing joined her seven delightful look-alikes just as they were making their entrance behind Mr Max Bygraves singing his hit...

> *I'm a pink toothbrush,*
> *You're a blue toothbrush.*
> *Have we met somewhere before?*
> *I'm a pink toothbrush,*
> *You're a blue toothbrush.*
> *Did we meet by the bathroom door?*

Chapter 1

Man on the Beach

Maspalomas. March 2000

It seems to me, Michael finds himself saying, not quite aloud, my future depends on meeting the Right person. Wearing nothing but a pair of khaki shorts, Michael is striding along a deserted Spanish beach. Bending his thoughts to the tune of Gershwin's "Funny Face", his bathroom baritone rings out in the emptiness,
Betraying Mona Lisa,
You're going to be replaced,
By some other god-dam sexy face.
Only the sound of the sea answers. 'Some other god-dam sexy face,' he belts out again to the vast blue heavens, the sunny blond sands, not a soul to bear witness to his oath.

Relishing the scorching sun on his body, a glorious reward for the last three months of hell and heartbreak, he inhales deeply, savouring the ozone. Terrific! Gran Canaria was definitely the right choice.

Surveying the Technicolor vista, the immaculate skyscape, his exhilaration becomes almost a delirium. Royal blue waves crash and foam dazzling white, dissolving to impotent ripples lapping his pale English feet. To his right the creamy sands become Sahara-like dunes, ahead the coastline curves away to that mysterious haze between heaven and earth, sky and sea, death and infinity.

This, his first morning, awaking to purple bougainvillaea on his hotel balcony, the London winter banished, the emotional pain in his sternum stilled, he is able for the first time in months to view his life as a new adventure. He reflects that though twenty-three years of marriage are shattered, his wife and daughters with another man, the loneliness impossible to fill, he is confident and determined to heal. He feels clear-headed and vital. After all, a unique springtime could lie ahead. A rejuvenation. A second chance!

"Playa Nudista," announces a notice stuck in the sand, across it, in red graffiti, like blood, is scrawled the word, "Sida"... AIDS.

I *will* be happy, he tells himself, leaping over a rivulet of sea water. Maybe I could sing Cole Porter and Gershwin in Tokyo? He smiles at the absurdity. Why ever not? Anything is possible now.

At the opening launch of a colleague's art gallery in Birmingham the other week, he was told by a Malaysian dancer he'd chatted up, there was a market for mature men who could sing in Japanese nightclubs. 'I just finished working over there,' she'd said, sipping mango juice. 'You're just their type. You wear the right gear,' she added, holding eye contact, 'you'd do great. Dishy middle-aged guy like you. Make a packet, no problem.'

No longer a family man, he'd felt free to be forward, 'Does that mean I stand a chance of getting laid?' It paid off. He had taken the girl to bed that night in his over-heated Holiday Inn hotel room, a Gauguin repro appropriately hanging on the wall. With her killer body and long shiny hair, Kiany was the first girl he'd had since his wife left. The experience was special enough to invite her home into the marital bed for a repeat performance, where the sex was even more adventurous and vengefully comforting.

Oh yes, being free has its advantages. Being 'available' again

reminds him of his youth, the larks, the chase. Today he feels as randy as ever, now it's just him again, his brain and his cock. Every stranger he meets he regards with carnal interest and excitement. Yes, she has done me a favour. No way will I take her back now. He sings out... *Pick yourself up,*
Toss yourself off,
Start all over again.

Chapter 2

Nemesis

Further along the beach a beautifully made young man emerges from the sea, as he flings himself onto a blue sunbed, crystal droplets of sea water glisten like sequins on his lissom twenty-seven year old naked body.

A black Dolce and Gabbana T-shirt hangs above him gently flapping on the spokes of a blue parasol, next to it a matching pair of 'Hustler' shorts. Stretching for the Ambre Solaire, he applies factor three around his neat slightly snub nose and pretty face, then flagrantly around his crutch, protecting the goods that until recently have earned him a jet-setter lifestyle as a model. Lifting rounded arms, the result of three workouts a week at a gym in Notting Hill, he combs back a wet mop of bottle blond hair and lies supine, one arm resting seductively over his head. His manicured hand holds on to the comb, the thumbnail tweaks at its teeth. Ioan Williams is also reflecting on his ambitions and desires.

Time out... figure... Dosh... and how to get it? Am I really up for this? Back to being a student? Hell! It's too much... been over it a hundred times. I'm on holiday, for Christ's sake! He plugs "The Chemical Brothers" into his ears and allows his thoughts to drift.

Jonathan will be back at school now. God, wish he was here. Together on this fab beach. Wow! He conjures Jonathan's toffee coloured crisp hair, doe eyes, peachy down-like angel face. Good enough to eat. Ioan contemplates an al fresco wank as he re-runs their first meeting.

It had occurred at his parent's pub in Canterbury, "The Olive Branch". Ioan had been staying the weekend. Dad introduced him to a group of customers and suggested he take their underaged son out of the licensed bar to the tables outside in the Butter Market.

Jonathan, wearing a soft brown windcheater and distressed denim jeans, carried a Coke with a straw. He'd laughed and pointed to the odd shape of a Smart car, 'Elephant's roller-skates!'

The silver Honda Ioan had borrowed for the weekend was gleaming opposite. 'Fancy that?' he said.

'Wow!' The boy's eyes lead him across the road. 'Wicked! It's the new S2000, isn't it?'

'Actually it's a NSX.'

'That is tops! Tops man!' The kid gawped in admiration. 'Is it yours?'

By way of reply, Ioan grinned, fished out the key, unlocked the door and ushered him in. Jonathan relinquished his Coke and squirmed his arse on the black leather upholstery, his innocent alabaster hands gripping the wheel.

'Wicked! Way to go! Can we go somewhere?'

Jonathan's father, Colonel Court-Smyth with his wife Margaret were watching with Ma through the pub window, they waved. The Colonel's crony Geoffrey White, Chief Constable of Kent was also in the group. Ioan waved back cheerfully. 'Can't. Sunday lunch in a minute,' he said.

Jonathan was playing with the C.D. player on the dashboard. 'Wow! This is so cool. I guess it pays being a model?'

'When it's hot.'

Jonathan blinked. 'You mean in the summer?'

'Thought you were a dude, man. When it's hot, a classy contract. When it's a high class product I'm advertising.'

'Oh.' Jonathan, looking button cute, switched on the car stereo.

'You get the perks,' said Ioan, lowering himself to his haunches and bringing himself at eye level. 'I'll tell you a secret. Actually, it's on loan from Honda, I did a job for them Friday.' He was not about to admit how he'd negotiated the loan, which had involved attending a private drinks party, a little E, and subsequent sex with the rep, and a probable repeat performance when he returned the car on Monday.

'Oh,' said Jonathan, changing radio stations, 'I see.'

Ioan was glad he didn't.

The kid turned off the radio and blinked his dewy eyelashes at Ioan, 'Can I ask you something?'

Ioan wondered for a moment if the kid was flirting.

'When you do the modelling, don't you feel funny, I mean all that posing?'

'God no! It's kickin'.'

'You live in London, don't you?'

'Notting Hill. Share a flat with a mate and his girlfriend. Have to move out soon, they're getting spliced... mad fools!'

'Only get to London in the hols or half term. Got a mobile? I've got a pager.'

Five days later watching late night TV, Polly and James out as usual, Ioan's mobile bleeped. It was Jonathan.

'I'm at Victoria Station. I just missed the last train back to Canterbury. Could you put me up for the night?'

Oh Christ! thought Ioan.

'Please,' pleaded the boy.

'It can only be in an armchair, or you'll have to sleep with me.'

Jonathan was on the doorstep within half an hour, grinning from ear to ear.

Preparing for bed they had a pillow fight in underpants, Ioan won and sat on the boy. They stopped struggling and looked into each other's eyes. The movie music that swelled in their ears could have been written by John Williams it was so very arousing.

Of course the boy had planned it all. He admitted as much the next morning as Ioan cooked him breakfast.

'Bacon?' asked Ioan.

'Four slices, please, and my eggs over easy... like my men!'

'Sit,' Ioan ordered, indicating the bench. Last night he had discovered just how uninhibited this particular public schoolboy was. 'And less of the smarty-pants. My flatmates will be up soon.'

Jonathan obeyed, sitting up to the table and helping himself liberally to muesli.

'How old, exactly, are you?' asked Ioan, reaching into the fridge for an egg.

'Fifteen in six months. Why?'

'Fourteen!' yelped Ioan. 'You're bloody jail bait you are. You deliberately set out to seduce me, didn't you?'

'Course,' replied Jonathan calmly pouring in the milk. 'Why else d'you think I got your mobile number? I saw you walking down Canterbury High Street months ago, I swore I was going to get you then. When your parents told my parents you were staying last weekend, well, that's why I came over.'

'God!' said Ioan, preparing to break the egg. 'You're worse than I am.' He broke the egg and as it sizzled in the pan, turned to dump the shells. 'You are a little tart!' and he made a mock gesture as if to slosh the boy.

Jonathan ducked. Looking up innocent, he said, 'You hit me, I'll tell my Dad of you. And what you did to me last night.'

Ioan arranged matters so they did it again and again. They couldn't get enough of each other.

Ioan's Mother was delighted at having him home more frequently.

'Lovely you're here, dear,' she'd said, 'but you're always off somewhere!'

Ioan's thoughts blend from the schoolboy he'd been having an affair with for the last three months, to his mother, the only other person close to him.

He'd felt a bit selfish leaving her, considering the circumstances. But, typically, she'd said, 'I'll be fine, Lovely. You go and enjoy yourself for heaven's sake. You've worked for it.' Which is exactly what he hadn't. For the truth was, work had not been coming in as it used. They were using more teenagers and blacks these days. But then everything was changed now. He pulls out his earpiece, The Chemical Brothers had died.

What the fuck's that row? He looks up. Some asshole in khaki shorts was walking along the water's edge singing… but loud!

The man stops.

Ah seen me? Embarrassed man? No, the guy starts bawling out again, some other unrecognisable song. Oh Pleeease! Is this some loony or just an eccentric? Looks like a pale new arrival. Chest hair narrowing in a line to his belly button then down the love channel into his shorts. Hairy Sean Connery types didn't appeal to Ioan. Young models shaved off chest hair. Glad his own body was smooth, his taste was sleek young men of twenty-seven or so, not unlike himself, he'd bend the rule only if to his advantage. Jonathan was the exception, but then Jonathan had fallen into his lap as it were. With his twenty-twenty vision he examines the face of the man on the beach. Fanciable? Silvery black crew cut, moustache. Ancient. Has to be gay, crooning like that. Hetero shorts, maybe not. Ralph Lauren beach bag, mmm… Gold flashed on his chest… Oh no, not Medallion Man!

Chapter 3

Peroxide Angel

Can't do duets, thinks Michael, cheerfully switching to Johnny Mercer. Deep breath...

I wanna be around, to pick up the pieces,
When somebody breaks your heart...

When his wife, Nichola, left the 'Dear John' note explaining she was dumping him to live with a fashionable actor, she placed it under a fried egg magnet attached to the frost-free fridge in their farmhouse kitchen in Wandsworth. Then, carrying her black Glamma mink coat over one arm, her cream leather jewel case in the other, she walked, in skin tone Kurt Geigers, out of their front door and his life for ever.

Upstairs, shaving in his bathroom, Michael heard the front door, thought it was Nichola returning from taking the children to school, half expecting her to walk in with a cup of tea, he considered himself the happiest of married men.

However, after he went downstairs to the refrigerator for his breakfast yoghurt and found the note, a curious process occurred, a process centuries old, a process that began when Paradise was lost and Lucifer revolted from God, his love turned to hate.

After an initial desire to kill his wife, a far more gratifying notion took hold. Kill her fucking lover!

Michael took out a contract. He had a friend, a distinguished and worldly painter, Wilfred Abery, who, acquainted with villains in the East End, fixed it up for £5000. He paid £2500 in cash to

'Wilf,' the balance to be paid on completion. Not death, just scar the pretty boy for life, maybe remove an ear or nose, enough to curtail the anticipated glittering career.

Emotionally he confessed all this to his psychotherapist, an eighty year old witch who practised in Maida Vale to whom he had recently become a patient. She sharply told him not to be such an ass, and talked him out of it, incidentally incurring a 100% loss on his deposit.

Setting him on the road to recovery, her treatment was not only timely it was to alter his whole perception of himself. Late in life, he learnt the hard lesson that happiness that relies on another human being, can never last. That nothing is forever. That if you love, there will always be the death of love. Or as Tennessee Williams put it, 'We have to distrust one another, it is the only defence we have against betrayal.'

Michael began to confront the fact that he had denied his true growth. Whatever else she had done, his wife had now set him free. At forty-eight he was fit, more than comfortably off, but alone. His father had died of T.B. when he was a boy, a wealthy but dominating mother, of cancer two years ago. Now, his own family unit was smashed. Inside Michael was scared, he did not want to be a lonely old man. Well qualified to empathise with Johnny Mercer's song, he continues singing...

> *When somebody breaks your heart,*
> *Some somebody twice as smart as I.*
> *A somebody who will swear to be true,*
> *Like you used to do with me.*
> *Who'll leave you to learn that mis'ry*
> *Loves company, wait and see .*

He stops, hardly believing his eyes. A beautiful naked youth is looking at him from underneath a bright blue parasol. He looks for all the world like some swish ad for sun cream or a David

Hockney fantasy with bright yellow hair.

Michael had noticed a group of parasols and sunbeds ages ago, but seeing no one in or out of the sea and lost in his daydream of being Tokyo's answer to Tony Bennett, had continued his repertoire uninhibited.

Now as the two men assess each other, neither can stop grinning. Michael's feet automatically change direction, he wants a closer look.

Pity about the hair... but a perfectly symmetrical face... what a body! A male Grace Kelly! Like the garlanded angel on the pin board in the office, Ghirlandio's 'Vocation of the First Apostles'. An angelic bad boy.

'Buenos dias,' he calls.

'You sound happy,' says the peroxide angel.

'Oh, you're English! Well, it's such a great day. And er... Would you mind looking after my gear while I pop in for a swim?'

'Sure, man.'

Michael drops his bag on the sand by the sunbed, undoes his belt and unbuttons his flies. 'It seems,' he says indicating the beach, 'we have it all to ourselves.'

'Everyone left after the Carnival.'

'I only arrived last night. Any good?' Stepping out of his shorts Michael deftly removes his underpants, tucking them swiftly into his bag.

The angel's gaze momentarily falters. 'Depends what you're into.'

Michael has to make a distinct effort to turn away from such compelling cornflower blue eyes. 'See you,' he says running to the sea, aware the angel is assessing his naked arse. God, was that Jude Law or what? What a marvellous looking lad. The sudden chill of sea water stimulates and refreshes his hot limbs. He dives into the waves, swimming crawl-style, then filling his lungs with air, submerges underwater. As his muscles push his body through the deep bluey-green world, he recalls the words of the witch of

Maida Vale. 'Survival, like the underwater swimmer, depends solely on you, on your strength, no one else's.' Bursting for air, he surfaces. Turning inland he looks for the boy on the beach. He's not there! Vanished. Michael tries to stand, but is out of his depth. Where's my bag? Oh Hell! Don't say he's run off with it. Why am I so damned trusting? Fool!

Suddenly the young man is beside him in the water pointing to something out to sea. He disappears under a wave just as the same wave crashes on top of Michael. Thrashing helplessly underwater he bumps into the boy's naked body, for a moment they curl round each other – not an altogether unpleasant sensation. They stagger up in the shallows laughing.

Blinding white foam and sun on the breakers dazzle Michael. They play the game of waiting for the biggest wave and diving into its heart before it breaks. Exuberantly they laugh and whoop with joy. Ioan catches the crest of a wave and body surfs. Michael tries to imitate him. His elation when he succeeds culminates in more wa-heyings and hoots of victory.

A pair of white frizzed matrons carrying green Corte Ingles bags paddle by.

'Nice to see,' says one to the other.

'Mmm, very nice!' giggles the other, toddling off.

The men emerge glistening from the sea, panting and dripping. They present an erotic contrast in male beauty. The older is slightly taller, has a cropped head of silvery hair, is well built and hirsute. The younger, with golden hair, is slim, tanned, and has startlingly black pubics.

As Michael pads towards his beach bag, he feels their energetic frolic has somehow sparked a bond between them.

It never occurs to him that he has been manipulated.

Chapter 4

Confidences

Combing his wet hair back sleek and straight, Ioan lies flat, forehead clear and noble. Tilting his chin up slightly towards the sun, his motives for joining the swimming stranger are concealed behind eloquent dark eyebrows and closed lids. Sensing movement too near, he opens them. The man is looking down at him.

'That,' says the stranger, 'was fun.'

Ioan treats him to his sensational and frequently photographed smile, 'Fab!' He reaches for his mirrored sunglasses to hide behind and watch.

The man tugs a towel out of his Ralph Lauren bag, something falls on the sand.

A fat Gucci wallet!

The same fat Gucci wallet Ioan had noticed earlier nestling in the top of the bag. The one he had extracted, examined and returned while its owner was swimming... and Bingo! Fifteen thousand pesetas, a Coutts Bank Card, an Amex Gold Card, a Harrods Gold Card, Driver's licence and a United Airlines Premier Executive Card. The dude was seriously cashed!

The dude picks up the wallet and returns it to his bag. Drying himself on a flamboyant beach towel, a scarlet and black repo of 'La Suerte suprema' – 'The moment of truth,' when the bullfighter positions the bull to make his final thrust – he rubs his head vigorously, leaving his hair standing up on end. 'My name's Michael,' he says, 'Michael Stanhope.'

'Hi! Ioan Williams.' Ioan leans up to shake the outstretched hand, amused at the proximity of such well hung circumcised masculinity.

'So, Ioan,' says Michael spreading his towel over the next sunbed, 'You must be a Celt with a name like that? You on holiday?'

'Right. You?'

'My first day,' and he lays back, arms tucked behind his head, as if sunbathing without a costume were an everyday affair. 'London was filthy yesterday, cold and vile. Now this. Bliss!'

'Live in London?' Ioan asks, knowing full well he does from his Driver's licence.

'Yes. But as a matter of fact, I just put my house up for sale.' Then, almost as if to himself, 'Have to find somewhere.'

'Why's that?'

Michael glances across for a moment before replying. 'Long story.'

'What else have we got to do?' Ioan immediately regrets his phraseology. Chill, man! He smiles again, flashing perfect white teeth. 'I mean, it'll pass the time. If you want.'

Michael leans up on his elbow, appearing to study him.

Ioan susses he's trying to penetrate the mirrors.

'If I tell you the story of my life,' says Michael, 'you have to return the compliment, O.K?'

'Okay, but I asked first. What's with the singing? You in show business?'

'Good God, no!' Michael laughs. 'Singing just makes me feel good. I love all those old Gershwin and Cole Porter songs.' He tucks his arms under his head again. 'No, I'm in the Art Game. Buy and sell paintings. I have a little Gallery off Bond Street.'

Ioan is hooked. 'Cool, man! Tate Modern stuff or classy old masters?'

'Classy modern. I like painting... Do you paint?'

'No way!'

'Good. Hard to be friends with painters. Hidden agendas. I have two beautiful daughters. One about your age, who is, I hope, at this moment helping to look after the store. I am also, alas, in the process of getting a divorce. No, I'll rephrase that. Not alas! Actually, I finally got my head around the fact that I'm free. You see...' and he's off. He doesn't draw breath for ten minutes.

Ioan, interested more in the man than his tale of betrayal and family break up, studies him. Art dealer? Thought they were swishy queens. He's quite dishy. Straight, I guess. Bit of a smoothy. Snogable mouth. Why's he pouring his soul out to me? He's old enough to be my Father.

'...in which case, you either pray,' Michael was saying, 'get religion, or become an alcoholic.'

'Been there, done that,' flips Ioan.

'You have?' Michael looks surprised.

'Hasn't everyone?!'

Michael's smile hovers.

Not wanting to appear shallow or lose adorability points, Ioan adds, 'Well, most everyone has in my business.'

'Which is?' Michael's thick eyebrows shoot up. 'Enough about me. I've been having counselling about all of this. Got me used to talking about myself. Forgive me.'

'No, no, it's interesting. Truly.' Ioan makes an extra effort. 'Does it work? Psychotherapy?'

Michael appears seriously to consider his question. 'For me? Yes, I think it does. It's like telling secrets. Sharing them with someone wise. Confessing to sorrow, shame, pain, helps. Of course it doesn't necessarily make them go away, but...' Then, as if he realises he's revealed too much, he suddenly rummages in his bag. 'This sun's cremating me!' Extracting a tube of sun cream, he squeezes some onto his palms. 'You want some?'

Here we go with the busy hands, thinks Ioan. Lying prone, succulent buns to the sun, his body language is instinctively importunate. 'Wouldn't mind,' he says, admitting to feeling just the tiniest bit curious. I wonder if he really is straight? Time to find out! He lowers his neck in preparation.

The shock of the cold cream hits. Michael's large masculine hands caress his shoulders, sensually smoothing the cream round his shoulder blades, down his back, around his waist, down, over his arse, the backs of his legs.

'You can do your front yourself!' says Michael sitting up.

'Cheers, man!' Oh! So... well... it's not as if I fancy the guy.

Ioan's conceit was that he could seduce anyone if he put his mind to it. If he was ignored, sexually, he felt challenged. Aware of the effect his looks had on all sexes, he was used to judging people on their perceptions of his comeliness, he'd been fighting them off or succumbing, as his taste dictated, since he was fourteen. Consequently he had few platonic male friends. So if the guy's straight, he thinks, I'll get him to buy me a dinner or two, we'll have some laughs. The old guy's quite hunky. He's certainly very open about his life. Simpatico! Ioan decides he rather likes him. Would have done so anyway, even if he hadn't have caught the plastic. Besides, he feels in need of a little psychotherapy himself.

'I've a bit of a problem to deal with myself when I get back home.'

'What's that?' Michael squirts a dollop of white sun cream onto his stomach. 'Your turn.'

Ioan wonders how honest to be. What the hell! 'Cash flow,' he grins. 'Funny, you can admit shit to a stranger that...' and he peters out.

'Ah now! Everyone's interested in cash flow. Good subject. Relationships, kids, a mystery. But cash flow, I'm your man.'

'Then you're my man,' Ioan smiles shamelessly. 'Can I do your back?'

'Thanks. That would be most kind.' Michael hands him the sun cream and rolls onto his front. 'I'd better be careful my first day. So tell me, Ioan. What is it you do?'

'Photographic model and catwalk.' He rubs the older man's shoulders as butchly as possible. What a hairy bastard!

'Interesting! I take it you've recently been the subject of some sort of hair commercial?'

Ioan gives his shoulder a thump. The bastard's sending me up. 'Thanks a bunch! No. This blond is just a Carnival thing. I did Eros on a float the other night.'

'Eros! Oh I see. I was wondering. So tell me, how did you get into modelling?'

'Talent scout spotted me my last year at Dulwich College.' Ioan presses his thumbs along Michael's spine. Not a bad body. Wonder if I could get him?

'Oh massage! You're good at this. Go on.'

Ioan does. 'It seemed a good idea at the time. There was nothing else on offer. I went along for the laugh really, and it's been fab. But, well, basically it's shit, y'know what I'm saying?

'Superficial world, I would imagine.'

'And some! At seventeen I was working in Milan, Paris, Rome, doing drugs, sex. Didn't know what had hit me. Oh, I made some bread, but man, being part of all that P.R. bollocks distorts values.' He wipes the remaining cream on his palms down Michael's calves, 'There. Done.'

'Ta, I appreciate that,' says Michael. 'Doesn't seem to have done you much harm. You seem aware of the dangers.'

'I'm a Celt, as you said. A canny Celt. Dad was a Welshman from the Valleys. My Mum's family were all coal miners. Grit's in me blood.'

'Grit in the blood,' repeats Michael, 'I like that. Go on.'

'Models learn one thing. Career as eye candy has the shelf life of a raindrop! New faces come along, looks don't last. I only ever did it as a temp thing, always knew one day I'd have to get real. I just never knew how, exactly. Not that is...' and for a moment a wistful look appears, '...till the other day.'

'Let me guess. You want to be a pop star?'

'Shit, no man! I'm not that crazy. I'm serious.'

'An actor?'

'Nooo!' shouts Ioan, laughing.

'What's wrong with being an actor? When I was your age, that's what I wanted.'

'Seriously?'

'Sure. After University I considered everything. Photography, Pop stardom, Portrait painting... but as I never managed to capture anyone's likeness onto the canvas, I realised there wasn't much point. Happily, circumstances propelled me into a career in the art world... OK, sorry. So tell me, what is it you want to do?'

'I need a fag for all this. I'm not used to this chat.' Ioan fishes in his bag.

'My shrink says chat is good for the soul.'

'Well. I had one of those soul-searching days, you know?'

'Oh God! Indeed!'

'I mean, Christ! I'm nearly thirty, and what have I done with my life? Where the hell am I going?' He finds his Fortunas. 'Want one? They're Spanish.'

'No thanks. I haven't smoked for years. But...' Michael hesitates, his fingers flicker, 'maybe today I just will. To celebrate.' He ceremoniously withdraws a cigarette and places it between his lips.

Celebrating eh? ...flattery! Ioan snaps his pebble lighter. Indulging himself in a frisson of pleasure by simultaneously feeling the hairs on the back of Michael's hand as he steadies the flame. Flirting is second nature. Despite the man's seniority, Ioan admits an attraction, a magnetism. Maybe it's the memory of their naked bodies bumping, thrashing underwater. He watches Michael exhaling appreciatively. 'Like it?'

'Oh God! It's been years.'

Ioan laughs and takes off his sunglasses.

'That's better, now I can see your eyes. So you were saying, when you were soul-searching, did you discover what it was you wanted?'

'I did.' He takes a long drag on his cigarette. 'The other week I was on a shoot in Barcelona. Guell Park. Designed by Gaudi, the architect. You know Gaudi?'

Michael smiles. 'Yes, I know Gaudi.'

'Well, I guess he kinda inspired me.' Ioan chatters on, not unlike Michael had earlier. Enthusing about the unfinished La Sagrada Familia, about Gaudi's balcony designs, rooftops and windows, even pulling out of his bag a book of photos and illustrations of the great man's works. 'This is the kind of thing. I mean, to be able to do that! I tell you, man, I don't remember being so excited about anything outside sex ever before, know what I mean?'

Michael nods, grinning.

'Course I know architecture's changed, but places don't have to look like great giant Portakabins. They all go on about curvaceous lines, like that place in Bilbao, you know?'

'The Guggenheim museum.'

'Yeah! Frank Gehry designed it. Expressionist modern shit! So boring! What about colour and ornament in design? I want to bring that back. Like hot sex, y'know? There has to be a way of combining art and beauty with high tech modern functionality. Everyone always dismisses that. I know it's down to money and all, but people don't want to live in cold depersonalised titanium towers. People want warmth, humanitarian values in their environment. Not so-called 'curvaceous' space age capsules, metallic flat pack stacks of container boxes.'

'Well, who would have thought. You're an old-fashioned traditionalist!'

'Hardly. More a modern humanitarian.'

'With Rococo angels?'

'Not exactly. But hell, yes, why not? If it's appropriate. You see those little golden angels on sale everywhere. That's what I mean. People love tradition.'

'Some. Others prefer something new. But I do see your point. You go for it, lad.'

Despite Michael's encouragement, Ioan's enthusiasm subsides. 'Yeah, but an architectural course takes seven years and a ton of dosh.'

'Which,' says Michael, anticipating the boy's predicament, 'you do not have?'

'Right. Last month we... well, we had a bit of a shock.' Silently he puts away the Gaudi book.

'We?'

'My Ma and I. Look, you don't want to hear all this. We're strangers.'

'Maybe not such strangers now. Come, tell me. What else do we have to do?'

'Touché! Isn't that what they say?'

Michael grins reaching for his bag. 'Want a drink?'

Ioan wonders if beer or something stronger might be on offer, but no such luck, the dude takes out Volvic. He shakes his head, holding up his cigarette by way of reply. Pushing back a thick lock of blond hair, he says, 'It's just that my Dad died.'

'Oh. I am sorry.' In the silence that follows, Ioan remains

motionless, eyes cast down. 'Was it very sudden?' asks Michael.

'Yes. Very.'

'Do you want to talk about it?'

Ioan shrugs, 'Don't mind. It's my Ma I'm worried about.'

'Naturally. Do you have a good relationship?'

'Yeah. She's great. Used to be a dancer. Not famous or anything, just end of the pier stuff. But she's still mad about showbiz. They run a pub in Canterbury... or rather used to.'

A series of memory flashes of his father's last morning project onto Ioan's mind. Since Dad went out that Monday and never came back, Ioan had examined every detail of their last moments together, now as he thinks about him again, it's like shuffling a pack of memorised photographs.

Dad in his braces and shirt sleeves breezing into the bathroom to have a pee, just as Ioan was at the mirror applying 'cover up' to a hickey on his neck. A hickey Jonathan had given him in the long grass the day before during a daring open-air sex session.

'Is that make-up you're wearing?' Dad had asked, 'You'll be sitting down to wee wee next.' Ioan had winced, but better a remark like that, than he knew the truth.

Dad in the pub cellar, uncorking the wood from a barrel, fixing the pipes to siphon the beer up to the pumps. Calling through the cellar flap as Ioan packed the 'empties' away and stacked up new bottles. 'Don't be namby-pamby about it, Boy. Get down onto your haunches.'

Dad at the breakfast table. Mum fussed, because she'd run out of marmalade. 'Sorry, I know how you both love it. Pop over to Sainsbury's, Ioan, do you mind, luv?'

Dad winking at him, 'I'll go. You stay with your Mum. You don't get to see her often.' Dad leaving the table saying his last words, 'Won't be a jiffy.'

Waiting for his return... longer and longer. Clearing away the table, leaving only his cup of tea, some toast and a plate. The photograph on the sideboard of Mum and Dad on their wedding day, Dad with red hair, burly and big, towering over Mum, a pretty blond teenager. Proof of how pin-up pretty she used to be.

Up in Ma's bedroom, still waiting, watching her make up as she sat at her kidney shaped dressing table with the rosebud chintz frills. Ma wearing a cardigan with all-over patch blocks of colour, peach, red, orange and blue. 'He's probably gassing with one of his billiard mates!' she'd said. The 'plop' sound her goldy lipstick cover made as she pulled it off to paint her lips pillar box red. Among her powders and potions, the small silver oval picture frame holding his portrait, aged eighteen, with the identical blue eyes as hers in the mirror. She still looks good, he'd thought, a bit hard boiled, forty-five years of stress and laughter lines discernible, but still pretty.

'You still got smashing legs, Ma.'

'The legs are always the last to go,' she'd laughed.

'You know, you could be a model if you wanted. For the older woman, obviously.'

'How sweet! Thank you, darling.'

'I mean it. You should get some stills done. I know a guy. You could make some dosh.'

'Your Dad is quite generous enough with his 'dosh' thank you,' she said, opening her white leather jewel case. 'Anyway it's been far too long since I shook a leg in front of a camera.' Choosing a pair of pearl studs, she eased them into her pierced lobes. 'Come and help me with my hair. It's being hopeless this morning.' She handed him her hair brush and he'd brushed it, following a childhood routine. 'Where the hell could the man have got to?' she'd said, looking at her wrist watch, 'The bar opens in half an hour.'

'You should try it up in a French pleat,' Ioan said, sweeping her hair on top of her head. 'Show off your earrings.'

'Don't you start! Betty Haag's been going on at me for weeks.'

'Why don't you go for the full blonde?'

'Because with these eyes, I'd look just like a tart, that's why!'

'Who's Betty Haag?'

'You've met her downstairs in the bar. Works in "A Cut Above". This,' she said, plucking at the grey strands of her hair, 'was once known as my golden crown I'll have you know. It's all your fault. Once you were born, it lost its curl and grew out straight. It looks like some pathetic grey mouse.'

'Ma!' he laughed, 'It's not that bad!'

A buzz from the intercom.

'Ah! That'll be him,' she said. 'He won't have time for his bath now.' She crossed the room to the phone on Dad's side of the bed. But it wasn't Dad. It was Valerie, the barmaid. A customer was downstairs asking for her. Returning to the mirror to check her reflection she applied a quick puff of powder to her retrousee nose. 'Time to greet the customers,' she said and gave him a dazzling smile. 'Bit like going on stage, isn't it?' Her expression changed suddenly as she looked him in the eye. 'Have you really got to go back to London this morning, darling? Couldn't you stay a wee bit longer?'

'Sorry. I've an appointment this afternoon,' he lied.

'Bring your Father's racing paper, will you,' she said collecting her empty tea cup and her "Hello" magazine. He did so, and together they'd left the safe womb of her boudoir to face the good burghers of Canterbury and the evils of the world. Their lives would never be the same.

His recall had only taken a moment. Michael, still leaning on his arm on the sunbed is watching him. 'So what happened?'

'Oh,' said Ioan, flicking ash from his cigarette onto the sand, 'Some insensitive old cow rushed up to Ma in the bar and blurted it out. Told her Dad was dead. Just like that.'

Ioan could still visualise the woman, standing by her shopping bag on wheels in the bar. Her fat round face flushed with the excitement at being first with the bad news, the abominable words spilling out of her phoney compassionate blubber lips. 'Oh, Mrs Williams, I'm ever so sorry to be the bearer of such bad news, but I just saw your husband hit by a car. He's dead.'

Ma standing paralysed. Her hand flaying out to his. As he held it, she staggered, almost fell. He managed to grab a chair with his other hand and transfer her. Holding her shoulders they listened to the woman gabbling on. 'I was just coming out of Sainsbury's with this lot,' she said, 'and there was this man in front of me. I thought, that's Dave Williams from "The Olive Branch". He was just crossing the road and this car crashes slap bang into him. Right over the bonnet he went, like a rag doll. Right in front of me! Awful! I've never seen anything like it, never in my life. Going far too fast it was. Just ghastly! Blood all over the place, dribbling into the gutter it was! Someone rang for an ambulance. It wasn't me. I couldn't do a thing. I was too stunned. Shaking, I was. A policeman was there, and some poor woman driver sobbing. She was in a dreadful state. "He stepped right in front of me," she says. Anyway the emergency people weren't long. Ever so good they were. But like a fool, I didn't think to ask where they were taking him. Least ways not till it was too late. But there're only the three hospitals locally. Shouldn't be difficult to trace him, dear. I thought I'd better come and tell you, because, well, I mean... Oh I'm so sorry to be the bearer of such dreadful tidings.'

Ioan, his eyes on vacancy, stud persona for the moment on hold, says, 'She loved telling every minute of it. It wasn't her life crashing apart. It was Ma's. Ma actually thanked the woman when she left. "It's very good of you," she said. We both had a brandy and I started phoning the hospitals. The second one, 'The Chaucer' had him. He wasn't dead. Quite. I rushed us over there like a fucker. Dumped everything in London of course and the two of us just sat either side of his bed waiting for the kill.' Ioan idly smoothes a pattern in the sand still holding on to his smouldering Fortuna. 'When his breathing stopped,' he continues, 'Mother kissed him. She asked me to do the same.' Suddenly Ioan viciously pushes the tip of his cigarette into the sand. 'Lying there with a grey tube stuck in his mouth, he looked even less appealing than he had in life. I couldn't bring myself to do it. Was that awful of me?'

'If,' says Michael slowly, 'that was the way you felt.'

'It was,' says Ioan, brushing the sand off his hands.

'Then it would have been hypocritical. Had you never cared for him?'

'Never. There was never anything but air between us. I don't remember ever speaking to him about anything important. Not even like us now. I guess we just weren't each other's type. He was like a kind of sawdust man to me. Oh, hells' hearty, popular, people loved him. I didn't. He played football and all that. I hate football. He didn't play my game, tennis. We tried billiards once... disaster!'

'I play tennis.'

'Great. Maybe we could have a game later. If you're up for it?'

'Sure. Why not? So go on.'

'Well, Ma cried, and there was nothing else to do but leave the hospital. As I helped Ma out, the Matron gave me an envelope of Dad's things, his watch, signet ring and wallet. When we got into the car, I gave them to her, and thought no more about it. The next morning Ma put a snap into my hand. A black and white photograph of a girl in a summer dress standing in a suburban garden. 'What's this?' I asked, 'Who's she?'

'I was hoping you could tell me,' Ma said. 'I found it in your Dad's wallet. Do you recognise her?'

'No. Am I supposed to? Don't you know her?'

'No,' she said, 'I don't.' She started pacing about the room, talking half to herself and half to me. 'Why on earth would Dave carry a picture of her around? Who is she? It's obviously been in his pocket for ages, look, it's dog-eared. Who could she be?'

'Anyway,' Ioan continues, 'I made all the funeral arrangements, supported Ma as best I could. Then came the reading of his Will.'

'Ah ha!' says Michael, 'Was it his mistress?'

'Wait,' says Ioan, who, to his surprise, is rather enjoying sharing the ghastly tale. 'Mother and I were at her solicitor's office in Herne Bay, and this lawyer dude, a Mr Nicholls, starts reading Dad's Will. It turns out he's left practically the whole friggin' lot to some illegitimate daughter of his in Leeds! Four hundred thousand quid! Mum only gets what's left after tax. I get zilch! Well, we were flabbergasted. Mr Nicholls said it was all quite legal. There'd be no point in challenging it, the Will had been drawn up years ago. There was nothing we could do. Ma didn't cry. She just sat there, her mouth kinda pursed. She did say though, when we got outside, "That'll help me get over his death. I'm not wasting anymore tears on him!" She couldn't believe she'd lived all those years with him not knowing the truth. It goes to show, doesn't it. You never know anyone.'

'Indeed you don't.'

Michael's ironic tone causes Ioan to flick him a glance. Was that bitterness in his voice?

But Michael smiles back candidly, 'You and I aren't doing so badly though, eh?'

Ioan nods, 'Strange, isn't it? I've not told anyone about this.'

'Secrets,' says Michael.

'Yeah. Well, you were so straight about what had happened to you.' With a toss of his head he flicks his blond mane out of his eyes. 'So, I guess it's all change in both our lives.'

'Mmm,' agrees Michael. 'I take it, this Will of his, affects the financing of your studies?'

'I'll say! And Ma will probably have to leave the pub. It's a Trust House, they like married teams as tenants. She's with my Aunt in Cornwall right now but oh...' he sighs, 'I don't know'. He reaches underneath his sunbed for some Evian, taking long gulps. Despite being in the shade it's warm. 'Luke-Matthew-Mark!' he mutters, lusting for a proper drink.

'Luke? Oh luke warm! Right,' Michael grins. After a moment says, 'I tell you what we should do. First we should have a swim, then go and investigate those.' He points inland to a backdrop of milky blue mountains. 'What do you say? We'll pick up some beers. I'll rent a car.'

'Great!' Ioan laughs, 'Aventura!'

'Then,' Michael taps his nose, 'I'll give you some tips on how to become an architect.'

Ioan swings his legs over the sunbed onto the burning sand. 'Ow! It's boiling!' He starts running to the sea, calling, 'Last one in's a poof!'

Springing up, Michael races naked after him, splashing, diving into the sparkling cool sea.

Fifteen minutes later, towelled and dressed, beach bags slung over their shoulders, they stroll away chatting amiably, involuntarily in step. Neither had noticed the numerous and disparate holiday makers decamp around them, so engrossed had they been with each other. One with his purposeful therapy, the other, with what by now, was a little more than the answer to his loneliness.

Chapter Five

The Old Vicarage

Cornwall. April 2000

The Cornish rain lashes the kitchen windows panes, as Rosie sits at the breakfast table reading a letter, her spectacles on the end of her nose. Sitting opposite is her sister Liz, drinking tea. Between them lay the remains of breakfast, a woollen cosyied tea pot of 'English Breakfast', a jar of thick cut 'Chivers' marmalade, a yellow tub of 'I Can't Believe It's Not Butter', and a ceramic jug from Liz's pottery of semi-skimmed milk. The two latter dairy products being Liz's perennial attempt at slimming. At her feet, under the scrubbed pine table, lies her golden retriever Sally, snoozing. A homely smell of burnt toast hangs in the air.

Rosie lifts her teacup and sips as she reads. The sudden death of her husband had shaken her to the roots of her being. Subsequent events had left her in an even more bewildered state. Her vitality, her good looks and the glamour Ioan had admired are nowhere to be seen as she sits bundled in her pink woolly dressing gown. Not that she looks middle-aged, more like a worn thirty-five year old, than her true forty-five years. Since her dancing days she has always remained an athlete, playing tennis at the Canterbury and Barham Health Club regularly, up to two months ago. She also has had enough feminine nous to take good care of her face, creaming it religiously every night with cleansing cream, so her skin is still fine and clear. Nevertheless, her customers in 'The Olive Branch' would have been shocked by her appearance. To them she had always displayed an open cheerfulness, even a certain sophistication, for she possesses an innate good dress sense and allure. At the moment though, she is frozen by worry and fear of the future, which seems to bode nothing but loneliness and poverty.

The Angelus clangs through the rain from the village church opposite.

'Are you up for it?' asks Liz, head slightly to one side, unconsciously fingering her Mam's gold crucifix hanging around her neck. 'I'll understand if you're not, but I shall go.'

'Do you mind, cariad?' says Rosie, frowning. 'These letters.' Then with a one-sided smile, 'I've rather had enough of God, for one month.'

To which Liz raises a quizzical eyebrow and drops the crucifix.

A complicated and disturbing letter lay open by the toast rack, it has a Leeds postmark and had been forwarded by Rosie's solicitor, Mr Nicholls from Herne Bay. She had just read it aloud to Liz. Unable to decide what to do about it, she had opened her second letter, the letter she now held in her hand. It had also been redirected, from 'The Olive Branch,' Canterbury, to 'The Old Vicarage, Sennen, Cornwall.' The handwriting was in neat copperplate.

School House   *21st, March 2000*
King's College
Canterbury
Kent

Dear Mrs Williams,
I was very sorry indeed to hear from Joan of the sudden death of Mr Williams. It must be a very difficult time for you. He was

always so nice to me when I came over to the "The Olive Branch" and gave me a free Coke. I just thought I would like to write to you to say how very sorry I am and to express my deep sympathy.
Yours very sincerely,
Jonathan (Court-Smyth)

What a sweet boy, she thinks, how kind. Odd that the son should write and not the parents who, after all, are much closer. Maybe they're abroad. Rosie had received many letters of condolence from customers over the past weeks, but nothing from the Colonel or Margaret. Curious.

Warmed by the Aga, the sisters sit thoughtfully in the vast kitchen of what used to be 'The Vicarage' before Liz bought it as an artist's colony some seventeen years ago. As the eldest unmarried daughter, Liz had inherited and subsequently sold their parents' house in Pontypridd, that, added to the sale of her own little cottage, enabled her to afford this rambling five bedroom nineteenth century country mansion. Set in three acres with high oaks and laurel bushes bordering a gravel drive, it has a touch of the gracious and rather like its owner, is large, untidy and welcoming. Over the years, Liz had introduced white doves into the dovecote, added a pottery, a kiln, an outside studio, converted the garage for picture framing, built a covered swimming pool with a vine, yuccas, and a massive fatsia japonica, which has since grown up to the glass ceiling. Under the trees, alongside the pool, a line of eight brick and timber chalets have recently been added. Each self-contained with its own kitchen and shower unit, for protégés, lost souls and the inevitable lame ducks that seem to accumulate around Liz. The affluent Victorian atmosphere of the house has cast its subtle spell over Liz, imbuing her with a more conservative outlook on life. When she had been a school mistress, she'd been regarded as something of a rebel, holding liberal leftish notions on matters ranging from Welsh Nationalism, education and disarmament, to capital punishment and sex. Nowadays, with the onset of weight and middle age, she has become as warm and cosy as her Aga, yet she is no soft touch. There is no 'free lunch' in her commune, a quid pro quo operates, quids in cash her preferred quo. Notwithstanding, throughout the artistic environs of Penzance, her popularity, strength of character, and undoubted talent as a potter has earned her the affectionate sobriquet of 'Den Mother.' To her extended family she is happy, with only the smallest reservation, to include the only member of her blood family left, her bereaved younger sister. Nevertheless, for the bedroom Liz has allocated her, Rosie insists on paying twenty-five pounds a week 'Towards the groceries.' It's a wise sister who knows her own.

Biting her lip, Rosie indicates the letter lying on the table, the one from Leeds. 'So what do you think?'

'Let's have a gander.' Liz lifts the glasses attached to a chain resting on her bosom. Rosie hands her the letter. The handwriting is flowing and in bright blue felt tip.

Dear Mrs Rosie Williams,

It seems ever so strange writing to you after all these years. I've always wondered about you.

It's a good feeling to make contact at last, even though in such sad circs.

Last week I had a letter from 'Saunders and Nicholls,' of Herne Bay who were Dad's solicitors. They told me he had died and I had inherited his estate. Well, it made me feel like I'd won the lottery, I can tell you. It really is a life changing thing for me, and I am so grateful he remembered me in this way, it makes up for the past.

Then I got to thinking, maybe it's not very nice for you, I mean the whole thing of me and the money might be a bit upsetting, coming on top of Dad's death too.

So this is why I am writing, please forgive me for being so up front (I'm a bit like that, so they tell me, and I don't just mean my chest size!)

I would like you to know, my Mum died when I was little, so I don't remember her much. I was brought up by me Gran, who works at Marks and Spencers in Leeds, and of course she's really been my Mum.

Dad said he was happy with you, but it was impossible I could live with him. Anyway I would not have wanted to leave my Gran.

Here's the thing, I would really like to meet you and Ioan, Dad showed me his picture in a magazine once, he is very good looking.

I just passed my entrance to Leeds College of Art and Design, so that's a good result too.

I send my best to you Mrs Williams, and hope you will agree that we could meet up soon. I have wondered about you so much.

Sincerely yours,
Julie Williams (Miss)

Because of my hair my friends call me 'Red.'

Liz puts down the letter and sucks her teeth thoughtfully.

'I think she's got a bloody nerve,' mutters Rosie.

'I think,' says Liz, 'you should see her.'

'What!' says Rosie astonished, her teacup frozen in mid air. 'Why on earth should I?'

'She is, after all, your step daughter. And it'll be something.'

Rosie crashes the tea cup into its saucer. 'What the hell do you mean by that?'

'Now don't get touchy.' Liz lays her finger tips on the edge of the table. 'I'm just being on your side. You can't go on just, well, treading water forever.'

'Good God, Liz, I'm grieving! You told me to grieve. Now you're telling me I'm treading water, what's going on? I'm here trying to work out how the hell I'm going to get my life back on track, how I'm going to face the rest of my life living alone, and you... you...'

'Living alone, let me tell you, is not the worst thing that can happen to a person. The only difference about living alone is that you learn to value your own company as well as everyone else's.'

Rosie rips a piece of toast apart. 'I'm not quite ready to fade away into old age yet!' She butters the toast and chews it crossly.

Liz silently reaches out to touch her sister's arm. 'Cariad! Of course you're not. What I mean is, this might be an opportunity to take an interest in something outside of yourself. In life... in stuff!'

Rosie gulps down her tea. 'Stuff!? Stuff does not interest me. I'm not like you, I can't pot and paint, be on my own for hours on end. I'm used to running a bar, meeting people, socialising, having fun.'

'Exactly. Well, here's your chance. This Julie-Red girl or whatever she calls herself, is people. Practise your social skills on her. Have fun with her, for Heaven's sake. Look, I love having you here, darling, you know. But you must shift yourself.'

'Shifting myself,' says Rosie, 'is different from having Dave's bloody illegitimate daughter condescending all over me, waving her money, my money, in my face.'

'Actually, my darling, strictly speaking, it wasn't your money. It was David's. To do with as he wished. It's not as if it was the money you'd earnt together working in the pub, it was the money he inherited from his grandad.'

'Oh, thank you so much for pointing that out! That's very helpful. You can be so bloody maddening at times. I thought you just said you were on my side.'

'I am, cariad. I'm just trying to help you understand, to make you see reason.'

'I don't want to be reasonable, thank you very much. I feel very emotional, and I think I have every right.'

'Indeed you do, but... Well, I've said my piece,' says Liz rising. Under the table the golden bitch stirs. 'If anyone wants me, I'll be about half an hour. Ask her down, it might be fun.'

'Your idea of fun is clearly very different from mine these days,' says Rosie pursing her mouth and clearing away the dishes. 'She is, after all, responsible for making me penniless.'

'Hardly her fault, darling. You can't blame her. Look, I'm out of here.' The retriever emerges looking hopefully up at Liz. 'You stay, Sal,' says Liz. 'Good girl. Stay with Auntie Rose.' With a 'Bye Bubba!' and an instruction to 'Think on,' Liz hugs the door, swiftly slipping through and shutting it before Sal can follow.

With Liz vanished into the hall, Sal grizzles.

'Bye,' calls out Rosie. 'Put in a word.'

'Always do,' calls back Liz.

'Pray I win the lottery!' mutters Rosie with asperity.

While Liz puts on a sou'wester and scampers through the rain over the driveway to pray for them all, Rosie rubs Sal's floppy velvety ear. 'Alone again,' she murmurs. 'Maybe I should get a lovely dog like you.' Rosie regrets her faith in the Almighty is no longer as strong as her sister's, in times like these she knows it would be a comfort. After sixteen years behind a bar, running pubs in Croydon and Canterbury she has come to believe, as the bar stools philosophers put it, 'If there is a God, he's got an awful lot to answer for.'

As a girl she'd been taught her to say her prayers and had attended Sunday school. At eleven she even wanted to be a nun. Her dilemma was short lived, choosing between a nun's habit and a pink tutu there was no contest. So she added to her prayers, 'Please God make me a good dancer.' After marrying David she altered it to 'Please God make me a good mother and wife,' and later, when their existence in Wales after the mines closed became intolerable, to 'Please God find David a good job.' Her prayers had been answered, but each time there had been a price to pay, a catch.

David had been an unbeliever, attending church only for christenings, weddings and funerals. 'If you expect me take part in that mumbo jumbo,' he'd said, 'you've got another think coming.' Over the years, with the loss of her career and a convenient but mundane marriage, her faith, like so much mist, had evaporated. As a barmaid she had listened and sympathised with many tales of woe coming across the counter and come to believe in a mixture of Fate and wind blowing chance. Now her sheltered life had disintegrated, she does not pray. Destiny, she feels, must have something in store, it owed it to her. She feels she has so much more in her heart to give, but to what and to whom, she has no notion. Only her love and belief in her son remain intact, that is indestructible. His presence and their talks after David's death had consoled and soothed her, as well as proving his growing maturity. 'Ma,' he had told her, 'belief in destiny, or a god that fixes your life for you, is for Bible-belt Americans. Life is what you make it. Believe in yourself. Nobody is going to help you now, but you.' Remembering this and saying to herself, Get a grip girl, she battles with her desire to move on. But the practicalities of doing so, coupled with her anxiety and grief, though mitigated by the fury she feels toward her dead husband, paralyse her. She recalls Ioan's advice, 'Don't make any decisions yet. Give yourself time.' So she merely kisses the top of Sal's head, who pads over to her basket in the corner.

Absently she picks up the letter on the table, vaguely aware she should answer it. Pondering how, she opens a drawer in the dresser, pulls out some sheets of Liz's headed note paper and sits again. Without making a rough copy she writes...

"Dear Julie Williams,
Thank you for your letter. I confess to being surprised to hear from you, especially as I only recently heard of your very existence. Mr Nicholls, who is my solicitor too, obviously neglected to inform you of this fact. It is incredible to me that my husband never told me about you, I suspect guilt was the reason, so I cannot blame you. But I will not hide from you that the news was a profound shock, mocking as it did my twenty eight years of marriage."

Rosie's mobile on the sideboard trills. Sal lifts her nose.

'Hallo,' says Rosie.

'Hi Ma! How's it going?'

'Darling! You're back. Thank Heaven! Did you have a good time?'

'Wicked! Fab weather. How's it going?'

'Not so bad. It's raining down here. Are you brown?'

'All over. How's Auntie Liz?'

'Same as ever. Drives me mad of course, but she puts everything into proportion. She's at morning service right now.'

'Religious nut!'

'Ioan! She's not nearly as bad as she used to be. Darling, I've got a letter here from...' she hesitates, 'from the girl in the photograph.'

'Wow! What does she want?'

'It's extraordinary, she wants to meet me. Do you think I

should?'

'Do you want to?'

'Not much.'

'Then don't.'

'What do you think she wants?'

'Well, it can't be the dosh, she's got that. Perhaps she feels guilty, wants to give it back.'

'We should be so lucky. Unfortunately people don't do that, even little girls.'

'I think little girls can be made to do anything.'

'Now, what do you mean by that?'

'Nothing. Why not check her out?'

'I'm afraid I don't feel very generous towards her.'

'Me neither. But aren't you curious?'

'Mildly.'

'I am. She's my half sister!'

'Liz says I should ask her down here to stay. Oh, we'll see. How's work?'

'There's a possibility of an Australian trip. A shoot on The Great Barrier Reef.'

'How thrilling!'

'It's not a definite offer, I'm waiting in Maisie's office right now. Might be fun.'

'Fingers crossed. What about the architect idea?'

'It's looking good. I think I've found myself a sponsor.'

'A sponsor! Who? I mean, how? Who?'

'A company, Ma. A firm that would take me on and train me.'

'Oh, do they do that? Well, that would be wonderful.'

'You made any plans yet?'

'I don't seem to be able to concentrate. I shan't be going back to the O.B. Not by myself, I couldn't.'

'No, of course, I understand. Something will come up, you'll see. I'll ask Maisie if she's got any jobs for senior model dames.'

'Don't you dare. I'm not fit to be seen by anyone these days.'

'Rubbish! Must run, honey. See ya. Love to Auntie Liz.'

'Bye darling. Love you.'

The phone clicks. Rosie presses the Talk button off, envying his busy lifestyle.

Sitting back at the table she picks up her pen, after a moment's thought she continues her letter.

> *"However, having got used to the idea of you, I admit to being curious. And to hear in your charming letter that you would like to meet me. Well, it would be churlish to refuse, and I hope I am not that kind of woman. So why not? Maybe we could fill in the blanks for each other. I shall be staying with my sister at the above address for the foreseeable future, so if you feel like it, pay us a visit. It's calm and peaceful here, almost a retreat. There's a studio for artists too, so you might find yourself feeling quite at home. You would be welcome. Just telephone before you arrive.*
>
> *Yours sincerely, Rosie Williams."*

Rosie folds the page into quarters and slips it into the envelope. 'Walkies?' she says, as she copies out the address. Sal bounds about wagging her tail, scampering and barking excitedly. Rosie collects her coat, a headscarf and umbrella, and off they go together in the rain down to the village post.

Chapter Six

Assignation

Ioan is not actually in Maisie's office, as he'd just told his mother, he is waiting to see her, sitting on a leather sofa in the reception hall of International Models Ltd, Soho. He is leafing through a "B.A.F.T.A. Academy" magazine, playfully trying to win the eye of the attractive thirty-something receptionist sitting behind a smoked glass desk. She ignores him, she is far too busy dealing with incoming calls on the switch board, anyway she's blasé, used to the beautiful people trooping past every day. An opulent display of fresh flowers, four foot high and changed twice a week, stand in a vase on a bleached refectory table. On the wall facing him, is a massive corporate, spot-lit, blue oil painting. The chequered floor is in cool marble. The place stinks of money.

Impatient and feeling randy, he decides to call Jonathan. They haven't spoken since his return from Gran Canaria. He'd left a message on the boy's pager, but it hadn't been returned. Dialling Jonathan's home number on his cell phone, he has a moment's concern. What if one of the parents answer? Could be tricky. Jonathan's mother, Margaret Court Smyth, had been effusive in her thanks to him for putting Jonathan up after he'd missed his train, but there seemed no logical or specifically 'virtuous' reason for them to continue to hang out together. Fourteen year olds and twenty-eight year olds seldom make ideal partners, though this one, he mused, made an ideal bedfellow.

'Hallo. Court Smyth residence.' The voice was a secretary or daily woman's.

'Could I have a word with Jonathan please?'

'Certainly, I'll get him for you.' He hears Jonathan's name being called then female voices talking low in the background. The phone is picked up.

'Hallo. Who is this, please?'

'It's Ioan, Mrs Court Smyth. How are you?'

'Ah yes, Ioan. Jonathan's out, I'm afraid.' She sounds very curt.

'No, I'm not,' Jonathan shouts in the background. A hand is placed over the instrument. Dim mutterings. Then Jonathan's clear young voice, 'Ioan! Hi! You're back. Great! How are you?'

Ioan lowers his voice to a tone promising lovemaking to come. 'Hi, sexy. Listen, I'm going to suggest some times and places. Say if you can make it or not. Okay? Are you with me?'

'Okay,' says Jonathan.

'Just say yes or no. Your Ma might be listening.'

'It's okay,' whispers Jonathan. 'She's just gone into the study Hold on, she's left the door open.'

Ioan waits for the click of an extension being picked up. It does not come. But his instinct is right on the button, though even he is unaware of the level of Mrs Court Smyth's suspicion.

In a drawer in her husband's desk in front of her, is Jonathan's scrap book full of pictures of Ioan, including a 10" × 8" semi-nude art photograph, signed "To Jonathan with love." She had found it under her son's bed. She and Jonathan's father, with their lifelong friend Geoffrey White, the Chief Constable of the County of Kent, had held a council of war about it.

'Do we confront this monster?' she'd said. 'We can't just pretend it doesn't exist!'

They had decided the best way to deal with the problem was a warning. No direct confrontation. Not without proof. The photograph, by itself was simply not enough. Personally, Margaret had found it quite enough, every hair and pore on Ioan's body was clearly in focus. But Geoffrey, who apparently had experience of this sort of problem before, advised caution. 'The only way a successful prosecution can be achieved is to have incontrovertible evidence. 'I tell you what,' he'd said. 'Let me have his walking shoes for a day. We'll keep tabs on the lad.'

Ioan, with his Filofax open beside him on the sofa, is suggesting days of the week. So far, Jonathan had answered 'No' to the weekend, and to Monday. 'What about Tuesday?'

The receptionist looks up from behind her desk. 'Mr Williams. You may go up. Miss Collins is free now. Second floor. You know the way.'

Ioan nods thank you, and stands, his cell phone clamped to his ear. Jonathan is replying to his last question.

'Great! Perfect! We're going to London that day anyway. At your place, Tuesday.'

'Fab!' says Ioan, 'See you.'

He enters the lift and presses the button to ascend to Maisie's office suite.

Chapter Seven

Happy Memories

'On the right please, driver. The house with the "For Sale" sign.'

The taxi draws up by Michael's impressive Grade II listed house in Wandsworth. He hauls off his bag and pays the driver. The estate agent's sign is a shock. It seems tangible proof his 'family life' is over. Looking at his beloved house, he is unable to stem memories. A wave of grief threatens to engulf him as he inserts his key into the front door and pushes it open. Moving swiftly to the Banham security box to press the code he suddenly halts, gives a sarcastic roar, and punches in the code – Nichola's birth date – ironic or what? He recalls why he hadn't changed it – on the day he left, he'd wanted her back.

A holiday can change your life!

No dogs jumping up, no children calling 'Daddy', no hugs, no wife. Two letters lie on the mat. One from the estate agent. He tears it open. They've had an offer at the asking price, £1,850,000.

Well, that's something! He'd bought the house for £460,000, just before the 80's boom, then it was considered expensive. Aware of the iniquity of English divorce laws, and the fact that the courts can do anything they want with your money, it occurs to him, that if Nichola demands any of this, there is going to be one almighty battle incurring even more legal fees. Lord! He idly wonders why successful people ever bother marrying, divorce laws are such a disincentive. The second letter is an invitation to speak in a debate at the Institute of Contemporary Arts, entitled

'Beauty and Horror in Contemporary Art. Are we being conned?'
'Yes' he mutters putting the letters with the accumulated mail, pizza ads and junk that Mrs Burgess the cleaner has piled on the refectory table.

In the chilly farmhouse kitchen he puts on the kettle and switches on the central heating. He makes a mug of Nescafe and takes it through to the living room to admire his Utrillo. The curtains are drawn, a watery light filters through. It looks as if a spell has been cast over the room. It is full of dead happiness. He turns on the painting's over light.

"The Church at Deuil" was insured for £25,000 but must be worth far more. He'd bought it with the spoils of his first year as a private gallery owner. Choosing a Mozart CD. 'Soave sia il vento' from 'Cosi Fan Tutte', he presses the button on his Bang and Olufsen and sips his coffee, contemplating. The decor reflects his taste, not Nichola's, who, indifferent to her surroundings, was more interested in decorating her person. The painting's grey and white patina is carefully echoed in the room's furnishings. Pearl grey silk curtains, which Michael makes no attempt to open, a fitted thick cream carpet, two huge cream sofas with plump cushions, separated by a vast double-layered glass coffee table, TV remote controls underneath and glossy books on top. "History of Art", "Italian Journey", "Beatles Lyrics", and "Britain from the Air". The Beckstein grand in the bay window, echoes the shadowed black doorway to the church at Deuil.

Michael notices the silver is tarnished. Mrs Burgess is getting lazy, probably thinks, 'why bother without the mistress around.' He sighs, reflecting the elegance and comfort of his home no longer gives him pleasure. He lights a cigarette, a satisfying hostile action toward Nichola, who forbade smoking in this or any other room. Almost as satisfyingly hostile as having his Malaysian dancer Kiany, upstairs in the marital bed. He considers calling her, but realises she won't have received his postcard yet. Smoking is another reminder of his youth. Ioan had given him a packet of Fortunas last week. Eight left. Twelve smoked in six days. Six days in which he'd come to some major decisions. On the plane home he'd made a check list. He takes it out and studies it. On the top, the name of his lawyer.

1. Oliver. Get divorce.
2. Sell home. (No don't tick it off yet, he thinks.)
3. Put furniture into storage. Subdivided into
    a) Property to keep.
    b) Property to auction or give to N.

Yes, Ioan had offered to come and help over that.

'It's simple,' he'd said, 'You put blue dots on the stuff you want to keep – the good stuff – and red dots on the tat for her. You get them from Smith's. I'll come over, I'll sort you out.'

His remark had been the first indication to Michael their relationship might continue after Gran Canaria. They'd been playing tennis on the hotel courts. Ioan, the winner, lay at his feet in white shorts, his right ankle resting on his raised left knee. Michael sat on a bench, plucking his damp T-shirt away from his skin, and holding an iced glass of Citron Presse to his neck. 'Tat?' he replied, 'Actually, I don't possess much tat.'

'Actually,' laughed Ioan, 'that's all I do possess. I sit on a biscuit box, it all goes on me back!'

Michael grinned. That was worthy of Nichola. He idly wondered how she and Ioan would have got on. Probably have 'adored each other, darling.'

Ioan was gazing up at the clouds. 'So, Mike, tell me, whereabouts in London do you plan on living?'

Michael had a suspicion where this topic might lead. 'Near my Gallery. I have my eye on a penthouse in Pall Mall.'

'Bloody hell, Mike. You don't half live it large, that'll cost a bomb.'

'Well, leasehold. I have a studio in Brighton too, but that's more of a warehouse for paintings. I must have a place in town.'

'A shag pad!'

'Don't judge others by yourself,' and he lobbed a lump of sugar at him. 'Why do you ask?'

Ioan rescued the sugar lump from the grass and examined it, 'It's just that I have to find myself somewhere soon.' He popped the lump into his mouth and sucked it, saying, 'Course, I suppose it depends where I'm going to be able to study.'

'First, you find a University that'll take you. They'll probably have Halls of Residence. Unless we can persuade some firm to take you on as an apprentice. I have a chum, Daniel, he designed my gallery, I'll ask him.'

'Fab!'

'You'll land on your feet.' Michael gazed at his friend sucking the sugar lump, his Fred Perry shirt was untucked, revealing a perfect tummy button and downy hair on a smooth flat stomach.

Michael's strength, ironically, was his greatest weakness. He recognised and valued beauty, that was his job. Equally he was a sucker for a pretty face, and Ioan had a very pretty face. Probably because his emotions were raw, he was more susceptible, vulnerable, even. Time spent with Ioan, was time without Nichola in his head, he was actually forgetting her for hours on end. His slightly middle aged behavior was changing too, and not just because he was on holiday. With Ioan he was window shopping, visiting clothes shops, boutiques, record and CD stores, something he'd not done since before he was married. Ioan was encouraging an altogther more youthful outlook. It was exactly what he needed. Ioan was indeed the golden boy. But love's a funny thing, one can lose one's heart and still be aware there is something fundamentally flawed about the object of one's affections. Michael had sussed Ioan was after the main chance, suspected he was gay, knew he was flirting with him, but he was amused by it, flattered even, grateful for such a handsome young companion. He preferred not to meditate too long on the consequences. Nothing warned him he was in peril.

It was while he was watching Ioan lying before him crunching the sugar lump and trying to blow a note on a blade of grass between his thumbs, the notion of sponsoring him took root. The boy needs help, I am in a position to do so, he told himself. I can certainly afford to promote, even support him in his desire to become an architect, a noble ambition after all. I should be proud to contribute to education, scholarship, and if the University College of London or somewhere does an architectural degree course... 'If we can find an apprentice position,' he said, 'I might be able to help you out, financially, I mean. If that would make things easier. Hell, you could even come and keep me company in my new pad, if it comes to that. As a lodger, I mean, for a bit, if you're stuck. The Penthouse has three bedrooms.'

Ioan looked up at him. 'Mike, that is so decent of you.' He was half smiling, astonished, shaking his head in disbelief. 'I won't deny I could use the dosh but we hardly know each other. I appreciate the offer, honestly. But Hell! Living together. Maybe we should think that one through a bit.'

Michael knew what he meant. He shrugged. 'See how it works out. Let's go and shower. Get togged up for the cocktail hour.'

That night, after dinner and a drink in a tourist bar, it was so hot they'd gone down to the beach, taken off their clothes and had a midnight swim. Michael had felt something like a catch in his throat seeing Ioan naked in the moonlight.

Three days later, after more relaxing, giving the other tourists wicked nicknames, more swimming, tennis, dinners, conversations about movies and music, art and architecture, on their fifth and final day, they reached the crucial moment, the moment of no return.

The sun went in. Clouds appeared, so Michael booked a riding session. They galloped along the windy beach, passing the spot where they'd first met. Back in the hotel, returning to his room after taking a shower, Michael found Ioan lying on the bed watching television, only a towel round his waist. He had a look on his face, an expression, that reminded Michael of his daughter, Susan. He felt that catch in the throat again, a great tenderness toward the boy. Lying beside him, the tips of his fingers touched Ioan's thigh, an electric shock fizzed, flinching, he pulled his hand away, hoping Ioan hadn't noticed.

Ioan looked across, his cornflower blue eyes penetrating. To Michael's utter astonishment he leant over and kissed him on the lips.

Michael tensed and pushed him away. Holding his shoulders, he searched his face. Ioan's magic eyes calmly returned his gaze. In that moment, some force within, love, lust, memory, whatever, told him he wanted Ioan. Slowly without a word he drew him closer, their lips met, tantalisingly their flesh came together, swiftly becoming a hungry lustful embrace. Their naked bodies crushed into one another, driving Michael into frenzy. Every hair on his body was electrified. He couldn't stop. Never had he felt such excitement, such intensity, not even in the early days with Nichola. He felt himself bursting, wanting to be part of the boy, inside him.

Ioan gently withdrew. 'God! Mike! You're some kisser. Phew!' He sat up and turned the television volume off with the remote. 'Oh God! I've wanted this since day one.'

Michael reached to draw the boy back to him.

Ioan pulled away again. 'Mike. I have to tell you something. It's important. I'm H.I.V. positive.'

Michael stared, his heart sinking. He was appalled.

'I'm on medication, it's OK, don't worry. I'm quite healthy at the moment. But you should know. Especially if... I mean, you know, I mean, if you're serious about this sponsorship idea, when we get back home. I don't want it to spoil anything.'

Michael glared back, angry, unblinking, uncertain whether to confess, yes, it did spoil everything, or whether to retain his friendship and explain that sex was not a precondition of sponsorship. An explanation of which, this very second, he was not at all convinced he believed. 'No, no... Of course not,' he stammered, 'But... How long have you had this?'

'Over a year. That's why I'm so careful. I mean, about not having sex. I've been up for it since the beginning, but you understand why we can't, don't you? It's tough. You're such a terrific guy. I want to please you.' Touchingly he laid his head on Michael's shoulder.'

Michael froze, unsure what to do or say next.

Ioan kissed his neck and stroked his chest, gently fondling his nipples. 'I knew you'd understand. Safe sex only eh?'

After a moment, a tingling physical pleasure flooded him, Michael put his arm around Ioan's shoulder and held him, but he was still uncertain. Silently he gazed at the mute television. After a while he turned and looked into Ioan's eyes. 'These last days have been great.' He leant forward and kissed his lips softly, lovingly.

This time Ioan did not pull away.

After their passion had subsided, an animal contentment enveloped Michael and he fell asleep, his arms wrapped around Ioan's shoulders.

He was awoken by his lover dressed and smiling, whispering into his ear. 'Time to go, if I'm going to catch that plane.'

Michael drove him to the airport in silence. Awkwardly they held hands for a while, occasionally grinning at each other. For the remainder of the journey, Ioan's warm hand rested on the inside of Michael's thigh. At Las Palmas airport they embraced, 'Call me when you get back to UK,' said Ioan.

'I promise,' said Michael, 'the moment I get home.'

During the solitary hours that followed his departure, Michael was euphoric. In his head, joining Nichola and his two children, there was now Ioan. Maybe, he thought, this is it! Maybe, after all, Nichola really has done me a favour. Released me to be more myself. He'd heard stories, gossip about people in mid-life, changing sexuality after a bereavement or divorce. His gay experiences had not been as limited as he would have liked to confess. Minor larks at public school, a love relationship with a man when he was a student, albeit concurrent with a heterosexual affair he was conducting. Recently there had been a young painter he'd signed for whom he'd felt an attraction, it had coloured his judgement. Michael had covered the 'gay/bisexual' subject extensively with the witch of Maida Vale, who, in her dogmatic fashion had opined, 'The best people are bisexual. Shades of grey. Sexuality changes like phases of the moon. You are in a period of profound change. It could happen, why not?'

Well, a period of profound change it sure was! So enjoy it. Rule nothing out.

As he 'people-watched' in cafes and restaurants, he noticed there were no single attractive women about. The out-of-season tourists were exclusively young families or gay men, none of whom he found remotely attractive.

Drawn by a high decibel Liza Minnelli singing "Cabaret", he strolled into a gay bar. A tacky, noisy room in The Yumbo Centrum in Playa del Ingles. A middle-aged drag queen by the door greeted him. 'Evening Mr Stanhope.'

Michael was astonished at hearing his name.

A raddled beauty with raven locks, in a glitter frock and high heels, perched on a stool with a bottle of beer. 'I know you,' she said.

Mystified, Michael hesitated, frowning and smiling simultaniously. 'How?'

'In "Peter Jones".' She inhaled her cigarette a la Bette Davis. 'Yeahs, I've often served you. You must excuse all this.' She adjusted her skirt over a bony knee. 'I came over for Mardi Gras. Don't think I'll ever go back. I'm having a ball. Cheers!'

Michael grinned, ordered a drink at the horseshoe-shaped bar and looked around. Well, if I'm going to swing both ways, I suppose I'd better get used to this. Through the cigarette haze, he searched the faces at the bar. Fat hairy Germans with handlebar moustaches, pink sunburnt northern lads shrieked, Max Factored moustaches on painted queens, no one nearly as attractive as Ioan. No, he decided, I have nothing in common with anyone here. Amusing, but not for me. He left. And Ioan would have done the same, he thought.

Proving just how little he knew.

Mozart comes to an end. Michael glances at the last two items on his check list.

No 4. Buy lease of 62A, Pall Mall.

No 5. Call Daniel re taking on Ioan.

He glances at the silver framed photographs of his two daughters on the piano. He dials the eldest, Susan's mobile. Her recorded voice on the machine comforts him. He leaves a message. 'How about dinner next week?' He calls the Gallery. Joyce, his co-director answers and laughs in her delicious ginny voice as she recognises him.

'Darling, everything's fine. The last two paintings in the present collection finally sold... yes, blessed relief. Knew you'd be pleased. The new stuff's arrived, looks fabulous! We must have a hanging session over the weekend. Sue was in last week, she has a new boyfriend. Bit scruffy, a pop singer, darling. Do you have a tan? God, I'm jealous. London has been freezing. When will you be in? Fine. Sort out your house and furniture while you're still fresh. Quite understand. Don't get gloomy, remember I'm just on the end of the phone. Bye for now!'

Now, the moment he has been waiting for. He dials.

Chapter Eight

Pop!

Ioan, no longer the golden boy, his hair – on Maisie's instructions – now professionally returned to it's natural coal black, is merrily sodomising young Jonathan under a full-length poster of Marilyn Monroe.

His studio/bed sitting room, is the front room of a second floor, once grand, but now shabby terrace house off Notting Hill. It boasts state-of-the-art gadgets, an uplighter – at present off – an impressive CD collection, a large Victorian mirror, an ample wardrobe – stuffed with designer gear, mostly nicked from photo shoots – shoes that would do credit to Imelda Marcos, a black leather armchair, and a sofa bed, at present withstanding heavy duty. His tanned arse works away rhythmically, finally, as the boy's moans and piglet-like squeals of ecstasy reach a climax, his pumping action subsides.

'God!' says Ioan. 'You're the best ever.'

'I love you,' pants Jonathan, squeezing, kissing and hanging on to Ioan as he shoots cum over their conjoined flat stomachs. They rest silent and sticky, the beat of Fat Boy Slim's 'Fucking in Heaven' thumping from Ioan's Aiwa sound system.

'You were in rhythm,' giggles Jonathan.

'Great timing,' says Ioan, reaching for a towel by the bed. Removing the condom, he wipes up, and lights up a Fortuna. As he stretches back, the boy settles into the crook of his arm.

They lie cocooned in paradise. No hint, or shadow of danger

dims their mutual post-coital bliss.

'Okay?' murmurs Ioan.

'Wicked!' Jonathan, saliva glinting on his inflamed lips, snuggles up cub-like. After a minute, he suddenly remembers. 'Ioan,' he whispers, 'I've something to tell you.'

'Mmn?'

'I think my Mum found your photo.'

Ioan knows at once which photo. A finger of fear jabs him. 'Which one?'

'The nudie one.'

'Oh no! When?'

'Just before you went away.'

'Oh, God!'

'It was with some others, ones from 'Attitude', y'know, in the swimming costume, and stuff I'd cut from magazines. It was in my scrap book.'

'Scrap book?'

'My wank book.'

Ioan frowns at him.

'Well, other guys have pin ups. I have you. Anyway, it's gone.'

'Jonathan! Where was it? What did she say?'

'Nothing. It was under my mattress but I can't find it.' His cheek rests on Ioan's chest.

Ioan inhales his cigarette. 'You should have said.'

'I couldn't. Your Dad had just died. Anyway when you called and told me you were going away, Mum and Pop were in the room, I couldn't say then.'

'That's weeks ago, nearly a month.'

'Tell me about it. That's why I needed my wank book.'

'And she's not said anything?'

'Well, Pop said he didn't think you were a good influence. Said he'd prefer it if I didn't see you anymore.'

'Oh fuck! What did you say?'

'I said, OK.'

'Oh, thanks a bunch!'

Well, how's he to know when we see each other? Anyhow, they made me promise.'

'Babe!' Ioan kisses the top of his head. 'I thought she was a bit funny on the phone the other day.' He stubs his cigarette out on the bedside ashtray. 'Was she listening?'

'Don't think so. I told her you said your Mum had missed them at your Dad's funeral.'

'Is that why they didn't come?'

'Probably.'

'Oh fuck! How come you got away today, then?'

'I just came.'

'We know that, Squeeze! But where do they think you are?'

'On a school trip to the Dome.'

Ioan snorts, 'What are you like? They're bound to ask you about it.'

'I'll say I had a fantastic time and I'm totally fucked!'

Ioan leans over the boy. Looking into his eyes, he strokes his eyebrows, then ruffles his fringe. 'Sexy green-eyed truant.'

Jonathan wriggles with glee. 'Long as I'm on the 4.20 from Charing Cross Station with everyone else, it's sorted.'

Ioan stretches further over the boy to look at his watch on the table. 'Half past one. We've got three hours.'

'Fab,' says Jonathan and nibbles Ioan's nipple.

'Nooo don't!' he giggles 'it's sensitive.' They snuggle closer. 'Don't know when I'm going to get to Canterbury next. Mum's leaving "The Olive Branch", I'd have to stay in a hotel. Can hardly ask your Pop to put me up now. Do you really call him "Pop"?'

'He likes it. I can always come up here.'

'You be careful, now. I tell you what, if you do, I'll pay your train fare.'

'Yeah. Like a kept boy,' and he waggles his bum to the beat of Fat Boy. Ioan pulls up the sheet, Jonathan's creamy round arse fitting neatly into the palm of his hand.

The phone rings.

'Hold on,' says Ioan. 'Might be my agent. Hallo?'

'Hi there! Mike Stanhope here. I just got back from G.C. How's life?'

'Mike! Man! Great. Y'right?'

'Fine. Look, um, I'll come straight to the point, I'm sure you must be busy.'

'No, no, that's OK.' He feels Jonathan sliding down, taking his cock into his mouth. The boy is insatiable. 'Go ahead, go ahead.'

'About your kind offer to come and help me sort through the furniture.'

'Oh sure. Anytime.'

'I'm about to call Pickford's and wanted to check you're availability?'

'Whenever. Thursday or Friday.' With his free hand he tousles Jonathan's hair.

'Great, I'll fix it for Thursday, then. If I encounter any problem I'll get back to you. You have the address?'

'Give it to me again.' His hand leaves Jonathan's head to pick up a biro by the phone and scribbles on a pad. 'Got it.'

'Nine o'clock too early?'

'No. Nine on Thursday's fine. Cheers, Mike.' Ioan replaces the receiver. Jonathan stops working and peers over the sheet.

'Who's Mike?'

'Some millionaire I met. Wants to sponsor my studies. You're not the only kept boy!'

'Millionaire? Wow! What did you have to do?' and he applies just a little pressure to Ioan's balls.

'Nothing. Ow! Stop squeezing, you tart.'

Jonathan holds on. 'Tell me. What did you do?' he repeats, still squeezing.

'Nothing, he's ancient.' Half laughing, Ioan squeals, 'Nothing. He was married.' Jonathan releases him. 'That hurt, you bastard! He only took me for a couple of dinners. His wife had just dumped him.

'Bet you had him?'

'I did not! I hate old men.' Fat Boy Slim comes to an end. 'Not that he didn't try it on.'

Ioan's reinterpreted version of events suddenly seems important, said, as it was, without a musical accompaniment.

'What did you do?' says Jonathan.

'I told him I had AIDS.' They look each other in the eye and slowly grin. 'So shut up,' says Ioan, 'and carry on sucking!'

Jonathan slides down again.

As Ioan lies back, he thinks he hears movement outside in the hall, possibly Polly home early. Not that she would ever come in, but he hadn't bothered to lock his door, better do so now, he thinks, but Jonathan is doing so well, it seems a pity to stop him.

'Ioan, are you in?' It's Polly's voice, followed by a knock, 'There are some men outside who want to see you.'

The door opens and in marches Colonel Charles Court-Smythe, bristling military pomposity. He looks around, furious. Taking in Ioan and the bed, he thunders, 'Where is my son?' Three policemen follow him, the last one addresses Polly in the hall, 'Thank you, Miss,' and shuts the door.

'Yes, thank you, Poll,' calls out Ioan, 'So kind!' The astonishing sight of three uniformed policemen, plus the father of his fellatio-loving friend in his room at this precise moment in time is surreal. Almost laughing in disbelief, he regards the faces lined up by his bed. He recognises one. The officer with a peaked cap and white moustache is a friend of his Dad's from the pub in Canterbury, it's Geoffrey White, The Chief Constable of Kent, and, as it turns out, Jonathan's godfather.

Colonel Court-Smyth, his eyes screwed up and glinting with blood lust, stands four square at the bottom of the bed. Not for nothing did his grandfather fight The Boers in 1900. 'We know he's here,' he roars. 'We have a trace on him.'

Jonathan's head peeps over the top of Ioan's sheet. 'Pop!'

The Colonel's eyes indeed pop. Unable to contain the sight, they rapidly shut in horror. Pink with rage, he bawls, 'Get out of there this instant!'

Jonathan peers about, he spots his godfather. 'Uncle Geoffrey! Why are you here?'

'Get dressed,' orders The Chief Constable, staccato.

Jonathan shrinks back against Ioan.

The livid Colonel strides round the bed and reaches over to grab his son's arm. 'Will you get out of there!'

'Ouch! That hurt,' yelps Jonathan pulling away. His movement causes his father to momentarily lose his balance. He topples helplessly over onto the bed. For one gloriously bizarre moment the Colonel's face is squashed onto Ioan's naked chest.

Dreamlike, Ioan says, 'Do you mind!'

Embroilment ensues. Simultaneously the Colonel fights to gain his balance and his son. Jonathan and Ioan attempt to avoid him. The soldier recovers his balance, but in vain his son or his dignity. He snorts with venom. Glaring, he wipes away the nauseous sweat of Ioan's flesh from his face and hands with a pocket handkerchief. 'You vile paederast! I'll see you in prison for this.' Turning even pinker, he shouts at his son, 'Will you get out of there. Get dressed!'

Ioan, his arm protectively round Jonathan's shoulder, regards them all. 'Better do as he says.'

Jonathan sheepishly scrambles out of bed toward his clothes. The police officers take in his nudity, and turn their accusing eyes back on Ioan. The Chief Constable says, 'You too,' then nods at his subordinates. Immediately they commence opening drawers, cupboards and searching the bookshelves. Ioan guesses what they are after. It's not much, but in his Dad's old tobacco tin on the second shelf, behind 'Japanese Mythology' and 'Kings and Queens of England' is a chunk of marijuana, with it, in a Vitamin E carton, some ecstasy tablets. He'd never shared or even shown these to Jonathan, so, he guesses, this must be standard practice when arresting poofs. The Colonel growls, 'Hurry up,' to his son, then drags him half-dressed out of the room. Ioan gets out of bed and puts on his underpants, a sweatshirt and jeans. By the time he's tying up the laces on his sneakers, one of the cops has found 'Japanese Mythology' and is smelling the contents of Dad's tobacco tin.

'So what now?' says Ioan, resigned to the inevitable.

The cop glances meaningfully up at Uncle Geoffrey, who nods and silently exits, following the Colonel and Jonathan out of the room. The cop turns to Ioan, grasping his arm he says, 'I am arresting you for buggery of a minor, and possession with intent to supply Class 'A' drugs. Anything you say will be taken down and used in evidence.'

Ioan can't think of anything to say, he decides silence is best. He lowers his head and bites his lip. To his astonishment the cop suddenly grabs his hands and clamps on handcuffs. They're surprisingly heavy. Confounded, he looks at the cop, who shoves him out into the hall. Polly is standing by the front door holding it open. He meets her eyes. She looks away. He passes her without a word.

Polly sighs and closes the front door, shutting her eyes with relief.

Finding three uniformed policemen on her doorstep when she'd come home had horrified her. Her father, an eminent Q.C., had bought her the flat for her twenty-first birthday. He had given her three pieces of advice on leaving school; a) Never travel on the Underground without a ticket; b) Never get caught smoking dope; c) Co-operate with the police at all times. The latter she had just done.

Ioan's bedroom door is ajar. With feline curiosity she peers in. The room has been ransacked. Drawers and cupboards are open, clothes spill out, the bed is unmade, chaos everywhere. She steps over the mess toward the window. Peeking through the Venetian blind she spots the heads of the two white-haired gentlemen holding the boy in school uniform. They're climbing into the back of a police car. Then Ioan appears sandwiched between the two policemen. They push him into the back of a second police car. Both cars drive away.

She shivers and turns into the room. If Ioan were to be sent to prison, she thinks, what should we do with all this gear? The baby is due in August. Be nice to have a nursery ready in time. Do it all out in Laura Ashley. That would cosy it up. Make it look super. She notices a name and address on the phone pad by the bed and tears it off. Might come in handy.

Chapter Nine

Family Secret

Rosie is gazing out of the pottery window contemplating the arrival of her deceased husband's illegitimate daughter. Her breath mists over the window pane. She writes "R" with her forefinger and watches the haze evaporate, leaving her initial still visible in the dust. 'What the hell have I got myself into?' she asks Liz, who she blames for having got her there. 'I should never have allowed you to talk me into inviting her. The wretched girl's an heiress.'

Liz makes no reply. She is absorbed in the act of throwing a pot, and with wet creative hands is moulding a lump of clay into some, as yet, mysterious shape on her potter's wheel.

Rosie glares at the damp fields ahead, the rain has stopped, patches of sunlight drift across the folds of land, in the distance she can dimly make out the horizon line of the Atlantic Ocean. She turns the R in the dust into a circle, then with her palm she wipes it clear. She perks up. 'Oh look. A rainbow.'

'Where?' Liz cranes round to see. 'Ah, isn't that lovely! A good omen.'

'I wish. I must be mad. This creature has our savings, everything we inherited from Dave's grandfather, I've barely enough to keep body and soul together, and here we are offering her hospitality! At least, you are. I could wring that bloody David's neck.'

Liz peers over her glasses. 'Now, you know you don't mean that.'

'I bloody do!'

'Anyway, she's a child. Be interesting to get to know her.'

'Oh Liz, really! Not this rich one, thank you very much.'

'Be good for your karma.' Liz wets her hands. 'Besides, you must be curious to know her birthday.'

'Oh, don't! It's all a huge mistake. I must be dotty.'

'You are, cariad,' says Liz. 'You've become a worry guts.'

Rosie turns with a reluctant sigh and folds her arms. She watches the clay on the wheel transform. 'I'd have thought I'd have been the last person she'd have wanted to see. Why me?'

Liz presses down hard, drawing the sides in and upward. 'Because you are the Mother she never had. As,' and here she lowers her voice, 'she is the daughter you never could have.'

'Trust you to mention the unmentionable.'

The unmentionable, was the stillborn baby daughter Rosie had lost twenty-six years ago, the fatal cause of an early hysterectomy. After a reflective moment, Rosie says, 'How you do that always amazes me.'

'Anyway, she sounded rather fun,' says Liz.

It was Liz who had answered Julie's phone call that morning, and given her directions from Penzance. Rosie had made up a clean bed, and in order to keep herself busy, had made an apple pie. A proper Delia affair, with cinnamon, lemons and cloves. But neither the voice on the telephone, nor the photo from David's wallet, prepared either sister for Julie's actual arrival.

At four o'clock, as Liz is placing her fifth identical vase onto the wooden pallet, distant mechanical thunder echoes. Sal barks and scampers to the front door sending the hall mat flying. The sisters exchange looks and scuttle after her, Liz drying her hands on her apron.

A roaring Kawasaki Ninja motorbike tears through the village. Sunlight trembles on the cottage windows and teacups shake in their saucers. With a loud crescendo of sound the bike careers into the driveway of The Old Vicarage, its skidding tyres sending shingle flying. The engine is turned off. Silence. Rosie and Liz stand hypnotised under the front porch. Even Sal seems intimidated. Birds resume singing.

A sinister leathered figure alights. As it removes a crash helmet and shakes out a mane of flame-coloured curls – it is no exaggeration to say, she causes a sensation. Good God! thinks Rosie, a punk with purple lipstick and a ring through her eyebrow.

'Which o'yo's Rosie?' says the creature in a broad Yorkshire accent.

Attempting to cover her astonishment, Rosie overcompensates with a too wide grin. 'I am.'

'Well, I've arrived!' says Julie walking over and grabbing her in a bear-hug kiss.

'Whoops!' says Rosie regaining her balance. 'Welcome.'

'And this is y'sister,' Julie states, turning to Liz and doing exactly the same to her. Sal jumps up barking. 'And who are yous then?'

'Sal, get down!' shouts Liz, 'Get down! That's Sal.'

'Hi y' Sal! Look, same colour hair! A relation!'

Rosie laughs weakly. A relation indeed! Her hair is exactly the same colour as David's used to be. "Carrot head," had been his school nickname.

'Nice bike,' says Liz, grinning.

'Don't you luv it?' says Julie, balancing her helmet on the seat and unstrapping a bag from the back. 'Only got her last week. I'bin longin' f'one f'ages. Only taken me five hours door to door.'

'Just as long as I don't have to get on it,' says Liz, laughing. 'I prefer something less bracing myself!'

Rosie can't take her eyes off the girl. There's no mistaking the genes. She has David's face too, just the way he looked as a boy at Coed Y Lang Comprehensive.

Julie seems as fascinated by Rosie. 'Look at yous' eyes. What a colour! It's only Sharon bloody Stone! No wonder m'Dad stuck with you.' She suddenly yelps, 'Of course, I must paint you! Wouldn't that be great? Could I do that? Would you let me? Oh, please say you would?'

'Hold on, hold on,' says Rosie, not to be flustered. 'Can I carry something?'

'I brought me paints. Look.'

'Here, let me,' says Liz, relieving her of a paint-stained box and her helmet. 'This way. Follow me.' She leads them in single file away from the house, along the footpath under the trees. 'We've put you in one of the chalets.'

Sal follows too, swishing her tail against the tall grass.

'What a fantastic place this is,' says Julie, looking around with inquisitive chumminess. 'Ee, look at bluebells.'

Walking behind her, Rosie is unsure whether to be relieved or not, she may only be a child, but her earthy vitality is terrifying.

They show Julie her chalet, then wander over to the swimming pool.

'Ee, smashing!' Julie zips open her leather top.

'Would you like a swim?' asks Liz.

'Not brought me costume.'

'Not a problem. There're some in the changing room.' Turning to her sister she asks grinning, 'Fancy a dip, dear? Shall we all go in?'

On impulse they do, Rosie for the first time during her stay. All girls together, splashing and laughing. It's fun, invigorating. Rosie enjoys the sudden exercise and swims a length crawl-style. She becomes aware that Julie is swimming alongside her. It turns into a race to the other end. Rosie wins, arriving slightly ahead. She feels childishly pleased, the physical effort helps to dissolve her apprehension.

In the kitchen, Rosie opens a bottle of Nuit St George and raises her glass in a toast. 'Welcome.'

'To our side of the family,' completes Liz.

As the sisters prepare a prodigal dinner, Julie helps laying the kitchen table and lights a pair of candles. The sisters' kitchen teamwork, automatic since girlhood, produces succulent roast lamb, stuck with garlic, rubbed in rock salt, with redcurrant jelly, mint sauce, spinach, sprouts and roast potatoes. Rosie's apple pie is the pudding. David's name is not mentioned, the sisters exchanging only the merest glance at the disclosure of the girl's star sign, Gemini, and age, sixteen. They laugh a good deal, and agree to call Julie by her nickname 'Red'. Finally, egged on by Liz, Rosie surrenders to the girl's virtual demand to sit for a portrait.

The following morning Liz sets off on one of her missions, accompanied by Sal in the back of her Volvo, leaving Rosie and 'Red' alone.

Together they make their way past the laurel bushes, in bud and about to bloom, and into the garden studio. Sunlight pours through a high sloping window. Rigged up against a brick wall hangs a heavy faded red velvet curtain. In front of it, on a low rostrum stands a worn Victorian chaise longue. 'Bloody hell!' says Julie, carrying her canvas and brushes. 'Looks like sommat out of "Dorian Grey".'

'You do me a portrait like his, dear, I'll be your friend for life!'

'We're gonna be friends for life anyways,' says Red, fixing her canvas to an easel. Her carrot curls are tied up in a yellow bandana, over her jeans she wears a mysterious purple top.

'Now where,' asks Rosie, making a bee line for the chaise, 'would you like me?' Tucking a stray lock of hair into her French pleat, she sits cross-legged, poised. Dressed in a soft navy trouser suit with white at the throat and wrists – as advised by Joan Crawford in Mam's "Life Stories of the Stars", which, as a girl had been her bible – she twists one navy-blue high-heeled ankle this way and that, matching the movement to her profile, left, right and centre. The idea of having her portrait painted would seem to have caught fire, but this is only half true, for in the pit of her stomach she has a gnawing pain that has something to do with David, being alone with his daughter, and fear of what might transpire. 'Where should I look?' she says, for she has made up her mind, in Ioan's jargon to "cool it."

'At me,' says Red. 'Look, this is not gonna be some realistic shit, you know. I don't paint that way. Background's no matter to me. That's all old-fashioned crap. Just be so as you's comfortable. Just stand, natural like. You're of today, woman!'

'Well,' says Rosie, feeling her "cool" blown, and most unlike a woman of today, 'you're the artist.'

'Got sommat blue? Colour of your eyes? Earrings or necklace?'

'I've got a T-shirt upstairs.'

'Better!'

'Hold on a mo,' says Rosie and vanishes.

Five minutes later she's back. Red instructs her to stand by the chaise longue, and she takes up her position. The cornflower blue T-shirt looks less showy and indeed emphasises her eyes, which are twinkling with laughter. Rosie is having a fit of the giggles, 'Sorry,' she says. 'This whole situation is so bizarre. It's hysteria.'

'Y'daft, woman. Don't look me in't eye, I can't concentrate. Look over me shoulder.' Red's own eyes are firmly focused on her canvas.

Red's professional manner pulls Rosie up. She stands upright taking deep breaths, trying not to feel self-conscious and persuading herself she is indulging a child. With hands clasped and eyes gazing at a clay pot on a shelf behind Red's hair, she says, 'I don't know if I can stand like this for long.'

'Take off your shoes.'

'Maybe I will.' She removes her high heels, placing them neatly under the chaise.

'Think I'll do y' blonde. A nice bright yellow. I like yellow. Did you ever go blonde?'

'I used to be blonde when I was your age. Yours is a lovely colour.'

'I help it along a wee bit.'

'My hairdresser's name is Betty Haag. I was going to see her the other day.' She stops, not wanting to remind herself, or Red, of the way, or the day, David died. But, she thinks, we're going to have to talk about him sometime.

'Betty Haag. Great name,' says Red. 'I'll do it for you if you like. Get a kit from the chemist, dye it proper. Make us look a right couple of tarts!' She gives an uninhibited hoot of laugher.

'What a tonic she is, thinks Rosie. Tentatively she says, 'Red, do you think we could talk about David?'

'Sure. I'd like to. But only if you want to.'

'Now we've broken the ice, I think we should try.'

But neither speak.

After a while, Rosie says, 'Did you... how can I put this? Did you always know he was your father?'

'Oh yeah. He came t'house when I was wee. Gran said he gave her some cash. He used to send me postcards.'

'Really? When did you... first get to know him?'

'When I was about six, seven. First I remember was when I came out of school. He took Gran and me to tea in a posh hotel. Told me 'e opened a bank account for me, savings, you know. First of the month, 'undred pounds.'

Rosie swallows hard. The bugger! She recalls David's eyes looking into hers, deceiving her, over dinners, over pillows, over years.

'Sorry. Does it upset yous... to know that?'

'It's a surprise, certainly,' says Rosie, playing bright. If she's sixteen, she calculates, then when she was six... that was when Ioan left Dulwich College. School fees stopped and times were easier. We'd given up the Croydon pub and moved to Canterbury. David inherited his great-grandfather's money about then, too, about the same time he must have made his Will. But why give so much to this girl?

Rosie had known why, of course, deep down, right at the beginning, sitting there in the solicitor's office in Herne Bay with Ioan beside her. The twin surge of horror that had flooded her mind on hearing that David not only had an illegitimate daughter, but that he'd left her the bulk of his estate. There would barely be enough left to live on. The wondering why. Then the dawning of suspicion, then the comprehension. But how could he have known? He would never have cut her out of his Will on a hunch, a mere guess. Liz was the only person in the world who may have guessed the truth and she would never have told him. If she had, and she never would have, then David's Will was retribution. On top of a hundred pounds a month for ten years! Rosie needed no calculator, after years behind a counter pounding a till her maths was instant, twelve thousand pounds. She disguises her thoughts with a smile. 'He must have loved you a great deal.'

'No,' says Red. 'That I don't fool meself. More like guilty conscience. Thought m'be that was one of the things you could tell me. Why d'y think 'e did it? Leave me all that dosh? Didn't you two 'ave a good relationship?'

How to answer such a question? One she'd been dreading. How do you explain twenty-eight years of marriage to a child? What's the point of raking up the bad times? They'd finished up happily enough. Yet her perception of their time together was refuted in the face of such tangible or rather intangible evidence to the contrary. Rosie keeps her bright smile firm. 'Yes, very,' she answers. It rings false. 'Leastwise,' she adds, 'that's what I thought. Dave was a dear. Oh, difficult, unimaginative, a typical man. A man's man. Football mad! But,' she says with a shrug, as if it explained everything, 'he was my childhood sweetheart. My one and only boyfriend.' She checks herself. No, no, that's going too far. Untrue and an insult to the others. For a moment the ghost of a certain boy's face flits across her memory, she can't recall the features exactly, but she remembers his name, the other one too, the teacher who emigrated to Canada. 'To answer your question,' she resumes, 'and it's one I've asked myself every day since, I don't really know.' Staring unseeing at the cluttered shelves on the studio wall opposite, some subconscious thought bubbles up. Without her deciding to vocalise it, she absently breathes the word, 'Retribution.'

'Retribution?' frowns Red. 'What's that? Like revenge?'

Horrified she's opened Pandora's box, Rosie improvises.

'Well, after all, David sacrificed a good deal to educate Ioan. Paying Public School fees was a big drain on us. Especially after the mines closed, and he lost his job. Do you realise there were a hundred and thirty thousand men without jobs in Wales in 1982. It was a terrible time. He had no work. We had to move away. He had to accept some job with the Liverpool Victoria in Croydon. By then, of course, Ioan was at school age. He started at Dulwich College when he was twelve...' The realisation hits Rosie afresh. That was when this girl she was posing for must have been conceived. She'd worked it out with Liz in front of the Aga last night after dinner. 'And all that time you,' she continues, 'his own flesh, were in greater need.' She hesitates, worried she's drawn attention to some disparity in their class. But Red either hasn't noticed, or doesn't care. Ridiculous, thinks Rosie, now our financial status is so completely reversed. 'After Ioan was born,' she says, obfuscating, 'David and I could never have children. Oh, it was my fault.' She strengthens her voice, attempting to cover up her emotional turmoil. 'Maybe he simply thought he'd given Ioan and me enough. Maybe he simply thought, now it's your turn.'

'Aye. M'be. I'm not complaining, mind. I think it's fun-fucking-tastic! But I know for you it's...'

'Right,' says Rosie, determined to shake away her introspection. 'For me it's...' she gaily raises her eyes to heaven. 'You would not believe!'

'Are you 'ard up?'

Rosie's facade drops. Oh dear. Did I overdo that? 'Well,' she says, 'I don't quite know yet.'

'Ow d'y' mean? You must know that.'

'I mean, I don't quite know yet... what I'm going to do. What work? Obviously I have to find myself a job, and somewhere to live. I can't sponge off Liz forever.'

'Bloody 'ell! Aven't you got a home, a flat or sommat?'

'No. We were tenants in the pub we ran.'

'Are you telling me you've not got 'owt?'

'Well...' Rosie shuts her eyes and gives up. '*Owt* about covers it. More or less. Look,' she says, suddenly feeling queasy, 'do you mind if I sit down?' and she sinks onto the chaise.

Red watches her for a moment. 'Y'know, I could let you 'ave some cash if you like. To tide you over, like.' With the stem of her paint brush she scratches her scalp. Returning to the canvas, she grins. 'Might have to give you a monthly allowance. Like he did me. That would be a turn-up, eh?'

Rosie looks in disbelief. The girl seems serious. What a thing! This punk rocker child is offering me help. She feels tears pricking. I can't accept, I can't possibly. But how can I afford not to? Ioan was right. I'm going to have to fill him in on all this. 'I couldn't. Really,' she says, 'I couldn't. Thanks, but...'

'It's done. Forget it. I'll get the lawyer, Mr Nicholls, to fix it up. If yous' always 'ad money, you'll miss it more than me. I've never 'ad it to miss.'

Stepping off the rostrum, Rosie puts her hands on Red's shoulders and looks her in the eye. 'You are a very, very generous and special person.' She kisses her. 'David would have been proud of you.' She wonders suddenly if that's true. 'On the other hand, he did want you to have it.'

'Yeah, well,' says Red, 'I'd feel better if you 'ad sum.'

'I don't deny it would help... just for a while, until...' uncertain when 'until' will be, she stops. 'Thank you. I'm truly grateful.' Turning back to resume her place she sees the canvas that until then has been hidden from her. 'Good God! Whatever's that?'

On the easel appears an incomplete cartoon. A navy-suited figure with gaudy yellow hair, bright blue eyes, and pink face and hands, on a background of purple and green scribble. To Rosie it looks like a child's effort hanging in a classroom.

'I think,' says Red, 'I'll put meself in, smaller, on t'other side. Here, like,' she indicates the area. 'What d'you think?'

Rosie is speechless. 'Sorry, I just wasn't expecting... Red, I know nothing about art. Liz is the one. She'll tell you.' She peers closer. 'I can see, though, that face does have a kind of expression of mine... a sort of...'

'You'd better like it, mate, 'else I'll cut you off without a penny!' Red roars with laughter, elbowing Rosie in the ribs. 'It's bloody brilliant woman! 'Ave to keep on the right side of me now, y'know. When it's finished they'll think we're mother and daughter. I'll call it "Family Secret", cause that's what I was, wasn't I?'

'Not anymore, you're not. You're moving way into the open.'

'Get back up where you was. Just for a wee bit longer.'

Rosie obeys. 'I'll have to tell my Ioan all about you.'

'Y'son, I know. He's a hunk! Dad showed me his picture once in a mag.'

'So you said in your letter. I'm surprised. They never really hit it off.'

'Why was that, then?'

'They were just, different. It was, well, a sadness.' Busy with her thoughts, she remains silent.

Red daubs. 'Shall I get to meet him?'

'I hope so. He'll probably come down soon. Stay a weekend.'

'It's funny, it's like I've got this new posh family suddenly. You and Liz, now 'im. Always fancied 'avin a big brother.'

'Oh, so did I.' Rosie considers confiding to Red the vicissitudes of having a bossy older sister. Instead she asks, 'Do you have a boyfriend?'

'Well,' Red flutters her eyebrows. 'Play the field, y'know. Anyhow, now I'll 'ave Ioan!'

Rosie's lips part, half in astonishment, half in amusement at this gaudy dragonfly girl.

'Well, half brothers,' says Red. 'That's allowed n't it?'

'No! It certainly is not. And before you get too excited,' says Rosie, 'he's gay.'

'Thought so. Wouldn't stop me!' Her exuberant laugh explodes again.

Can this girl be serious? thinks Rosie. She's making me feel older by the minute.

As Red studies Rosie's face, she says, 'Does 'im being that way upset yous?'

Rosie does not feel like going down that road. Enigmatically she inclines her head.

'It's nowt to be gay in Leeds. How did y'find out?'

'Red, do you mind? I'd rather not discuss this.'

'Why, did you find him in bed with someone?'

'Good Lord, don't! No, no.' With a reluctant sigh she says, 'He told me.'

'How?'

'Red! Really.'

'Well, how did he say it? It's interesting. I mean, how d'y tell your Mum that?'

Oh dear. This was one conversation Rosie had tried to forget and been in denial about for years. She'd never mentioned it even to her Lesbian friend Lily in "The Olive Branch", least of all repeated it to David. With his almost daily homophobic jokes, she knew just what his reaction would have been. Once only, with Liz one evening, when they'd been watching a television soap opera with a gay character, and Liz had said, 'It wouldn't surprise me if Ioan was gay,' had she confided Ioan's confession. Liz had shrugged, told her the world had moved on since their Mam's day, and if she didn't want to lose Ioan, she'd best be more open-minded. In the last eleven years she felt she'd achieved that, nevertheless it was still not something she liked to brag about. But here, standing before this purple-lipped punk, it dawned on her just how ancient she must appear. So, as they seemed to be on some sort of truth-telling jag, Rosie allows herself to remember.

'He was sixteen,' she says. 'It was a Sunday afternoon. We were alone in the living room listening to a concert on the radio. David was out at his billiards. Ioan was reading a book. I'd just asked him something about a girlfriend of his, and...'

'He has girlfriends, then?'

'Lots. Well, sometimes. I don't know. He said he would never make me a grandmother. I didn't understand him at first. Then he said, "Ma, I must tell you something. I'm gay." Just like that. My heart sank. Oh, I'm not proud of my reaction. I did not behave well. I should have told him I loved him no matter what. But I didn't. I cried. I regret that. Now, I hope I'm wiser. Well, you read so much about it in the papers, don't you? There are programmes on television. I hope to God I'm not that bigoted. But back then, it was, well, fear, I suppose. Ignorance. A confirmation of what I'd dreaded. There'd always been something sweet, gentle about him. There still is. I don't mean effeminate, he's not like that, not in the least. But he was never what his father wanted, a little tough-boy type for him to play football with, though he's a fine athlete, beats me at tennis every time. He used to be the cutest little boy you ever saw. He told me not to be unhappy because another woman would never come between us.'

Red has listened quite still. Now she returns to her canvas. 'Did you tell me Dad at all?'

'Good heavens, no. It would not have gone down very well, believe you me. He would have hit the proverbial ceiling. Your oh-so-generous Dad was a most conventional Welshman.'

'I'm living proof he wasn't,' says Red.

Rosie clenches her teeth. 'Mm. Well. Maybe it was me who was the conventional one.'

'Ah, that's old-fashioned crap! Y'not still prejudiced, are you?'

Their eyes meet for a second, Rosie glances away. 'Well, I'm hardly ecstatic about it. He'll not stand much chance of happiness. But you're right, it's a generation thing, the way I was brought up. It was only in a little backwater in Wales. When I first went into show business, heavens! was that an eye opener.'

'You were in show business?'

'Only in the chorus, for one summer season. Before I married.'

'Tell us about it.'

Relieved to be off the topic of Ioan's sexuality, she submits to another memory, a memory with an even deeper emotional undertow. 'Well, it was wonderful. Best time of my life. I was the youngest in the dressing room, and, golly, did I have to grow up quickly. First time away from home.' Rosie covers her face with her hands, she had long ago realised this period as a turning point of her life. 'I had dreams of dancing in musicals and films, but I also wanted children and a family. They didn't quite go together. At least, your Dad didn't think so. I was just a small town girl, never smart like you.'

'Don't believe that. Anyways, I'm not smart.'

'Well, streetwise. Isn't that the expression?'

Red blushes at what she takes as a compliment. 'You sorry ye gave up show biz?'

'Oh yes. Really regret it. Even more so now I don't know how I'm going to earn a crust. I was wondering, maybe I could be someone's cook. I'm a good cook.'

'Wish you'd teach me,' says Red.

'You're on. I will. Of course, back then, I had little Ioan to look after. It was a lovely time, grand, I loved that. Your Dad was a proper toff in those days, very important, he was. Managed the coal pit at Ty Mawr. Very well thought-of, he was. A good man.' The pain in the pit of her stomach heaves. 'He was good to me, he was,' her lip trembles. 'I did love him... so much, so very...' Her thoughts scramble and contradict her words. He couldn't have loved me, though. How could he, to do what he did? She swallows, trying to rid herself of the lump in her throat. Damn you, David, damn you. Choking back tears, she says, 'I'm sorry. I don't know what's the matter with me.' She searches for her handkerchief. 'He was always so steady... took care of me...' The dam bursts. All the emotions she's been trying to bottle up for the past weeks flood, cascade over. Her body shakes beyond her control and she sinks onto the chaise longue, weeping.

Red watches helpless. 'It's me, isn't it?'

'No, no,' says Rosie between sobs. 'Well, perhaps. Just a bit. Nothing personal. Just the fact of you. I'm so sorry, I didn't mean for this to happen. I can't seem to find a hankie.'

Red holds out an oily rag. 'Sorry, it's all I've got.'

Rosie looks at it. 'It's covered in paint!'

'Try this.' Red unties the yellow kerchief from her hair.

Rosie accepts with a quick smile, 'Ta,' and blows her nose.

The girl rubs Rosie's shoulders. 'He was a good man to us both,' she says. 'Think of it like that. Do you want to talk about it some more?'

Rosie is on the verge of confessing everything. Indeed, since the reading of the Will, her conscience has nearly burst. But no. Secrets are best kept. Yet, what's the point of keeping a secret when the person you have to keep it from is dead? Habit? No, no, it would achieve nothing and only give pain. 'It's a long story,' she says, mopping up her tears. 'Another day perhaps.' She blows her nose again and forces herself to smile. 'I'll keep this. I'll put it in the washing machine.' She decides she feels better for her cry. Thought I was tougher than that. Whatever's the matter with me? This widow business seems to have left me so weedy. Looking up she says, 'Sorry. Shall we have another go?'

Red gently smiles. 'If you're sure you're up for it.'

'Quite sure. I've got a grip. Promise.'

Artist and model resume their places. After a while Red starts to hum. Probably trying to dispel the atmosphere, thinks Rosie.

'Tell me,' says Red, 'has Ioan got a boyfriend?'

'Good heaven's, no! At least, I don't think so. We don't discuss that kind of thing.' Unsure she would enjoy such an intimacy, she changes the subject. 'I do know he has the possibility of an Australian trip coming up. He's saving to study architecture, says he's had enough of modelling.'

'Can't wait to meet 'im,' Red's eyes glint as if anticipating chocolate.

'He has this crazy idea of finding himself a wealthy sponsor to finance his studies, and to my utter amazement,' she adds, lowering her voice, in a characteristic she shares with Liz, 'he tells me he's actually found one!'

But at that moment, three hundred and twenty miles away in West London Magistrate's Court, the very last thing on Ioan's mind is architecture or his wealthy sponsor.

Chapter Ten

In the Dock

Like a dark Satanic angel, Ioan stands taut, tight, waiting in the dock. Dressed carefully in his matte black Armani suit, black shirt, black silk Ted Baker tie, his hair cut short and spiked with gel, he is motionless, apart from a slight dilation of the nostrils. The three Magistrates confer. Two elderly men and a pretty looking woman in dove grey and pearls. She studies him before whispering something to her fellow J.Ps. He recognises the look, it's the way all women look at him.

Inside, his stomach churns, it hasn't stopped for three days. Not since Colonel Court-Smyth aka 'Pop', swanned into the bedroom with the entire bloody Police force, hauled Jonathan bollock-naked out of bed, searched the room and found the stash. Three days spent wrecked. Avoiding Polly and James, drinking too much, clubbing by night, sleeping in cinemas by day. Three days since the shitty hours spent in Notting Hill Cop Shop. 'Tilly Truncheon' impressing the hell out of Uncle Geoffrey. The finger-printing, the mug shots – 'Hold this number. Face the wall'... – the DNA sample taken. The questions:

When did you first assault the boy?

How many times did you bugger him?

Where did you get sixteen ecstasy tablets?

Where did you get the cocaine?

Where were you going to sell it?

And down the corridor, Jonathan – some medico up his arse

no doubt, probing, examining. Uncle Geoffrey and bloody Pop, moral rectitude erect, making him say God knows what. What the hell had he said? What could he have said, poor sod? Two cops, Pop and the Chief Cunt of Kent had all but seen him giving head!

Ioan was facing four charges of Indecent Assault over six months and Possession with intent to supply Class A drugs. The duty solicitor, a tall, prematurely balding young man only a few years older than himself, had explained he did not at this stage have to enter a plea of either 'Guilty' or 'Not guilty.'

But Ioan knew the law, knowledge he'd picked up in fashion house changing rooms around the world. He knew that if the case went to a higher court, he might have to wait six months for a trial, where he could be given either five years for gross indecency, ten years for indecent assault, or life for buggery.

The Magistate in the middle turns and speaks.

'Your case will now be sent for trial to the Criminal Crown Court.' In that second Ioan's heart plummets, he realises his life has changed forever. He barely hears or comprehends what follows. 'Your preliminary hearing date will be in two weeks' time, that is on the 17th April. I am remanding you on bail with one condition. Not to contact Jonathan Court Smyth or any of his immediate family.'

'You may stand down,' says the clerk.

In the corridor he politely thanks the solicitor, who confirms he will accompany Ioan on the 17th April, and reminds him of the conditions of bail.

Outside on the steps, the air still has a morning freshness. It's only just turned 10.30am. He takes in a deep breath and switches on his mobile.

Two days ago he'd left a message on Jonathan's pager. 'Courage! An extra big up. Chill, man. Call me. Luv Ioan.' But he'd had no reply. They probably had the poor little bugger locked up in the family manse.

'You have three messages,' says the recorded operator. He presses No. 1.

'Ioan! Call me,' is all the voice says. He recognises it as Maisie, his agent at 'Models Incorporated'. He calls back. She has a 'shoot' for him on Monday morning. He takes down the details. 'Any news on the Barrier Reef job?' he asks, the idea of bolting to the Antipodes making that job even more attractive.

'Sorry,' she says. 'It went another way. They went for the blond look. Ironic, eh? Shouldn't have changed.'

'Maisie, I...' He considers confiding in her, but the words won't come. He resorts to 'Thanks. See you,' and rings off.

The second message is Jonathan's. At last! His voice is whispering, urgent, and quick. 'Ioan, Oh God! Where are you? I'm wrecked and pissed off my face. I have to speak to you. Are you OK? They're watching me all the time. They've even confiscated my pager. It's awful. I'm speaking on a mate's mobile in the loo at school. Look, I can get away after school, midday on Saturday. Any chance you can get here? Meet up? Say, in the Cathedral, by the Black Prince tomb? I'll wait for twenty minutes and hope you'll be able to make it. I have to tell you what happened. I'm thinking about you all the time. Bye. Love you.'

What was he like? The tomb of Edward, the Black Prince! The kid is a true romantic.

The second message is Michael. Shit! Today was the day I said I'd go over to help him move. Michael's voice sounds deep, calm and reassuring. 'Hi there! Don't worry, Pickford's haven't shown yet either. It's just gone ten. Did you oversleep? Maybe you're working. Anyway, they're coming tomorrow morning instead. Be a great help if you could manage it too. Come for breakfast. By the way, I just spoke to my architect chum, Daniel. He suggested you call his secretary for an appointment. Cheers! Look forward to seeing you.'

I bet you do, you randy old sod. What the hell am I going to do about that man? Wasting my time with something that can, no way, lead anywhere. Not if I have to go to prison. Oh Christ! His stomach wrenches again. All bets will be off with that scenario, career, becoming an architect, Jonathan, my whole bloody life buggered. Cool it, man, cool it. Think it through. Tidy stuff up.

He wipes Michael's message, and stops himself just in time from dialling Jonathan's pager. If they'd confiscated it, did that mean 'Pop' had read the earlier message? Shit! Ioan can't bring himself to call Rosie. Not now, later. How the hell am I ever going to tell her? Putting his mobile back into his pocket he feels something. A card. Embossed print announces "The Stanhope Gallery, Cork Street. W.1 Contemporary Art." The last time he'd worn this suit he'd been dining with Michael in Playa del Ingles. Better return his call, I suppose, get it over. Hell, it's starting to rain. Get back home first. Somehow explain all this to Polly and James. Oh God!

Chapter Eleven

The Stanhope

A fine drizzle drenches Bond Street. Springtime in Mayfair! To keep dry, Michael, elegant in Prince of Wales check, and navy silk tie, cuts through Burlington Arcade on his first day back at work. Despite Ioan and Pickford's non-appearance this morning, and the last two depressing days packing up home and house, he feels good. Susan, his eldest daughter, turned up last night, she'd had a spat with her boyfriend and needed a cuddle. He'd given her dinner, and as they packed books into tea chests, she'd talked… about her boyfriend, life at Camberwell Art College, painting, and, slightly more interestingly, how Mummy was losing patience with her lover, apparently the little charmer was short on domestic skills and was unable to control the boiler. Michael listened joyfully, realising he hadn't lost his daughter after all.

Passing the diminutive arcade shops selling expensive cashmere sweaters and jewellery, he comes to the one from which, twenty-five years ago, he'd bought Nichola her wedding ring. He'd passed it a hundred times, but today something in the window catches his eye. Gleaming on a black velvet pad is an 18 carat gold, blue lapis lazuli signet ring. It occurs to him how handsome it would look on Ioan's tanned hand. About to enter the shop, he stops. Don't be hasty, wait. Don't want to make the same mistake twice from the same jewellery shop.

Turning into Cork Street, it's still raining. Covering his head with 'The Times' he hurries past The Redfern Gallery, noticing that they have a Danny Markey exhibition. The Messum Gallery has a John Miller, a Cornish painter he admires. Further up the road he pushes open the brass-plated glossy black door of "The Stanhope."

Immediate sanctuary. Opposite the door, set back on the landing, behind a generous antique desk, sits Joyce, her make-up immaculate. She's on the phone, her attractive salt and pepper hair is brushed up, she wears a red suit, a double row of pearls and lots of gold. When she sees him, her eyebrows shoot up, her face breaks into a smile, and she blows him a kiss, immediately winding down her conversation.

Michael is surprised at how glad he is to see her. Even from across the desk he can smell her familiar perfume, 'Arpege', his present to her last Christmas. The memory of kissing her passionately at a New Year's Eve party some twenty years ago, when they were both happily married, pops into his head, he wonders if she still remembers.

'Darling, you're soaked!' Kissing him on both cheeks, she whispers hurriedly, 'Two Arabs in divine navy suits downstairs, looking for something for the harem.' Then in her normal gin tones, 'I love the tan! Did you have a wonderful time? Meet anyone gorgeous?'

He wants to tell her he has, but isn't entirely sure how the news of his shifted sexuality will be greeted. That will have to be handled by degrees. Though, as students they'd shared confidences about each other's love affairs, even his one gay one, confessions and intimacies of that sort had stopped years ago with their marriages. Joyce was now a widow, some would say, and indeed did say, a merry widow, and much of their business relationship was conducted from a flirtatious base. Now that he was 'available' again, some readjustment in their alliance was going to have to be made. So he does not answer her question, but keeps silent. Anyway, the Arabs are coming up the stairs carrying a canvas. Simultaneously the phone rings. He answers. 'Good morning. Stanhope Gallery.'

'Mike?' It's Ioan.

Michael's face breaks into a secret grin. He turns to the wall, speaking intimately, 'Hi! How are you, then?'

'Sorry Mike, I can't make it.'

'Oh! Well. No problem. Some other time perhaps?'

'No. No, Mike, it's over. I can't see you. I have a lot of problems right now. I don't want to discuss it. I just don't want to see you anymore. OK? There's no point. I mean, I'm sorry and all that, we had a good time on holiday, but it just wouldn't work now. I mean, well, quite frankly, I don't fancy you. So why don't we just drop it, eh? We don't have any future together. OK?... OK? I'm going to ring off now. Sorry. Cheers, man. See you.'

Michael is pole-axed. The disconnect tone buzzes in his ear. Joyce is being efficient with the Arabs. A sale is imminent... he hears the words 'Nine thousand, five hundred pounds' which helps somewhat to re-focus him. She introduces him.

'This is the Gallery owner, Mr Stanhope.'

Michael shakes hands with the two princely gentlemen, avoiding eye contact by looking at the canvas. He switches into automatic sales mode, unaware he is quoting from the brochure he's written. 'Ah yes. Taylor and Burton in "Cleopatra". Good choice. Fritz Hahnmann, one of Germany's best-known artists. In a direct line from Cezanne, Monet. Motifs drawn from Hollywood, and his hero, Van Gogh. He converts the images to his personal vision, masterly handling of the paint, both impressionist and expressionist. Excellent. Good investment. Mrs Howard will er... Joyce, would you be good enough to... Excuse me.'

He escapes downstairs to the loo, he has to be alone if only to kick himself for being such a fool... he feels sick. What an idiot!

What a naive, stupid, ass I've been. Falling for a pretty boy like some old queen in "Death in Venice"! What the hell am I doing? What has happened to me? He lights up the last of Ioan's Spanish cigarettes, hurling the empty Fortuna packet into the bin. I have got to get myself laid. And quick... and by a bloody good woman.

Upstairs Joyce is being perfectly charming to the Arabs.

'I visited Bahrain with my late husband years ago,' she's saying, holding on to a National Commercial Bank of Saudi Arabia cheque for nine thousand pounds. She'd dropped five hundred as policy, anyway, she's sharing commission with another gallery. 'Alas, I never managed to reach Saudi Arabia. I hear Riyadh is quite beautiful.'

'Thank you. It is,' says the eldest prince, nobly inclining his head. 'Modernisation without westernisation. Unlike this,' he smiles, suddenly delighted at his purchase.

'Our Mother,' says the younger prince, 'is a confirmed film fan.'

'Then, I'm sure she will love it,' says Joyce. 'It should reach Riyadh within ten days. I'll see to it right away. '

The princes, with small courteous bows, depart.

At the computer she taps in the details of the sale and shipment, then leans back in her chair, concerning herself with Michael.

She had previously encouraged his holiday break, hoping it would help him get things into perspective. Yet here he is again, looking desolate and uptight. Could that have been Nichola on the phone just now, she wonders? The woman had called the gallery twice last week, inviting Joyce to her new house-warming party.

'Mustn't lose touch, darling,' she'd said.

Joyce wasn't having any. Her loyalty was to Michael, whom she'd adored since he was a long-haired student, studying History of Art at "The Courtauld", twenty-five years ago. Then, they'd both been under the tutelage of Tom Howard, the professor Joyce subsequently married. Michael had made such a witty speech at their wedding, and had been her occasional 'walker' ever since. Nichola had never quite been her cup of tea, Joyce thought her superficial, coarse, and not nearly good enough for Michael. Nevertheless, she'd been as dismayed as everyone else on hearing that she'd bolted.

When Tom died five years ago, leaving Joyce needy but with an impressive art collection; including Ben Nicholson, L.S. Lowry, Stanley Spencer, Victor Pasmore, Graham Sutherland, and John Piper, Michael had offered to release the equity by selling them on without commission, which was how the gallery idea was born. Joyce, as her husband had, has a passion for all the arts, and takes great pleasure in other people's enjoyment of the discovery of art and literature. She has also developed, if not a passion, then something very akin, for Michael. In fact, when her son, who studies hotel management in America, telephoned, and was told the news that Uncle Michael had been dumped by Auntie Nichola, he'd said, 'Now's your chance, Ma!'

'You are dreadful!' she'd answered. 'Michael's in crisis. I'm just being 'there' for him.' Privately she'd hoped, yes, and one day, maybe he'll be there for me, when the time is right.

She smiles at him as he comes up the stairs, then frowns. 'Mickey! You're smoking.'

'Sorry. Yes.'

'Your shop, darling. But the smoke alarm.'

'Yes, of course.' He absently stubs out the cigarette in a bowl on Joyce's desk.

'Darling!' she yelps. 'That's my Bernard Leach. Are you alright?'

'Sorry. Preoccupied. Listen, I have to pop out. Have to collect the keys to the new apartment. See you. Bye.'

'But it's pouring,' she calls to his retreating back.

He absently waves as he closes the door.

He'll catch his death, she thinks.

Watching him through the window as he hurries down the street in the rain, she wonders whether the time will ever be right.

Chapter Twelve

Appraisal

In Cornwall, the wind howls and whistles around "The Old Vicarage." It's dusk. The tall oaks wave and creak as their branches collide and scrape one another. In the garden studio, Rosie has just cracked open a bottle of wine to celebrate the completion of the "Family Secret." Neon strip bulbs cast a merciless light onto the unframed and still sticky painting under examination.

Liz, holding a fluted glass of red wine, stands back from the easel, shrewdly appraising Red's work. Artist and model hover behind like excited kids, waiting for her judgement.

'Ah!' says Liz. 'So that's why you did your hair that extraordinary colour.'

Rosie's hair is now as sunny yellow as Ioan's was in Gran Canaria at Carnival time. The identical lemon gold shimmers in the painting. 'This,' says Rosie, 'is life imitating art. Maybe we did overdo it a bit in the bathroom, but I love it. Makes me feel sixteen.'

Subjectively, she may be right, for her eyes do indeed shine and her smile sparkles as she fluffs out her newly-bleached locks. Liz, a more objective observer, thinks it makes her look cheap. Red has trimmed Rosie's hair shorter too, the effect is more fashionable, and reveals a new tender area of flesh around the sides of her face and neck. Red's companionship over the last four days seems to have wrenched Rosie out of the cocoon of her grief, but the emerging butterfly seems more fragile.

'Sixteen?' repeats Liz, raising an eyebrow cynically and glancing at Rosie. 'I do hope not. I remember what she was like.'

'What *was* she like?' asks Red, grinning at them both. 'Go on, do tell.'

'A chubby little ball of fire who wouldn't let anyone or thing stand in her way.'

Was I really, thinks Rosie. How marvellous. Wish I was like that now. 'What about you then?' she says. 'Miss Bossy Boots, the school Ma'm!'

'My schoolteacher was a cow,' says Red. 'Wish you'd schooled me.'

'Flattery will get you nowhere,' says Liz, but she grins as she returns to the painting. She sips her wine. The picture now has two figures, the central one has a mop of yellow hair, bright pink hands and face, with an expression that makes Liz smile, it's so like Rosie. The smaller figure also has a pink face, but her hair is flame red. The background is dark blue and green. The whole effect is striking, cartoon-like, and altogether charming. Liz examines it minutely. 'Mmn. You've certainly caught a comic strip likeness. It's simple, yet has a depth. I love the colour. It's fun. You're a clever girl. Yes, I could live with that!'

'How much?' asks Red, a little too quickly.

'Oh no, I'm not buying,' says Liz with a laugh. 'I think you'd be better off exhibiting. I tell you what. We have a rather exclusive Art gallery in Nylwen, of which I am one of the directors. I think I'll take it in. Try and persuade them to hang it. See what sort of reaction we get. You up for that?'

'You bet.'

'You didn't bring any other work down with you, did you?'

'No. Got tons at home.'

'I'd like to see it. Sit down, do some sketches for me.'

'Oh no, cariad,' says Rosie. 'Not now. She's been here four days, and not even seen Sennen beach yet. We promised ourselves an outing when it was finished.'

'It's vile out. Look, nearly dark. You can go for a walk tomorrow. This is important.' She takes Red's wine glass and sits her down with paper and charcoal. 'Draw that,' she says, pointing to a collection of books, jugs and a bust of Julius Caesar. 'I want to see depth, tone, and form. Back in thirty minutes.' So saying she grabs the wine bottle, tucks her arm through Rosie's, and sweeps her out into the wind and rain. The pair duck under the trees, dash past the soaked laurel bushes and scamper into the back door. 'Sorry,' says Liz, arriving wet and windswept in the flower room with its goloshes and buckets under the sink. 'I want to see just how clever she really is. Make certain that painting's not a one-off. I think we may have captured ourselves a little star.'

Chapter Thirteen

The Tomb of the Black Prince

'Canterbury East, please. A daily return.' Ioan buys his ticket and makes for platform 1. The 10.05 from Victoria to Canterbury is supposed to take an hour and twenty minutes.

He finds an empty carriage, but a pretty girl joins him. Sitting opposite, their eyes meet for a second, he senses interest. No way, Babe! Fixing in earphone studs, an Orbital CD thumps in his head. Last night he went clubbing solo, trying to lose himself, get high, forget the events of the court room, the slagging match with Polly. What a cow she turned out to be, demanding I bloody leave. Even James, my old school mate, taking her side. Only a week to quit. Where the hell am I to go? Find an agency, I suppose. Hell! Sort it later. Must see Jonathan.

Gazing out of the window, graffiti comes into focus, he ponders briefly on the dexterity, height and reasoning of what must be an army of delinquent writers. As dirty brick and concrete give way to fence and field, to trees and springtime green, he reflects on his situation.

Here I am travelling to an 11th century Cathedral, the centre of the seat of English Christianity, to meet my fourteen year-old lover by the tomb of England's most idyllic example of chivalry. The Black Prince, champion of the battles of Crecy and Poitiers, what were the dates? Thirteen hundred and something? Jonathan would know. Jonathan knew all about it. How boys of fourteen, sons of knights, became pages in the castles of other knights, learning horsemanship, military skills, yeah, and the other. What a kid! And I might have go to prison for loving him.

In the last three days Ioan had decided that he definitely loved Jonathan. It would all be unbearable if it were merely lust. It was true that no one had ever made him feel such a stud before. By a perversity of fate, Jonathan had made him feel stronger, smarter, and safer than any previous lover. They'd ambled around Canterbury Cathedral a dozen times, swapping information on history and architecture. Maybe it had been just somewhere to go to get out of the rain, but it had the effect of lifting their aspirations onto a nobler level.

It was that damned photograph that had buggered it. I should never have given it to him. 'Mummy' finding it under his bed. The dreaded 'Pop' must have attached some fiendish military tracking device onto his clothing. One of those American T Decs, aspirin-size things, they fixed into the soles of shoes. How else could they have traced him to the apartment? I wonder if Jonathan's sussed that? They might be tracking him still. Then Ioan remembers, Canterbury Cathedral was also the scene of the murder of Thomas à Becket.

The train pulls into Canterbury at 11.30. He's excited, even getting an erection – a novel experience at Canterbury railway station – but he's in the grip of romance, in a Utopian state.

The sun is trying to shine, a chilly but exhilarating east wind blows. Head high, he hurries towards the Cathedral through the narrow lanes. He reaches the old Butter Market, it used to be called Bull-stake, when bulls were baited here, he remembers. A useless piece of information he'd picked up, that had fascinated Jonathan. Glancing into the corner at the pub his parents used to run, "The Olive Branch" looks exactly the same. Strangers living inside now though, no Mum, and definitely no Dad. Maybe the flowers in the window boxes are different but the same empty tables and chairs stand outside in the cold by the grey stone war memorial.

He joins the milling tourists and students making their way through the ancient main gate into the precinct, past the familiar 15th century houses to the left facing the lawn, and there it is. God, what a pile! A shaft of sunlight catches the front spires. Fucking magnificent! He'd only seen it two months ago, but can't help marvelling again, wondering about the forgotten stone masons, what an achievement. Intoxicated, he inhales deeply and makes for the entrance.

A policeman is on duty by the door. Ioan can't remember having noticed one there before. Am I being paranoid? Inside the vast stone space, the acoustics alter. The organ is playing. Out of sight, a service is being conducted. Someone says, 'Is there a shop?' A tourist says, 'Shush' loudly, and points to a notice urging them to be respectful. Hushed voices echo. Ioan looks up at the elegant stone pillars of the nave, then high above to the device of spherical triangles used to confer unity between clerestory and triforim.

He crosses toward the south aisle behind a crocodile of tourists, past the memorial plaques and up the steps. He reaches the transept, hurries over, and there, further up, standing alone, silhouetted against the deep purple and blue stained glass of the far east window is Jonathan, standing in his school uniform by the black railings of the tomb of The Black Prince. Ioan stops, fixing the picture in his memory.

Years later, when he looked back on what happened next, he saw it all in slow motion, like in a movie. Rays of coloured lights from the window falling onto Jonathan's face and hair as if he were waiting at the end of a rainbow. The boy turns, smiles, and glides toward him.

Face to face, neither speak for a moment. They grin happily at each other.

'Hi, Babe!' says Ioan.

'Wicked! You're here!'

Ioan wants to hug him, instead, self-consciously, he holds out his hand.

Jonathan takes it, formally shaking hands.

Two giants in bomber jackets materialise. 'I'm a police officer,' says a bald one, holding Ioan's arm in a vice. 'Please come outside, sir. Let's not have any fuss.'

Jonathan backs away. 'No. No, how did you know?' he cries.

'Never mind that,' says the other cop, seizing Jonathan. 'You too, sonny. Now!'

'Sanctuary,' murmurs Jonathan, then shouting loudly, 'Sanctuary!'

People stop and look. But do nothing.

'Yes,' Ioan tries to be calm, 'how about respecting the sanctity of this Cathedral?'

'How about respecting the age of this lad here?' snaps the cropped-haired cop, digging his fingers painfully into the crook of Ioan's elbow. 'Come along, mate.'

Vaulted nave, ancient flags, stone and masonry swirl with fury inside Ioan's head. Thinking he's going to faint, he fights to control himself... can't let go in front of Jonathan. He feels himself being frog-marched, pushed firmly through the oncoming trail of tourists. They're forcing him back down the south aisle towards the entrance. Jonathan in his wake.

The uniformed policeman in the entrance vestibule is talking into his shoulder phone. Once outside in the precinct, Ioan is grasped in an arm lock high behind his back, the pain forces him to thrust his head forward. He's separated from Jonathan, propelled onto his knees, face in the grass, hands behind his back, he's handcuffed. Allowed up, he's surprised by his helplessness. A crowd of onlookers gather. A police van appears from nowhere.

Shoved into the back of it, he turns, trying to see Jonathan.

'Over here!' shouts Jonathan. One of the shaven giants is restraining him, but the boy is jumping up and waving.

Their eyes meet for an instant before the van door slams, blotting them from each other's sight for many years. Memory will sentimentalise the moment, but Ioan will never forget Jonathan's pretty downy cheeks and tear-brimmed eyes smiling a heart-breaking good-bye.

Within seconds the van is on its way to Canterbury police station where Ioan is charged with breaching his bail conditions. His pockets are emptied, prior to being bagged and labelled. Seeing his mobile phone on the table jolts him from his paralysis. He remembers from movies he can ask for a phone call.

'One only,' the sergeant warns. 'Keep it short.'

Shit! Don't have that duty solicitor's number. Ma? For a moment he wrestles with the problem of telling her. No. Can't. Maisie? His agent's office number at International Models is programmed into the phone. Damn! Saturday. She won't be there. He calls her home number, it's engaged. Michael's business card faces him on the table, reluctantly, he starts to dial the number. No. Don't give him the satisfaction. He cancels. The sergeant is placing his CD player, Omega watch and return ticket to Victoria into a plastic bag. In desperation he presses number three – his land line at home.

'Polly! Hi! Look, sorry about last night... Yes. Actually I am leaving the flat today. It's cool but, er I've been arrested... Yes again... Canterbury. Listen, will you contact Maisie for me, you know my agent, the number's by the phone... Yes. Let her know... No idea. I haven't had a bloody trial yet! Oh God, Poll, I don't know, put it all into storage... No, no. Please don't do that. I'll call my Mother myself... Thank you. I appreciate it. Bye.' He turns off the phone and gives it to the sergeant, who's face says a good deal, but who bags it without comment.

The remainder of Saturday is spent locked in a cell. Lying on the bench, he replays in his mind every incident that has lead him here. Those cops must have been trailing Jonathan. Tipped off by "Pop", no doubt. That damned pager message. They'd been expecting me.

Accompanied by church bells on Sunday morning, tasteless food arrives. Boredom and impotence are already setting in. Staring at the ceiling for an eternity he eventually dozes off. He is awoken on Monday morning by the door being unlocked.

When he is ushered into the corridor he complains of the discomfort.

The duty officer snaps on handcuffs. 'That's a walk in the Park, mate, compared to what's in store for you.'

Chapter Fourteen

Finding Out Whores

Michael, still mad at himself for being so affected by Ioan's phone call and on a quest to get laid, parks his BMW on a meter in Curzon street. He's known the whereabouts of the Shepherd's Market brothel for years, he'd passed the door many times, but never imagined there would come a day when he would require the comfort provided in the shop-worn pink heaven. At the desk, he chooses the most conventional offer he can find from the bizarre list of options available, "Wild Sex with a Romanian". He pays a £100 with his credit card and he is shown upstairs to a bedroom. A plump raven-haired tart sits at a table doing a jigsaw.

'Hallo!' she says, cheerfully professional, with a slight foreign accent. She casts off her silky dressing gown revealing voluptuous flesh barely covered by a brief pink slip.

About as wild as raspberry jam, thinks Michael, saying, 'Hi.' Glancing at the jigsaw, which seems to be of a country cottage and flower garden in full bloom, he says, 'Interesting.'

'You too! Just a hobby. Passes ze time. Businessman?'

'Kind of.' He takes off his coat and sits on a chair by the door to untie his shoelaces. 'I work just round the corner.'

'Oh! What you do?'

'I'm er, in the picture business.'

'Films, oh! You know Tom Cruise?'

Michael smirks, 'Fraid not,' and he drops his pants.

Minutes later, he lays back on the bed flaccid.

The whore uses her required skills for a further excruciating five minutes – to little elation. Michael feels totally unerotic and demeaned.

'No worry,' she says. 'Relax. You like to help me finish jigsaw?'

'Sorry. I'm er, having problems at home.'

'Of course,' she shrugs. 'Zat is why you here, no?'

'It's okay. If you don't mind, I think I'd better go.'

'Up to you. But no refund. You come back when you feel better, yes?'

Seriously alarmed he leaves with his tail between his legs. Never before has such a catastrophe occurred. His world is crumbling. Outside, sat at the wheel of his BMW, he feels even more wretched and unhappy. A traffic warden approaches. Although he still has thirty minutes left on his meter he drives off. His frustration turns to anger at Ioan. He makes up his mind to confront him. He remembers the address; 31, Dawson Place, it's near the Portobello market. He knows Dawson Place well. Finding it easily, he searches for number 31. He stops outside. Looking up he wonders which is Ioan's room. A light goes on. A woman lowers the blind. He turns on Radio Four and drives back to the empty shell in Wandsworth that used to be his home sweet home.

The evening is spent packing. He divides up the furniture as Ioan suggested, blue stickers on stuff to go to the penthouse, red stickers on things for Nichola. Then he checks each room in readiness for tomorrow's move – the finality of it is getting to him. Taking a bottle out of a packed grocery box, he pours himself a stiff brandy and calls Malaysian Kiany in Birmingham.

'How are you, Gorgeous? Can you get your beautiful arse down here for the weekend? I'm moving into my new apartment.'

'Mike! Darling. Tomorrow I have two shows.'

'Of course. Sorry. How's about Sunday? Come and help me

hang some pictures? Get laid on the new carpet!

'Lay the new carpet?'

'No, no. Get laid. Never mind. Could you be here for Sunday lunch?'

'Sure.'

'Great. I'll book us somewhere. We'll go to St James' Park. Have tea and crumpet.'

'I know English enough to know that's rude.'

'Yes, but it's a bun too. Look, doesn't matter. I'll pick you up at Euston? What time?'

'No, no. I'm getting a lift.'

'OK, but don't go to the wrong house. I want to christen 62, Pall Mall. Bye, honey.'

In his bedroom, Michael sticks two red dots on his ornate brass bedhead, once he and his wife's most valued possession. This, I can live without. Leave it to the betraying bitch and her toy boy. With that generous thought, he falls asleep. His last night in the palace of the dead.

Twelve hours later, on Saturday afternoon, Michael stands surrounded by tea chests and furniture in his unfamiliar new apartment. Pickford's men are tipped and vanished. Where to start? He yearns for his lost daughters. Ioan too. Looking around he wonders if this will prove a safe haven from where to build a new life, with or without a loved one? A day to wait till Kiany arrives. He knows perfectly well she's not the Right Person, but in his present mood, someone is preferable to no one. He checks that 'The Church at Deuil' is undamaged, but can't face unpacking anything else. Saturday afternoon, what to do? Of course, lunch down the Portobello Road. I could buy myself a house warming present.

If it's a reason or excuse, he doesn't care. He drives straight to Notting Hill and 31, Dawson Place. Parking in a resident's bay opposite, he sits watching. Why not just check it out? There are three bells by the door. Beside one is typed, "Taylor, Stewart, Williams". He pushes it.

'Hallo?' A distorted female voice.

'Is Ioan in, please? I'm a friend of his.'

'Who is it?'

'Michael Stanhope.'

'Who?'

'Michael Stanhope.'

'Hold on.' There's a buzz, and the door clicks. He pushes it open and climbs the stairs. On the second floor a slightly pregnant ex-deb type is waiting by her open front door. 'He's out,' she says.

'Oh! I had a rather strange call from him yesterday. I was worried. Is he okay?'

'Well, actually, no, he's not. Look,' says Polly. 'There's a bit of a drama going on. I was just speaking to him on the phone. Would you like to come in? As a friend of his, you may be able to help us.'

Michael steps into the apartment... Ioan's apartment. Polly shows him into the living room. 'This is James,' she says, 'my fiancé.'

A tall embarrassed young man rises from an armchair. 'Hi!' They shake hands.

'Do sit down,' says Polly. 'Well...' As always with girls who want something, she gives away more than she intends.

During the next five minutes, the scales fall from Michael's incredulous eyes.

Chapter Fifteen

Liz's Secret

Rosie is screaming like a girl on a roller coaster sitting pillion on Red's motorbike. Speeding along a Cornish country lane she waves to Liz in her Volvo Estate as they overtake her.

The three of them are on their way to Nylwen Art Gallery, Liz has an appointment with the curator, Simon Barclay at noon. The "Family Secret," now dry, framed and loosely wrapped in brown paper is by her side. Sal is sitting on the back seat, nose propped on the open window happily sniffing in the passing breezes. Liz waves back, laughing at Rosie's white mackintosh flapping behind in the wind, she's also mulling over an intriguing piece of information her sister had let drop as she mounted Red's Kawasaki in the driveway.

Rosie had said, 'I haven't been on one of these for nearly thirty years.'

'Bet it wasn't a Ninja Turtle,' Red had shouted, revving up.

With mock hauteur, Rosie replied, 'No. It was a Harley Davidson. Swept off me feet for a dirty weekend to Paris, I was!'

'Thought you said you didn't 'ave any boyfriends before me Dad?'

Liz had noticed Rosie flinch.

'Oops! That just slipped out,' said Rosie, 'sorry!' and she glanced guiltily at Liz.

'She got around more than she likes to admit,' Liz joked.

'Only frogs!' Rosie laughed, but her smile faded falsely, like a comedian's when he's failed to get his laugh.

Watching her flapping white Mac disappear round the bend, Liz ponders. Thirty years ago? Paris? That must have been with that boy in the theatre. My dear sister, she's still the ninny she always was. At least she looks happier than she did when she arrived. But, oh dear, the baggage of memories and the guilt she brings.

Sisterly emotions are vile, much more painful than love affairs. Liz's conscience is giving her a hard time, which is why she's doing all she can to rehabilitate Rosie. She has a pretty shrewd idea of why David left the bulk of his estate to Red, and not to Rosie. Liz had known David well. She had loved him.

When Rosie and Liz were little girls, they'd been inseparable. Being her senior by four years, Liz had looked after and guided Rosie, handing down clothes – 'Second hand Rose' was the family joke – and even sharing pals. Disastrously in the case of young David Williams.

David, a lusty red-haired teenager, 'Carrot-head Williams' was considered quite a catch at Coed y Lan comprehensive. He was great grandson to Walter Williams, one of the original pioneer mine owners in the Rhondda. Despite the 'black gold' glory days of the mining industry being over, he still stood to inherit a good deal from his grandfather, old Walter Williams' son. In the early sixties, when David started school, the industry was facing pit closures. So he had not attended his father's expensive Public School. The local secondary was deemed more prudent.

Liz developed a crush on him during their last year at Coed y Lan, enjoying the usual groping and snogging, everything but the last couple of inches. Frustrated, David's eye had turned to her blossoming nubile sister. It started innocently enough. Rosie pleading to come to the pictures with them. It was not a problem for Liz, so Rosie joined them. When Liz moved on to Bangor to attend a three year degree course at the Teachers' Training College at the University of Wales, Rosie continued to go to the pictures with David – sitting in the back row. By the time Liz returned for Christmas, and to welcome in 1972, David had clearly transferred his affections to the sweet seventeen and more yielding Rosie.

Liz pretended she didn't care, and everyone believed her. Anyway, she'd matured a good deal in Bangor, actually in Holyhead, where she'd virtually thrown away her virginity to a burley Irish sailor after a weekend crossing to Dun Loaghaire. Her new life as a schoolmistress and sometime church organist was busy, she acquired a golden retriever, Sally – mother to Sal – and appeared to be happy. Only on lonely evenings, after correcting her pupils' exercise books, did she feel like the elder spinster sister, a role she gradually began to absorb, telling herself marriage was unnecessary, valuing trust and friendship higher, the burley Irish sailor a distant memory.

When Rosie confessed she was pregnant, and asked her help by persuading David to visit her in Bournemouth, Liz crushed down the old tinge of jealousy to a more acceptable emotion, that of sisterly responsibility and family respectability. Rosie and David were, after all, the two people closest to her. So she did as her sister asked, and drove David down to Bournemouth, on the fatal weekend he proposed to Rosie.

During the wedding ceremony that September, her Mam said, 'There, you see, Lovely, you've not lost your friend after all, you've gained a brother-in-law!'

She had attended Ioan's birth, and the sisters chief joy became his development. His blue eyes and healthy complexion making for admiration in all who saw him. When he started nursery school, Rosie gradually got her young life back, but with David away working all day she became restless. She returned to her dancing classes, yearning for the days of her lost summer season. David, who came from a long line of chauvinists, absolutely forbade a return to the stage.

'You'd be buggering off to work just as I was coming home. No bloody fear! No wife of mine is going on the stage.'

Rosie found herself at twenty, at the end of her career before it had begun.

Around that time a handsome new supply teacher came to Coed Y Lan Primary, Liz's little school in Pontypridd. Liz tentatively started an affair with him. Rosie found out and wanted a share of the pie. When she got it, Liz was furious, Rosie had pinched her boyfriend yet again. The sisters had an emotional scene, the upshot of which was, the teacher dumped them both and emigrated to Canada.

David, oblivious to Rosie's boredom, was under pressure managing the troubled pit at Ty Mawr. One evening, a little drunk, he knocked on the door of Liz's flint-stone cottage, wanting, as he graphically put it in his deep Welsh tones, 'A wee trip down memory lane, cariad?'

Where David was concerned, Liz was putty. She opened the door, and in a mood of retaliation to Rosie, gave way to his advances, guilt lending frenzy to her passion.

'It was always you, annwll, always,' he breathed into her ear.

Lost in David's brawny arms again, was exactly what Liz needed. She realised she loved him, always had, and minded very much losing him to Rosie.

'May God forgive me,' she whispered. 'Rosie must never know.'

And Rosie never did know. Liz and David had always been friends, so no-one suspected. Their clandestine affair passed unnoticed. Liz's open persona as a dedicated teacher and church goer, sister to the vivacious ex-chorus girl, ensuring her respectability.

With the subterfuge and intense passion their affair engendered, inevitably, Liz, more cerebral than David, forced a confrontation about honesty and marriage.

'I cannot go on like this,' she told him. 'We have to stop. We have to tell her. It's more than I can bear. You only married her because she was pregnant! You've said, often enough, that Ioan no more takes after you than a lump of coal! Well, maybe he isn't your son, did you ever think about that? I know for a fact, she was sleeping with some theatre type when she was in that summer show.' Immediately she'd said it, she regretted it. 'Please,' she said, 'you're turning me into some bitter vengeful woman, which I'm not. You know I'm not. But I cannot go on like this. You must choose. Me or Rosie? Which of us are you using?'

'Using?' he said. 'You mean, like she used me?'

'Don't.' Liz hung her head. 'You are the two people I love most in the whole world.'

'Me too,' David said, holding her close. 'Me too. Don't make me choose, cariad. And don't say that's why I married Rosie. It's not true. I married her 'cause I loved her. I love you both.'

'That's impossible. You can't love two people at the same time?'

'I do,' he lifted her chin to look into her eyes. 'You know you were saying about reincarnation the other evening? Well, I been thinking, maybe I was an Arab, a sheikh with lots of wives, in one of my previous lives!'

Liz , despite herself, laughed. Her love for him was such that she couldn't give him up, and her love for Rosie was such that she couldn't force David to leave her, which he probably wouldn't have done anyway. So David achieved his objective. Maintaining the status quo, keeping both wife and mistress. Despite the guilt, the pain and the lies, their affair rumbled on. Until one morning, Liz had a phone call from her sister. Their Mam had died during the night.

After the funeral, on a holiday visit to St Ives to stay with an Art teacher friend, Liz decided to change her life. To have nothing more to do with love. It was too paralysing. Too time consuming. There was so much more she wanted to do with her life. It also meant giving up sex, of course, but as that had never been important to her, it was no great sacrifice. So Liz left Coed Y Lan Primary – where five year old Ioan was one of her pupils – and with the help of her Mam's inheritance, moved to Cornwall, hoping her absence might improve David and Rosie's marriage. Which it did. Their struggles during and after the pit closures, seemed to draw them closer. By the time they moved to Croydon, Liz, in Cornwall, had organised a completely new life. By offering herself as organist to the local church, she was soon woven into the very heart of the community. She had mourned for David many years before his actual death. On hearing the terms of his Will, she was as shocked as Rosie, but after she'd thought about it, she was not that surprised.

Judging by Red's age, her mother must have come along about ten years after Liz had left Wales, about the same time David had come into his inheritance. Twenty years of Nursing Home fees had depleted most of grandfather William's fortune – he was ninety-five when he died – but David still inherited some healthy investments, most of which now belonged to Red.

And if I'd been a different kind of woman, thinks Liz, a tougher type, maybe today I'd be rich and Red would be my daughter. And there she is. Sitting on her motorbike with Rosie, waiting at the cross-roads not knowing which way to go.

'Take the A 30,' Liz calls out, pointing, 'then take the signpost to Nylwen.'

'See y' there,' calls Red, and off she zooms.

I wonder who her mother was, Liz ruminates as she drives.

What could she have been like? At least David didn't leave her anything! Red is definitely gifted. Where does that talent come from? The good Lord, of course, as he gives to all. From David? Dear solid, stolid Welshman that he was, maybe he wasn't the most emotionally connected of men, but he did have a beautiful bass voice. A picture of him singing at the National Eisteddfod in Cardiff appears in her head, with his great grinning face and 'Carrot' head. Yes, David was an artist when he sang. Be wonderful if I can really do something for his daughter. Oh, I do hope Simon likes her painting.

The Nylwen Art gallery is a weather-beaten building, built in dark Cornish stone in the late nineteenth century. It is the last house at the end of the village, or the first one you come to, if you are approaching from Penzance, a large area of tall grass is at the side. Three worn steps lead up to a sealed front door, a new glass entrance has been built at the side. Large windows back onto the sea, giving the interior a particularly sympathetic and airy atmosphere. Arriving in the vestibule, Red and Rosie decide they'll wait in the adjacent Art shop, but Liz shoos them off. 'Take Sal for a walk, or something.' She's had dealings with Simon before over one of her protégés, she likes him, but suspects he might be tricky. Her instinct tells her, she'll do better on a one to one basis.

Simon Barclay greets her with a kiss. 'Liz! To what do I owe this pleasure?'

'Simon, I want your 'candy' opinion on this, please.' She unwraps the "Family Secret", placing it on the floor, carefully resting the back of the frame against the wall.

'Candy opinion eh? That's a new one!' He takes out his horn rimmed glasses from the top pocket of his tweed, leather-patched jacket. Looking enigmatically at Liz, he polishes the lenses with a hankie for much longer than seems necessary, he places them on his cadaverous forty-something year-old face.

'Where have you been hiding this?' He steps back. 'Ah! It's a story picture.'

'How can you tell?'

Simon shrugs. 'Are they sisters? No, mother and daughter!'

'Something like that. The artist calls it "Family Secret".'

'Interesting!'

'Really?' asks Liz, betraying her apprehension. 'Seriously?'

Simon turns to look at her. Without responding he bends down to closer inspect the brush work. 'Why is this one so important?'

'Long story.'

'You must tell me one chilly night!'

'I might do that. What do you think?'

'Who's the artist? English?'

'Leeds.'

'Mmn,' he stands up. 'So it would fit in with my British abstract theme. Do you want me to sell it?'

'Just dip your toe in the bath water for me, would you mind?'

'You're such a wily bird, Liz! Are there any others?'

'I could get some if you're interested.'

'Have to wait a month till the Basil Beattie's over.' He nods vaguely in the direction of some oil and wax abstract canvases on exhibition. 'Good colour! Yes, it's fun. With pleasure. I'll need a biog.' Taking off his glasses and turning his hooded eyes to look Liz full in the face he says, 'So, what about Wednesday night for dinner?'

Liz could not have been more surprised if he'd hit her with a wet kipper.

With eyelids half closed, he adds, 'It is about time.'

'Yes,' says Liz, trying not to twinkle. 'Maybe.'

'I'll call for you at seven, then. How would that be?'

'That would be lovely, Simon. Thank you. Till Wednesday then.'

Liz walks away feeling distinctly tingly behind the ears. She'd known Simon casually for some years, but presumed him involved with the brunette who always accompanied him to the various functions at which they met. This was something new, and very welcome too, she decides. Maybe she misses sex more than she admits. As she walks down the road looking for her sister and Red, she can't help thinking, Mmn, best keep him away from Rosie.

She finds them, looking like a couple of kids, they're devouring ice-creams in a tiny cream shop along the road. Liz relates what happened, omitting the sexual chemistry part, and everyone is delighted. Red is due to start at Leeds Art College tomorrow, so as today is her last day, a shellfish lunch treat is planned. Buttoning their coats and tightening their scarves against the wind they set off along the prom to the restaurant. Sal pulls ahead on her lead. Dogs are forbidden on the beach by order of the Penwith District Council, along with feeding the seagulls, notices appear announcing this fact along the promenade rail. Through a break in the clouds, a beam of sun spotlights St Michael's Mount across the choppy sea, it's a postcard view. As Liz spots "The Lobster Pot" sign, she says, 'There it is,' and they cross the road. But it's closed. A board outside reads "For Rent".

'It's fate,' says Red. 'There's your restaurant. Perfect!'

Two nights ago after dinner, Liz and Red had encouraged Rosie to make a list of all the things she liked best in the world. Their idea being to try and discover an interesting way for her to earn a living. Top of Rosie's list was Musical Comedies. Second, Films. Meeting people. Romantic novels. Biographies of film stars. Clothes. Cooking, and Giving parties. The most practical, if tenuous conclusion they had drawn, had been 'Restaurateur.'

Peering through the grubby glass window, glimpsing oak beams, an inglenook fireplace and an old newspaper on the floor,

Red says, 'You could do cream teas!'

'I've been here often,' says Liz, restraining Sal, who is more interested in a passing Pekinese. 'It's charming.'

'How much do you think they'd want?' asks Rosie.

'Call 'em,' says Red, pointing to the notice, 'Look, there's the phone number.'

Liz rings it on her mobile.

It turns out to cost £50 a week for the shop, £75 for the accommodation upstairs. £120 for both. Rosie bites her lip. 'Somewhere to live too. It's tempting. I wish Ioan could see it! He'd know what to do.'

'Call him,' Red nudges her. 'Call him now.'

'Later. Yes, I will. It would have to be decorated,' she says.

'Go for it!' encourages Red grinning. 'Remember, Dad's estate's gonna pay you a hundred quid a week!'

'I think it's perfect,' says Liz. 'It's not genuine Tudor, of course, but it looks very attractive. We can always ask the bank manager for a loan.'

'Be a start,' says Rosie.

Retracing their steps, they discuss the pros – which are many, and the cons – of which there seems only one. Hard work. Rosie says wistfully, 'I could call it "Rosie's Tea Shop."'

'You could do your apple pie, like the one we had the other night,' says Red.

'Cornish cream whirls. Florentines.' Rosie's eyes sparkle. 'Cornish Pasties!'

P.A. Wilkins Estate Agents has a shop front in the high street. A helpful Mr Wilkins proposes a six month lease on both the shop and the accommodation, explaining that if they want to buy, the vendor would accept £7000. Rosie decides to take Red's advice and 'Go for it.'

So impressed are they by their achievement, they go to a pub for a celebratory drink. Eventually, laden with tuck from Liz's kitchen, Red mounts her Kawasaki. Rosie seems really sad to see her go. Liz instructs her to work hard, to treat The Vicarage as a second home, and Red promises to visit her two new Aunts soon, so with hugs and kisses she heads back to Leeds.

The following Wednesday evening, Liz, dressed in a short sleeved black rayon crepe frock with a border of whimsical giraffes on the skirt, waits to be collected by Simon Barclay. He arrives punctually and drives her to an intimate, but very expensive county restaurant. Over dinner they discuss visiting the Picasso/Matisse exhibition in London, which leads on to whose works they would most prefer on their walls; Simon is for Picasso, Liz for Matisse.

Simon rather overdoes his 'art connoisseur' role, but Liz deals with that easily enough. Slowly she perceives in him a rather sweet, professorial, cuddly personality. When, over coffee, he invites her to see his private collection, she accepts. She'd already made up her mind. She'd been loverless too long.

A fortnight later, Rosie makes the big leap. Moving from under her big sister's protective wing, to the solitary bleak flat above "The Lobster Pot". Electricians, plumbers and painters are employed, and life is suddenly busy again, which is just the way she likes it. Excited, she's at last moving on.

Then Ioan's letter arrives.

Chapter Sixteen

At Her Majesty's Pleasure

When Ioan left Canterbury police station, he was incarcerated in a sweat box – virtually an upright coffin – for almost four hours as the police van made it's way to West London Magistrate's Court. There, he was refused bail, returned to the sweat box and taken to HMP Wandsworth, where the huge jaw-like doors of that fearful place opened greedily to devour him.

At the time, Her Majesty's Prison, Wandsworth, happened to be in the news – a highly critical documentary with accusations of overcrowding, bad hygiene, and a glut of suicides had been shown on television. A tabloid newspaper had featured an emotive story of a lad hung with his own shoelaces from a pipe in his cell. The management was being condemned at virtually every level by Sir David Ramsbotham, the Chief Inspector of Prisons.

Ioan was processed with seven other men through Reception. The Victorian stone floor was covered with rubbish and old food, two overflowing dustbins stood against a wall smeared with gunge. This was nothing like any prison movie Ioan had ever seen. Reality was filthier. A 'screw' in a white short-sleeved shirt ordered him to undress, shower and put on prison clothing. Second-hand underwear and socks, a sweatshirt, and brown regulation denims. Remembering the times he'd been handed Armani, Farhi, Versace, Gaultier, and Yves Saint Laurent to model, a bubble of humour arose in him, he couldn't resist saying, 'Does it come in other colours?'

'Blue when you're convicted, shit head! Move.'

Following the warder up an iron staircase his gut churned, it hadn't stopped for the last three days, but now it was worse. They turned into the balcony on the second floor landing. As the guard opened a heavy steel door, he grabbed Ioan's arm.

'Want to go on the numbers?'

Ioan, uncomprehending, frowned. The guard motioned him inside.

Three dormant but dangerous looking men lay on beds. Their bullet eyes bored into him. The metal door slammed, the noise crushing, unmistakably his 'time' had begun. Daylight filtered in through a small closed heavily barred window. Three uncovered buckets stood in the corner, no sink, no toilet. Ioan was incredulous. This in 2000! The cell smelt of rotting feet, shit, and unmistakably, of crotch. Ioan stood rigid with dread. These were three ugly yobs.

Ever since his father had taken him to a football match at fourteen and he'd witnessed a dart pierce a neighbour's skull, Ioan had a latent fear of hooligans, even when passing a pub with lager louts sitting at a street table, he felt threatened. One of the reasons he'd signed on at his gym was to learn how to handle himself. He had a feeling he was shortly going to find out how well he'd learnt his lessons.

'Got any burn?' An enormous man with massive shoulders, and a swallow in flight tattooed across his cheek, spoke.

'What's burn?'

'Bloody 'ell! Tobacco, boy. Y'first time in bird?'

Ioan nodded. A huge Negro with a shaven head, on the top bunk to his left said, 'Welcome to Wanno, man. Take the bottom, I prefer d'fresh air!' and hooted a deep chested laugh. A mattress, with urine and blood stains covered the empty bunk underneath. Without taking a step Ioan dropped the bag of prison issue clothes and bed linen he'd been handed in Reception. He took out his Fortunas.

'They're Spanish.' He offered them round, scrutinising each face in turn as its owner greedily took a cigarette.

'Thanks, man,' said the Negro, pleasantly enough.

'Ain't that nice,' said the tattooed man, taking two. He grinned, showing an absence of teeth. 'I'm Lennie. That's Ossie.' He indicated the Negro, jerking his thumb upwards. 'The mad fucker up there's Den.'

'Hi. I'm Ioan.'

The mad fucker Den, a swarthy rat-like bit of work with a pigtail, nodded.

On the Underground, Ioan decided, he would not have sat next to any of them.

As they lit up, he said as casually as possible, trying to make conversation, 'The warder just asked if I wanted to go on the numbers. What did he mean?'

The three looked at each other, then back at him.

'What you in fer?' asked tattooed Lenny.

'Theft.' They stared. Carrying out his previously thought-out plan, hoping to add verisimilitude, added, 'TV and a Hi Fi.' It was futile.

'Hoisters,' sneered a dangerous looking Lennie, 'don't go on the numbers. Are you a fucking nonce?'

Ioan had no idea what he meant, but the tension was unmistakable.

'You're a fucking nonce, ain't cha?' Lennie nodded to his mates. 'Fuckin nonce, they've put with us.'

'Why you suppose they done that, Lenny?' said Rat Face.

'So we can all 'ave a good fuck tonight!' rasped Ossie rubbing his head stubble and crutch simultaneously. The others snorted and leered.

'Promises, promises!' Ioan brazened out, turning to undo his bag. 'What's a nonce?'

'Bloody hell! Sex offender. Child molester. Z'at what cha are?' Lennie demanded, peering at him. ''Cause if you are, mate...' and he pointed a threatening finger. 'I'm gonna squeeze your balls to pulp.' Ioan felt his colour rise. Employing his best macho body language, he lit his last cigarette. How the hell do I deal with this?

A deadly mocking smile appeared on Rat Face. 'Ossie, I fink you got somethin' there. Ee's very pretty, ain't he?'

'Fuckin nonces should be hung up by piano wire,' muttered Lenny, taking a deep drag on Ioan's fag. 'Dirty filthy bastards! Hang the cunts.'

Rat Face sprang down, suddenly facing Ioan, menacing. 'Dodgy baby-faced killer are ye then?' he taunted. Ioan turned away, affecting indifference, but his heart thumped. 'Naw! He's a fuckin pervert, y'can see it. Look at 'im. Fuckin poofta, we got 'ere. Hey Ossie!' he whispered. 'Fancy a bit of bacon, do ya?'

Blinded suddenly by a towel thrown over his face, Ioan was punched in the kidneys. He sagged to the floor in agony. His arms were grabbed, he couldn't breath, someone was on him, sitting on his face pinning him down, struggling was useless. His jeans were opened and yanked off. His ankles grabbed, lifted and pulled apart, he felt his anus being prised open, invaded.

He tried to scream. The towel was stuffed into his mouth.

They took it in turns to rape him. The rat-faced Den thrust into him as he lay on the floor. Lennie hauled his shoulders into the bottom bunk, pinned him to his knees and fucked him like a dog. Oz stood him up against the end of the bunks, kicked his legs apart, smacked his arse and forced in his huge black member. It hit Ioan's prostate gland, rubbing again and again, causing him to ejaculate. The other two jeered as they watched his spunk spurt.

'Filthy nonce likes it!'

When Oz finished, he flung Ioan onto the floor like a discarded rag doll. The others sneered and laughed, kicking him under the bunk.

Ioan had been in prison barely an hour.

Consciousness returned with a bolt of pain. Crowd noises filtered through to his brain. What's happening? His eyes flickered. His face was pressed against a wall. Unaware of being under a bed, he attempted to move, his shoulders hit a mesh of steel slats. A spasm shot through his body, he couldn't discover where hurt most. One thing he did know, he had to get to a lavatory. By pushing against the wall, he slid from under the bed. Turning round was agony. To his surprise he saw he was alone. The cell door was wide open. Staggering up, he saw blood on his hands, his nose was bleeding. He clambered to the door, clutching a blanket.

Outside, in the central well, men holding plates were collecting food and returning to their cells along the balcony corridors. Nearby, hurrying them along was the same guard who had earlier locked him up. Ioan shuffled toward him.

'Please, I need the toilet.'

'Please, Guv', the guard said, emphasising the last word, refusing to look at him.

'Sorry. Please Guv. Where's the toilet?'

'Tea, lavatories closed. Use y'bucket,' and he turned. Seeing Ioan's bloody face and half naked body, a flicker of something crossed his plump features and piggy eyes. Knowingly he nodded, 'Thought we'd have trouble with you.'

'I don't have a bucket, Guv.'

The screw looked at him impassively. 'Get bloody dressed!' He followed Ioan as he limped back to the cell. 'Use one of them,' he shouted, pointing to the buckets.

Feeling he was about to be sick, Ioan crouched before the bucket of faeces and urine. The smell hastened his action, he wrenched and threw up. After a while he stood, wanting to pee.

He glanced at the door. The warder was still watching.

'Told you, you should have gone on the numbers,' he smirked turning into the corridor. 'Bring your gear. Y'mates'll be back soon.'

Ioan peed, trying to keep the stream quiet, unsuccessfully. He noticed there was blood in his urine. With difficulty he struggled into his denims and gathered up his prison issue bag. Following the guard, he spotted Lennie and Den at the bottom of the stairs holding plates of food. They noticed him too, and glared. Ioan was going to have to pass them.

'That's a fuckin' nonce, you got there, Guv,' shouted Lennie. 'Takin 'im to be plunged, then, are ya?' Everyone turned to look and laugh.

Later Ioan was to learn what 'plunged' meant. It was having boiling water and sugar thrown over your bollocks.

The guard lead him safely past his adversaries, and out of the area. Ioan followed, through corridors and sliding gates which the screw unlocked, till they reached the Senior Officer.

Sat at a high desk in the alcove of a long corridor, was a handsome grey-haired man of forty or so. He was very clean, and wore a white short-sleeved shirt with HMP epaulettes.

'Name?' he said.

'Williams 2935, sir.'

The S.O. jotted it down on a pad. 'What's this about?'

Ioan, trembling and in pain, told the S.O. everything. No way, could he return to that cell with those sadistic bastards. Grass up the buggers! But he knew he was commiting the unforgivable prison sin of being a 'nark'.

Deadpan, the S.O. listened. 'You're a homosexual, right?'

'Yes, sir.'

'So what was done to you, was not the first time, right?'

'Sir. I was raped!'

'Was any weapon used against you?'

'No. But...'

'Witnesses?'

'No.'

'So it's your word against theirs?'

Ioan's head bowed.

'Williams,' said the S.O., leaning back on his high stool, 'if you are making this an official report, I will have to call in the Police. I'd rather not do that. If I do, and they find you're telling the truth, your cell mates will be charged with GBH and sent to the segregation unit, the Block. You will be sent to another prison. You will also be making a lot of trouble and enemies. Or...' and here his mouth creased into the semblance of a smile, his eyes, however, remained steel, 'you can go on Rule 43. I'll apprehend those concerned, and that will be the end of it. What's it to be?'

'What is Rule 43, please?' asked Ioan.

The S.O. looked him in the eye. 'To quote the book,' and he took a breath, 'Involving the removal of the prisoner from association, in the interest of good order and discipline, removal for reasons of the prisoner's own protection. Deprivation of the opportunity to participate in recreation, including physical education, entertainment, or classes or work.'

'I think,' said Ioan, after a moment, 'that would be best. Yes.'

'I think you've made a wise decision, Williams.' He nodded to the guard. 'Get him cleaned up.'

As Ioan walked away the S.O. turned to his subordinate.

'On a bloody busman's holiday!' Screwing up the paper on his pad, he added, 'Can hardly report that. We're in deep enough shit as it is! Better see the buggers in his cell, I suppose.'

Again, Ioan followed the warder. He was allowed a shower, then lead downstairs through labyrinthine corridors to the basement. The dungeons. A cell was opened and he was locked inside.

A huge bald monster of a man glared.

Chapter Seventeen

On Examining Art

On Sunday morning, Michael wakes early in his Pall Mall penthouse. He stretches out, luxuriating in his new double bed. He'd noticed Joyce smile when it was delivered, but he had no intention of buying a single. That would have smacked of chucking up the sponge, throwing in the towel.

His Decree Nisi had become Decree Absolute, so pain at losing Nichola clouds his mind. He is aware, though, of it diminishing, rather like a pendulum swinging back and forth in his head losing momentum. Preferable, is the sensual lovesick pleasure he derives from thinking about Ioan. Astonished as he had been by Polly's revelations about him, which he could scarcely credit, he understands now Ioan's rejection of him. Obviously the boy was ashamed, and rather than admit guilt, had cut and run. But Michael is paying for his insight. Paying monthly.

When Polly had expressed her worry over Ioan's belongings, he'd magnanimously offered to finance their storage – if she would arrange it – to which end, he'd handed her a Pickford's card he happened to have in his pocket. Polly was ignorant of where Ioan was incarcerated. But, Michael supposed, one could easily find out, his lawyer, or maybe even one of Wilfred Abery's East End villain friends – after all, they still owe me £2500.

Michael gets out of bed and pulls up the blind. Dull for June. The gold clock on Clarence House opposite says 7.45.

What time should I leave for Glastonbury? Why do artists

have to live in such weird places? Michael had arranged to visit one of his contract artists, Bernard Kay, whose work he felt was becoming jaded. Bernard was due to exhibit later in the year. Michael wanted to check up on what he was going to get for his money.

He showers and prowls around his apartment barefoot. Newly carpeted, freshly papered and painted in a cool grey, favourite pictures, familiar ornaments in elegant place, it was complete, but wrong. Too neat, a show flat, not home. Down-scaling had seemed wise, now he feels cramped. Joyce had helped with choosing colours and drapes, but last week, with the apartment finished, she'd driven off for a break to the West Country. He missed her. Kiany was busy this weekend too. Sundays are the worst! Must get Susan and Katy over next weekend. They'll be with their Mother today – Nichola playing happy families with lover boy over Sunday lunch.

As a wealthy singleton he was now in demand by hostesses giving smart dinner parties. But he declined their invitations, wishing to shun the company of married friends he'd shared with his wife. They appeared either embarrassed, smug, or, worse, sorry for him. Their sympathy, particularly from Nichola's girlfriends, he found insincere and treacherous. He tried recalling old friends and lovers before his marriage, on the back wall of his memory there was a girl or two, but where were they now? To please Nichola he'd ritually burnt his 'little black book' years ago. All his pre-marriage friends seemed to have vanished.

He flips through his new CD rack. Choosing Montserrat Caballe's "In questa Reggia" from "Turandot", he places it on his Bang and Olufsen, now fitted into a recess by the fireplace. Across Marlborough Road and The Mall he glimpes the tops of the trees in St James' Park. On a walk yesterday, he'd noticed the rhododendrons and delphiniums blooming. From his new high tourist aspect, he looks down on the Clarence House guard changing, their precision is faultless, but he and a few pigeons are their only admirers.

Tidying away his "Welcome to your new home" cards on the mantlepiece, he finds an embossed invitation to a Preview. "Sandro Botticelli's illustrations to Dante's 'Divina Commedia". It's for today! Ah, something to do. He dresses in charcoal grey trousers, blue shirt, navy tie and tan suede jacket. Walking briskly up St James's Street, past Lock's hat shop, he turns right into Piccadilly, then, as everyone knows, turns left into the courtyard of the Royal Academy.

Upstairs, on the airy fifth floor are the usual assemblage of the great, the not so great, and the pretentious. All in their expensive casual Sunday best. They cluster eagerly around ninety-two framed masterly parchment sheets depicting Dante's tour through Inferno, Purgatorio and Paradiso.

'It's a Spielberg horror movie!' A Kensington voice gargles.

'He's probably bought the screen rights!' says her companion.

A head moves close to Michael's ear. 'Contemplating a heist, ducky?'

Michael turns. A leathery lined face grins behind a pair of sunglasses on a Roman nose. Wilfred Abery's brawny body is coated neck to shoe in black leather, his hair colour matches, suspiciously.

'Wilf!' says Michael.

'Must be worth ten K each!'

They clasp hands, talking as they do so. 'Good to see you.'

'Poor old sodomites,' Wilf imparts, in a voice roughened by too much smoke and liquor. 'Upside down with feet on fire!' – which exactly describes the picture before them – 'What a masochist old Botti must have been. 'Cause he was one, you know. He was accused of seducing one of his apprentices.'

'Exactly the sort of fascinating fact I would have expected you to know,' Michael laughs. 'I was only just thinking about you!'

'Looking at this? Oh ta, Mike. Thanks.'

'No, no. Earlier this morning.'

'Why? Want to reconsider knocking off the wife's lover?'

'Sssh!' Michael smiles sickly. The remark was a shameful reminder. But the pique that had propelled him to contemplate the action six months ago, has dissolved to a shadowy folly. It causes only a moment's discomfort. 'Look,' he says, 'can we have a drink after we've taken in these?'

'What, with all the posh totty in the Friend's Room downstairs? You want to drive me into a frenzy, mate!'

'Prefer the anonymity of a Soho bar?'

'No, no. I may despise this lot, most of them anyway, but I love the fact they have to accept me. Besides those deep leather sofas compliment my archaic depravity!'

Later, in the exclusive, but presently packed Friend's Room, the English establishment – whether they accept him or not – pointedly and politely ignore the infamous Wilfred Abery. After some whispered ribaldry, they sink into one of the said leather sofas. Wilfred, self-consciously nursing a delicate china teacup and saucer in his gnarled talented hands.

Michael suggests that whoever had profited by his unreturned deposit of £2500, and he isn't at all convinced that person isn't Wilfred himself, might return the favour by tracing a young friend's custodial whereabouts.

'Tall order, ducky! You should try the Prisons Department of The Home Office. What's his name? Does he live in London? Seven prisons in London. They usually confine them as near as possible to home. Try his solicitor? What's he in for?' Jotting down Michael's answers, Wilf says, 'Sex offenders are Category 'B'. Probably be the Scrubs, or Brixton. I'll look into it. I'll not ask why you want to know, none of my business, but always thought you was a bit bent, Mic.'

Michael laughs, but Wilfred's badinage rubs in salt.

Returning home, Michael sees the LCD light winking on his answering machine. It's Joyce.

'Darling! Sorry to have missed you. I'm in Penzance – such a relief, it's actually Summer down here! Came to visit Simon Barclay, remember? He's just broken up with Maggie. Terribly sad. I tell you, it's happening all over. Anyway, darling, enough of that. The thing is, I think I may have spotted us some talent. Simon was showing me over his gallery, he's got some amazing stuff down here, really excellent, and I spotted three paintings all by the same girl. Fantastic! Apparently she's still at Art School. But so promising, and commercial – of course that's your department, but I really think you should see them. I got quite excited. I offered to buy one, but Simon was being cagey. I think he may have some ideas of his own, so I could hardly ask for slides. Look, I won't go on, but call me, and think about popping down. We can always Box and Cox at the Gallery. Must dash. We're off to St Michael's Mount to see the John Opie landscapes. The causeway's only open at low tide... The joys of country life! Byeee.'

Michael smiles. Joyce loves finding talent, and why not? It's what it's all about. He packs an overnight bag, checks he has his Nokia, and sets off for Glastonbury in his BMW.

The evening meeting with Bernard Kay does not go well. As Michael had anticipated, Bernard's studio is awash with the same style paintings he'd been serving up for the past three years. Blue, blue and yet more blue.

'It's not good enough, Berny.'

For all Michael's professionalism and shrewd judgement, he loaths doing the tough bit, especially as he knows Bernard to be an artist of the highest rank. He is driven to do so by his experience of what his wealthy and cognizant customers will buy. It is Joyce who knows everything there is to know about painting, Michael doesn't know quite as much as her, but he does know about selling, and has learned to trust his intuitive eye. 'Sorry old man,' he says, 'but we'll not get the prices for these. We still have some of last season's stuff we can't unload. I want something new. I can't show this.'

Bernard is very upset. 'But this is my style!' he chokes.

Michael knows him to be an emotional man so remains silent.

'I can't change just to fit some vagaries of your idea of fashion. This is me, a year's bloody work.' His arm sweeps round a studio full of canvases. 'This is literally my blood sweat and tears – in Technicolor!'

'Bernard luv, I've seen it all before,' says Michael. 'Believe me, I understand. But we have to be practical here. You'll just have to dig deeper into yourself to produce something different, and it will be better. Of course it will. Sorry, but that's the business we're in. If you can't find it, well, at best I'll only be able to offer you a split show in the Autumn. Now, I suggest we drop the subject. It's late. I would appreciate heading up to bed. I've an appointment in Penzance tomorrow,' he lies. Upstairs in Bernard's damp guest room, he calls Joyce's mobile and corroborates his lie.

After an early and hurried breakfast with a miserable Bernard, not wishing to embarrass him further, Michael shoots off.

On the Exeter bypass, his mobile trills. It's Wilfred Abery.

'I've some news about your chum.'

'Blimey! That was quick,' says Michael.

'I got lucky – which is more than he did. He's in Wandsworth – and that's tough, believe me, I know. It seems he's fallen foul of a bunch of vengeful and bitter lags. You'd better warn him to be on his guard.'

'Wilf, you're a marvel, thanks. How on earth did you find out?'

'Come off it, Mic. You know about my early days in stir.'

So it was true, thought Michael, Wilf was a convicted villain after all. I suppose Wandsworth must have been his old nick. 'I never quite believed those rumours,' he says.

'Let's just say, I have connections in high places. Remember his mail is censored, so don't write anything incriminating. Now that you owe me, steer some of those rich Japanese clients of yours my way. I've come up with some amazing stuff recently. Come over, I'd like your opinion. Cheers ducky!' and he was gone.

Pleased to at least have Ioan's address, he drives on. Westward Ho! His impromptu decision to join Joyce in Penzance pleases him. He's not been to Cornwall since he was a kid with his parents. 'Aventura', as Ioan would say. He makes good time and reaches Penzance by midday. Taking the coastal road he cruises past Nylwen Art Gallery at 12.10. His meeting with Joyce isn't scheduled until one. He parks the car and strolls along the sea front. He notices a sign, "Rosie's Tea Shop", he smiles to himself, the name reminds him of an ex girlfriend.

He pushes open the door.

Chapter Eighteen

Rosie's Tea Shop

Seven weeks earlier, on a bright morning in May, Rosie had unbolted the old street door of "The Lobster Pot" and opened up "Rosie's Tea Shop". Delighted by the friendly 'tinkling' sound the overhead bell made – she'd had it installed especially – she wedged the door open and awaited her first customer. The appetising aroma of roasting coffee beans she'd placed on the hot plate, swirled over the tables and out to the pavement to tempt in trade. With Red's extravagant hairdressing efforts muted to a more natural blonde, she looked better than she'd looked for months. Dressed in a fresh green and white two-piece, with dolman sleeves and a flowing skirt, she stationed herself behind her brand new display case, filled with mille feuille, macaroons, florentines, and creamy jam doughnuts – all made on the premises. Some of her chorus girl sparkle had returned, now mixed with Welsh grit, grit she thought she might have lost. Standing alongside the old-fashioned cash-till, she resembled a certain class of chic Parisian, whose steel spine intimidates yet ensures survival.

Ioan's silence had been bothering her, she'd left messages on his landline and mobile, but her calls were unanswered. Reminding herself that their relationship was totally different to the one she'd enjoyed with her own Mam, who'd lived only a few doors away in the same village, she put him from her mind and concentrated on work. 'It's my name on that sign,' she said, 'and

I'm damn well going to make it swing!'

'A swinging Tea Room?' Simon Barclay had quizzically raised an eyebrow. 'Are we sure we need one of those!'

'You know full well what I mean.'

Simon had been most helpful, advising on local tradesmen and where to go for this, that and the other... the other, had not been forthcoming, Simon being taken up for the moment with Liz. Which was nice for her, she thought, it was about time she had someone in her life, even if he was a bit of a poseur.

Rosie had never been without a man in her life. The day to day administration of the cafe, she was confident of coping with, baking and cooking were second nature to her, but the the onerous boring book work, she was dreading. Many an evening, as she lay exhausted at the end of her day in the single bed above the shop, she yearned for the comfort of a masculine shoulder. Adjusting to independence, and the unnatural role of celibate widow, she channelled all her vitality into creating her new cafe, but, she was learning, it did not absorb yearning.

The local bank manager, Mr Anthony Bennet – 'Like the singer, my dear,' he'd said, ushering her into his office, his hand hovering around her waist – after granting her request for a bank loan, had invited her to join him at the opening night of the season at the Minack Theatre, a significant local event. But a worthy open air production of "Much Ado About Nothing" failed to ignite the hoped-for passion, either in Mr Bennet or, for that matter, in Rosie. On the other hand, the curly-haired young Cornishman who came to rewire the kitchen, succeeded, making a lusty and most appreciated pass. Alas he wore a wedding band. Rosie firmly but regretfully slapped him down, telling him she was old enough to be his Mother, then went and made him a cup of tea. A gesture she was mightily proud of, for she found him very attractive.

Whilst drinking the tea, he asked her what plans she had for the shop?

When she told him, he replied, 'Lotta olde world atmosphere here. Alus does well. You should meet my uncle. He's gotta farm up Marazion. Organic and all. He'll deliver y'groceries for you if you like.'

'I think I should like very much.'

'I'll send him along. Not that you deserve it, mind!' he said with a wink.

She had waited in vain. No organic farmer showed up.

Not, that is, until that opening May morning. A pleasant looking fellow in corduroys strolled in introducing himself as Joe Fudge, the electrician's uncle. At first Rosie barely noticed him she was so busy with her customers. Over a hasty conversation he cheerfully agreed to supply her with fresh vegetables and fruit, preserves and Cornish cream every Tuesday morning. It was not until his second delivery, that Rosie did a slow burn. Watching him sip a complimentary mug of chocolate, she realised he was quietly rather attractive. Fresh faced, sandy haired, well-defined mouth, very nearly as handsome as his nephew. As they chatted, Rosie discovered he was a widower.

Ioan's letter, when it arrived, was addressed 'c/o The Old Vicarage'. Liz recognised her ex-pupil's handwriting immediately, and drove the six miles to Nylwen to deliver it. Rosie read with her hand over her mouth. Liz watched in fascinated horror.

'Whatever is it, cariad?'

Rosie sat clutching her stomach, dazed. She handed over the two sheets of six-by-eight inch lined paper.

"When writing to Members of Parliament," Liz read, "please give your previous home address to avoid delay, in your case being taken up by the M.P." A Number was quoted. A Wing number. Name, "Williams", and on the right, rubber-stamped was...

"H.M. PRISON. WANDSWORTH"

Dear Ma,

This is a letter I never thought I would have to write, I have been putting it off for weeks. I guess the address says it all. Years ago I told you I was gay, I know you hated me saying it (believe me, so I did I) and found it difficult to deal with, which is why we've never talked about it since. But, that is why I am here. I was caught "inflagranti" as you would say, with Jonathan, and by his Dad, who has brought the action against me. Jonathan is under the age of consent. Which is probably why you did not hear from his parents after Dad died.

I am On Remand till my case comes up, but as it's being transferred to a Crown Court, I'm not exactly sure when that will be. My solicitor has advised me to plead Guilty, although it goes against the grain. The trouble is, if I plead Not guilty they would force Jonathan to appear in Court, and make him give evidence against me, and that is something I know he would hate. I don't think I could subject the poor guy to that. We were stitched up (you see I'm already learning the lingo) by his Dad and Col White, (that bit might be censored) who were witnesses. So I'm thinking maybe I will change my plea to Guilty and have done with it. On Remand means I'm allowed to buy extra cigarettes and have more visitors, and the time I spend here is subtracted from any eventual sentence, but please don't think of visiting me, Ma, I don't think I could bear the pain, maybe I mean shame. I'm sure it would be difficult for you too. So let's just do letters for a bit, eh? Sorry not to have been in touch earlier, I hoped you might think I got that job in Australia, but it never came up. Maybe you should tell people it did and that's where I am, if it's difficult for you. Polly knows the truth, so does my agent, Maisie, no one else, except, of course, Jonathan's parents. Just as well you *didn't return to The Olive Branch, eh?*

Life here is weird, and you can imagine I was a bit put-out initially, understatement! I'm doubled up in a cell with a strange man who hardly talks, so I spend my time reminiscing about my past adventures, home, food, and lifestyle. I'm reading a bit, and hopefully learning to grow up. My love to Auntie Liz and of course I send tons of love to you. Forgive me,
Ioan.

Liz read with one hand on her sister's shoulder. When she finished she closed her eyes, almost in disbelief, then knelt down and hugged her.

Rosie straightened up and retrieved the pages. 'I must go to him,' she said, trying not to cry. While Liz had read the letter, she'd been thinking about Jonathan, that sweet boy of Margaret Court Smyth's. She clearly remembered the Sunday morning scene in "The Olive Branch", when they'd waved to the two boys outside in the Butter Market as they admired Ioan's silver car. A shadow had crossed her mind even then, but she'd swept it away, as she always did, as she'd tried to sweep away Ioan's whole way of life. "You found my confession difficult to deal with," he writes. How could I ever have done otherwise? Grasping Liz's arm, she said, 'I must see him as soon as possible. No one must know, Liz. Not down here. Not with me having to start up all over. This must be between just the two of us.'

'Of course, cariad, I won't breathe a word,' said Liz, privately remembering promising Rosie something of the sort once before.

"*My darling Ioan,*" wrote Rosie, "*I have just received your letter. My dear son, I do not quite know what to say to you, except that I love you and will stand by you and help you in every way possible. Shame or pain, of course I will come up to see you, and as soon as it can be arranged. I am no* longer staying with your Auntie Liz, I am renting a little cafe nearby. If it is successful I might even buy it, but I'll tell you about that when I see you. If I do not hear from you, I will telephone Wandsworth prison and ask when they will allow me to visit.

I send you all my love, son. I am thinking of you constantly. Love, as ever, Mum. XXXXXXX.

P.S. I enclose a note from Auntie Liz."

> "Dearest Ioan. I was so shocked to hear the news. What a terrible thing for you. And how frightful you must feel. I have been trying hard to think of some practical advice to offer. All I can come up with is exercise, and how the hell, I can hear you saying, would she know about that, never having done any! But I do know the enzymes released when a person exercises, makes for an uplifting feeling, and you've got such a good body, it would keep it strong. Yoga, is my other idea, they must have some books on that in the prison library, if not I will send you some. It might help a lot. Chanting too, used to help me in hard times. Otherwise, my dear boy, I say to you, think positive and keep strong in your head. I know how you feel about praying, so I won't go all evangelical on you, however you won't stop me praying for you like billyhoe. Love love love, as the Beatles used to say. So do I. Auntie Liz. xxxxxxx"

After two days, impatient for Ioan's reply, Rosie telephoned Wandsworth prison, explaining that the six hundred miles round trip would involve an expensive hotel stopover. A sympathetic telephone voice told her she should have a Visitor's Order. But further discussion elicited a visiting time a week ahead, 'by then the necessary paper work will be complete,' the voice assured her.

Five days later the 'VO' arrived.

On the designated Wednesday, Rosie pulled down the blinds

and shut up shop. Dreading the experience, but armed with a novel, knitting, and a walnut and coffee cake for Ioan – his favourite – she boarded the first morning train from Penzance at 6.22 a.m.

The journey, in an open carriage with noisy children, and two inane giggling girls across the passageway, took five hours and twenty minutes. At Exeter, a black lad plonked himself opposite, and spent the rest of the journey shouting into his mobile, each call a tirade of abuse against a girl who had dumped him. Passengers caught each other's eye, collectively admiring the girl's good sense. Then, on the unfamiliar London Underground, two young men sitting opposite, about Ioan's age, kissed each other openly, full on! Astonished, she looked around. Nobody turned a hair. If this is the twenty-first century, she thought, I've had enough. At Clapham Junction, she hailed a taxi. Just after one o'clock, under a dismal grey sky, she looked up in dread at the high brick walls of Wandsworth jail.

Ushered through Security with the other prison visitors, mostly wives and children, her bags and person were searched. Finding the cake, it was explained, she was not permitted to bring in food. Directed to a functional classroom-like visitor's room, with two guards watching, she sat at a table. A haggard woman with two children at the next table applied lipstick. Inside Rosie was in turmoil but determined to appear cheerful. During the train journey she'd worried endlessly about what she would say, the whole moral aspect of his crime disgusted her. She'd decided she would not mention the homosexual thing at all, just stick to safe topics, the new cafe, Liz's art commune, and Red.

Ioan came in. To her surprise, he was grinning.

'Hi, Mum!'

As she kissed him, the lump in her throat exploded into a sob. Controlling it, she said, 'I brought you a coffee cake, but they confiscated it.'

'Ma! No blubbing. Okay? '

She nodded. Breathing deeply she sat down. 'You've got thinner.'

'You're looking great. Like your hair like that. What's all this about opening a cafe in Cornwall?'

From then on, she was fine. She told him all about it, how she'd bought a second-hand Honda Civic, how right he'd been about Red wanting to give back some of the money, what fun she turned out to be, and how Liz rated her as an artist... even about Joe Fudge, the farmer with the Collie dog who delivered cream to her door. She wanted to hug and cuddle him as she had when he was little. By talking fast, she didn't give him a chance to say much and thankfully the reason he was there was never discussed. She guessed, of course, that he was holding back a good deal, but then so was she.

Returning home – she caught the 18.03 from Paddington – she felt emotionally drained, but glad she'd made the effort. Outwardly Ioan had seemed unchanged, a little drawn, but not nearly in as bad a state as she had anticipated.

Life in Nylwen, became cooking by night and serving in the cafe by day, leaving little time to feel lonely or dwell on Ioan's misfortune. The tourist season was beginning and Rosie knew this was her make or break time. She sent Ioan postcards of Cornish views and felt guilty at not visiting him. The weeks flashed by. Occasionally a note from Ioan punctured the conveyor belt of her routine, they were hardly letters, they revealed nothing of his feelings, they were more like updates or bulletins, progress reports on his court case. The first explained that his case had been transferred, and not to bother to visit but to keep up with the postcards. The second, that at his second Crown Court appearance he'd changed his plea to 'Guilty'. Soon, he wrote, after something called a presentence report, he should hear his sentence. This would be his final Court appearance and he'd been advised to wear a suit and tie. Could she send him his Armani suit?

Eventually Ioan's landlady, Polly, returned Rosie's calls. She was agog with news of her trip to America, her pregnancy and eventually hollow sympathy for Ioan's imprisonment. Rosie cut her short with, 'Where have you put all Ioan's clothes?'

'Pickford's. The Fulham branch,' Polly explained.

In his next note, Ioan told her a date had been set for his sentence. Monday, the 26th of June, at 10.00 a.m. Rosie realised she would have to collect Ioan's suit the Saturday before, which would mean a Sunday stopover. Expensive and upsetting as the whole thing was going to be, she knew she had to be there. But planning a trip to London meant finding a replacement for the cafe. Fortuitously, Red telephoned saying she had completed two new canvases for Liz and Simon, and asked if she could stay the weekend of the 24th June?

'Of course, luv,' Rosie answered, with her eye on the diary. 'You're part of the management. As long as you don't mind holding the fort for me in the cafe. I have to go up to London on the Monday.'

'Waitressing and painting's me best thing!' said Red.

Rosie breathed a sigh of relief, her problem was solved.

At Red's end of the phone, she clenched up her fist in victory, silently shouting 'Yeah!' For she'd had an ulterior motive in making the request.

In her Gran's 1930's semi, just outside Leeds, Red's bedroom walls were covered with posters, but on one wall she'd made a collage. Her beloved "Mattise at the Baltimore Museum of Art" poster held pride of place, alongside it were other Fauve artists, Gauguin's "Promenade au bord de la mer," Van Gogh's "Bedroom at Arles" and a Kandinsky print. But on the collage, covering the wall by her bed, were sumptuous cut-out photographs of sexy young boys and men. Outnumbering the torsos, white teeth and shining eyes of Johnny Depp, Leonardo di Caprio and Robbie Williams, were hundreds of pinups of Ioan Williams.

Growing up as an only child, with no mother, an absent father, only her Gran for company, Red had yearned for a pal. As no cousins, aunts or uncles called to play, she'd make do with Gran's old Cocker Spaniel. When he died, she invented a friend for herself. Daisy was the perfect pal, quiet, a good listener, and totally trustworthy. Red confided everything to her, her most secret thoughts, even her ambition to become a famous artist. Red had drawn pictures from the moment she picked up a pencil. When Red disclosed her ambition to her Gran, and Gran had answered darkly, 'It's not what you know, but who you know in that game,' Daisy's shortcoming became apparent. Daisy knew nobody, and nobody knew Daisy. Daisy had no clout. But when David showed Red Ioan's photograph, revealing to her she had a famous brother, Daisy was forgotten. Ioan was real, he knew people, people certainly knew him. He was the grown-up big brother who would help her, who would understand, who would appreciate she was special, an artist, an artist that one day millionaires, like Saatchi and Saatchi, would pay vast sums to, like they did to that Tracy Emin. Red built a fantasy friendship around her model half-brother. Searching for his photographs, and finding them, in the glossy magazines in W.H. Smiths advertising colognes, wearing Armani and Gucci fashions, once even on a bus advertising "fcuk". She collected every advertisement she could find that featured him. When she asked David for Ioan's address, he promised that one day he might arrange a meeting, but until that day, she had to remain a secret. "Best be silent," he said, "it would be too much of a shock, and would make Ioan's mother deeply unhappy. I don't want that." Even as a thirteen year old,

Red understood, and was sensitive to the family situation. So, not wishing to disobey her father, the writer of the monthly cheque that Gran found so essential to their lives, she obeyed, and never wrote. After David's death and she heard of her inheritance, her first words to Gran were a thrilling shout of 'At last I'll get to meet Ioan!'

As she had worked on the two paintings that Liz and Simon had requested, Red decided that when she delivered them, this time, rather than stay with Liz at 'The Old Vicarage,' she'd try and stay with Rosie. There, she would bound to find out more about Ioan, like where the hell he was exactly? Although she hardly dared admit it to herself, Ioan was the reason she'd written to Rosie in the first place. So far, though, she'd not succeeded in finding out much. 'He's abroad, I believe. In Australia filming some commercials,' was the most she'd extracted from Rosie. On this next visit, Red promised herself, I'm bloody well gonna find out where I can get hold of him.

Thus it came about, that on the morning of Monday, the 26th of June, as Michael was strolling past "Rosie's Tea Shop" and popped in for a cup of coffee to while away the half hour before he met Joyce, Julie 'Red' Williams was serving behind the counter.

The bell over the shop door tinkles.

Red looks up from her sketch pad. She's in the midst of surreptitiously drawing two old ladies sitting by the inglenook fireplace – they're the only customers in the shop, and far too busy gossiping to notice that they are being immortalised. On the cover of her pad, Red has stuck an advertisement for eau de toilette. Having trimmed away the writing, she'd drawn an ornate yellow frame around the romantic scene, an exquisite moonlit seascape... emerging from the waves, a glistening male, a skin-pore sharp, soaking wet, semi-clad Ioan.

'What would you like, sir?' she asks, cheerfully closing her pad, and leaving it on top of the display case.

'Just a coffee, please,' says Michael. 'A cappuccino. And maybe...' he approaches the counter, 'a croissant?'

'A cross what?'

Michael enunciates, 'A Crois-sant.'

'You mean a bon?' says Red.

'A bon? Yes, well, I suppose 'a bon' would do,' says Michael. 'You're not from around here I take it. Is that a Midlands accent I detect.'

'Who are you then? That bloke from "My Fair Lady?"' and she flounces her red curls, turning to prepare his coffee. 'Which one?'

Michael grins. His eyes fall to some Battenbergs in the display case. His view is intercepted by an out-of-focus Ioan... sepia moonlit, picture perfect. He re-focuses his eyes. The picture reminds him of a certain night on the beach in Maspalomas.

'Excuse me, what is this?'

'What?' says Red turning. 'Oh sorry. Just me pad.'

'I know this guy.'

'Which guy?'

'This guy.' Michael taps the cover.

'You do?' Red looks at him with renewed interest. 'Honest?' Smiling broadly, she says, 'He's me brother. Well, half-brother, actually. Um...' She turns to noisily foam up the milk, when she's done, she places the cappuccino before him. 'Excuse me, but, er, are you in touch?'

It was all clicking into place in Michael's head. Ioan's half-sister. This must be the girl from his Dad's wallet, the girl he was telling me about. What on earth is she doing here? 'Actually,' he says, 'yes, I am. He's a friend of mine.'

'Is he in Australia? '

'Good Heavens, no. Though I'm perfectly sure he would like to be.'

'Knew he wasn't,' says Red. 'So. You 'avin' one of them bons?'

'That one, please,' Michael points to a pastry.

'That's a Danish,' she says gripping it with tongs and putting it on a plate. 'He's told 'is Mum he's in Australia. What's 'e bin up to, then?' She looks at Michael steadily, a smile hovering around her purple painted lips. 'Do you know 'im well?'

'Quite well,' says Michael meeting her gaze.

'Where is he then? Would you tell us? I want to write 'im.'

Michael is undecided whether to disclose the unfashionable address. She is very cute, he thinks, maybe she'd like my address too. 'Sadly,' he says, 'Ioan is in Wandsworth prison. But I'm perfectly certain he'd be delighted to receive a cheery letter from you. Are you living down here?'

'No. Just on a break.'

'Ah! How much do I owe you?'

'It's all right, sir,' says Red. 'Have it on me.'

That, I wouldn't mind at all, thinks Michael, sipping his coffee. Not at all.

Chapter Nineteen

On Rule 43

Today, Ioan will hear his sentence.

Lying on his top bunk he silently intones his mantra – Be strong – Hide emotions – Beyond my control. Be strong – Hide emotions – Beyond my control. Today will at least be different, have to leave the cell to go to Court. Might even see Ma.

Ioan is feeling at the limits of his endurance. Living in a cell five paces by three, twenty-three hours of every day, a toilet in the room without a seat or lid, waking every morning with a headache from lack of oxygen – the first thing he always did was to go to the window, stick his lips to the grille and suck in the fresh cold air – the constant artificial light that hurt his eyes, all were bad enough. He didn't know which was worse, the boredom or the strain of sharing the space with a mindless git of a giant.

Terry Boyce was a formidable six foot three, convicted killer. He seldom wore a shirt, exposing a beefy matted chest emblazoned with tattoos of big-boobed tarts and snakes. He rarely spoke, permanently scowled, and constantly fingered the black stubble round his mouth and chin. His only utterance when Ioan had entered was, 'You behave, or I'll do for you.'

'Frankly,' Ioan had answered, 'I'd be glad if you did.'

On his second night, Ioan had a nightmare. Rat Face and Denny were on him. He awoke with a cry of fright and a sense of danger. Dimly outlined against the cell window he made out the terrifying figure of Boyce standing over him, moonlight glinting on his bald head. Ioan could hear the man breathing. He held his own breath, not daring to move, his heartbeats pounding in his ears. Fearful of an attack, he braced himself. After a while, the man moved silently away.

He learnt Boyce's story from a prisoner in the exercise yard. Apparently he had owned a butcher's shop in Beckenham, had strangled his wife, chopped her into joints, and incinerated her. The tabloid press had christened him, 'The Butcher of Beckenham!'

The chaplain visited frequently, exhorting them to rid themselves of evil.

'I did already,' said the butcher.

'How?' asked the chaplain. 'What did you do?'

'I killed the wife.'

Ioan couldn't help smiling. Boyce caught him. To his surprise, he winked. The tension between them eased. The chaplain visited less often. Ioan, as a pragmatic gesture offered him a cigarette – the reaction was unexpected.

'I'm a lifer,' said the butcher, inhaling. 'Done five years in solitary. Bit dehumanised. Get panic attacks when I'm with people. You're my first mate.'

Being Terry Boyce's mate was somewhat intimidating, but Ioan felt it a matter of self-preservation. Slowly, over the weeks, the man became more amiable, and a certain mute comradeship replaced Ioan's initial fear.

It was Terry who taught him the useful trick of synchronising his defecating to slopping out times. Ioan hated sitting on the lavatory in front of him, he didn't much care being around when Terry shat either! Doing it sitting in a line with others wasn't so personal and had a macabre comic appeal. He remembered visiting the Colosseum in Rome and laughing at the collective use of the ancient public loos, so, here, he thought, I'm doing it just like the Romans.

It was Terry, too, who had urged Ioan to write to his Mother. 'Family's everything, boy. You ain't got family, you got nothing. My boys are strangers 'cause I killed their Mother. But you got a Mum. You write her. Your family's blood, lad, that's forever. Nothing else is. Ask her to come and see you.'

Sex, up until now, had totally ruled Ioan's life. Followed, in sybaritic order, by sunbathing, movies, clothes, pop music, getting high and getting hired. These things had formed the structure of his life. As he had explained to Michael three months ago on the beach at Maspalomas, he was aware that his life was shallow and had ambitions to change. Prison was doing the job for him, pushing him to discover the true depth of his morality, testing the very fibre of whatever strength he possessed. At this moment, he feels he has very little.

The gang rape had been ghastly, but God knows he'd been fucked before, that he'd coped with – though the lack of condoms worried him – Rat Face, in particular, had looked and smelt infected with disease. It was the kicking afterwards, his ribs still ached. Worse, was the horror of the daily threats. While Terry and he, with the others on Rule 43, were queuing for lunch, or on exercise in the small yard, they were spat upon from above, batteries and wrapped faeces 'bombs' were hurled. Animal screams of "You dirty filthy bastards," "Scum" and "We'll get you" were a daily dread. He found himself warily on the lookout for Rat Face and the others, but never spotted them. Escorted by guards into chapel, attended more as an excuse to leave the cell, than from any religious belief, he was jeered at and booed. Within a society composed of the lowest of the low, Ioan learnt the hatred that men on Rule 43 were accorded. Being part of this despised sub-group was loathsome. To survive, he knew he had to pull something out of his hat. To call upon some steel, the grit in his blood he'd boasted of, inherited from his tough but unloved father.

He had looked forward to Rosie's visit, despite the inevitable emotional strain. Getting gossip from her instead of tears, had been a relief. But after she left, he sank back into his protective numbness. Throughout, his self-control and composure had been odd. He'd not given way, lost his temper or cried once. Not during the five weeks waiting for his first Crown Court appearance, when his case was transferred to Middlesex Guildhall Crown Court in Westminster, not while having to wait another four weeks for Pleas and Directions, when he'd pleaded guilty to all three charges, not even during these last arduous three weeks waiting for the presentence report. Today, having to travel to Court to learn of his Lordship's final decision, he is less confident of his self-possesion. He is tormented by a mixture of fear and tenacious fortitude.

It was Terry again who had been responsible for reminding Ioan he should look good in Court. He had lectured him for not bothering with his looks on his last Court appearances.

'You wanna show the Judge you're a gent. You could look the dog's bollocks, boy. Don't lose your self-respect. You ask your Mum to bring you a suit. She'll come around.'

As she did.

When Ioan arrives at the Court House he's shown to a claustrophobic little room in the basement. There, on the back of a chair, is his Armani suit on a hanger, with a clean white shirt, a tie, socks and a pair of shoes. He changes and waits till his name is called.

Climbing the stairs up into the Dock, he is surprised by the sudden space and airiness in the Courtroom. It's a relief. He stands flanked by warders with 'Securicor' on their lapels. No longer the glinting dark angel of months ago, now a pale penitent handsome youth faces The Court. He scans the faces in the Public Gallery looking for his mother and wondering if, by some miracle

Jonathan might be there. He isn't. But someone else is. Jonathan's father, Colonel Court Smyth's face scowls down at him. Ioan looks blankly away. As he does so, he glimpses his Mother in his peripheral vision. He looks back – she's had her hair done, and is covering her mouth with her hand. She tries to smile. He nods an imperceptible 'thank you', and bows his head, breathing deeply, steadily, to calm himself. Be strong – control emotions – beyond my control. At least, he tells himself as he waits, this last three months will be subtracted from the sentence.

Finally, the scarlet-robed Judge speaks.

'You, Ioan David Williams, have been convicted of three offences on a fourteen year-old boy who held you in confidence. You have grossly abused that position of trust and confidence. There is only one sentence that this Court can pass. You will go to prison. I sentence you to eighteen months on each count, to be served consecutively. A term of four years and five months imprisonment. You will serve two thirds of that sentence before being released on licence. Your name will be entered on the Register of sexual offenders. Take him down.'

Ioan clenches his jaw and fists, refusing to break, he can feel his Mother's eyes. He forces himself to look at her, but cannot smile. A warder touches his arm indicating he should leave. Led downstairs, unaware of what he's doing, he signs forms put before him and changes into blue prison denims. After a while he is handcuffed to another man and driven back to Wandsworth.

That night, in his bunk, for the first time, he gives way and silently weeps.

'You'll be OK,' a voice whispers in the dark, so close it seems almost in his head. The butcher is towering over him. Ioan flinches. 'Sssh. You'll be OK.' He feels Terry's hand stroking his hair. 'There now. Come on now, you're a strong lad. No one's going to hurt you, not here. Not while you're my mate.'

'I don't think I can make it,' Ioan tries to choke back his tears.

The huge man cradles the back of Ioan's neck with his massive hand, gently pulling his head toward his chest. ' 'Course you will.'

Ioan's resolve utterly breaks. The anguish of the last two months finally pours out, shaking his body with uncontrollable sobs.

' 'Course you'll make it,' Terry soothes. 'If I can, you can. I done seven years already. We'll keep each other company. We'll do it together, lad. I'll teach you. The secret is, don't think about life outside, see, not in the free world, take each day as it comes. This is your world now. Our world, just you and me, here.' And Terry rocks Ioan to and fro like a baby.

Nestling deep in Terry's furry comforting chest, Ioan inhales his warm musk. I'm going to have to revise my opinion about hairy men, he thinks, letting his tears fall.

Chapter Twenty

Reunion

Rosie feels completely wrung out as Ioan leaves the Dock. While the next case is called, she closes her eyes attempting to collect herself. It becomes a prayer for Ioan. Accepting and overcoming her religious defection, she recants and silently prays. Dear God, forgive me. But it's not for me. For my son. For Ioan. Give him the strength to endure. Please God give him the strength.

The first thing that hits her when she opens her eyes is the smug bald head of Col. Edward Court Smyth standing a few feet away in the next row. She is not at all confident she'll be able to negotiate her exit without an encounter. The man sitting next to her picks up his briefcase, the buckle nicks her tights. Damn! That'll be a ladder. At that precise moment the Colonel turns and catches her eye. He bows icily. Caught off guard, she gives him a hesitant smile and glances at her watch, eleven o'clock. If she hurries she can make the 11.33 from Paddington back to Penzance.

Outside in the street, across the road from Westminster Abbey, just as she's trying to hail a taxi, Edward Court Smyth catches up with her.

'Rose. Please accept my condolences.'

Rosie is astonished. Speechless at his condescension.

'Margaret and I,' he continues, 'were both most grieved to hear of David's death.'

Heavens! thinks Rosie, I haven't thought of David for a whole morning. 'Thank you.'

'But, thank God,' says the Colonel, lifting his eyes to the spires of the collegiate church of St Peter, 'he never lived to see his son brought so low.'

Rosie is suddenly hot with fury.

'Watch it, Colonel,' she says, 'I do not condone what he did, but neither do I believe your son was blameless gold. Your boy hero worshipped my son, anyone could see that. By bringing this case, you have brought your own son low, and probably scarred him for life.'

Mercifully, a taxi pulls up beside her. She opens the door. 'St Pancras station, please, Driver. My regards to Margaret,' she says to the Colonel, slamming the door with a deal of satisfaction. As the cab takes off, she finds herself trembling, wondering where that little speech had come from, surprised, but proud she'd defended Ioan, she leans back. Leaning forward, she says to the driver, 'Sorry, I meant Paddington station.'

Just catching the 11.33, she finds a corner seat with her back to the engine. She'd worked out that if she faced the engine, what with the constant eye movement watching oncoming scenery, she got a headache – this never happened if she faced a retreating scene.

Since becoming a widow she'd taken up knitting again, although it didn't suit the persona she was aiming for, as a therapy it calmed, and, she told herself, was healthier than smoking. The needles click as her pink painted nails flash over the wool, her thoughts brood on Ioan. When she'd delivered his suit to the side door in the Court House basement, she'd expected to be allowed in to see him, but the official had told her "No visitors." At the time it had added to her anxiety, but with hindsight, and if she was honest with herself, which lately, without a man around, she was more inclined to be, she was relieved. She'd worried endlessly about what she would say.

A trolley of refreshments comes along, she buys herself a cup of coffee. Sipping it, she can't get Ioan out of her head. It is in this moment, for the first time, the notion of blame occurs. Not guilt, though that would come. Just the stray thought that, if she'd not blanketed out Ioan's confession years ago, as he'd reminded her in his letter, what might have happened? I should have reacted differently. What if I'd pretended to understand? Just tried? Might we have become closer? Would he have confided in me about his friends? At the time she'd told him, 'I don't want to meet or know anything about your lovers. The whole thing is abhorrent to me.' She shudders at the memory. Her reaction had been almost as bad as David's would have been. Maybe being around Red is broadening my vision.

To distract herself, she tots up her expenses. Three nights in a Kensington hotel at £100 a night, £40 to Pickford's for opening up Ioan's trunk, the return fare £55, plus the hair salon in South Kensington, £85, extravagant, but worth every blonde streak, and seeing "Gladiator" in Leicester Square after a visit to the National Gallery – with food, over £500! Can't afford many of these trips. I could have bought him a suit for less.

The train is due at Penzance at 4.55. Outside Reading, she calls Red on her mobile, 'I'll be home before closing time.' Then Liz, to tell her of Ioan's sentence. Liz is horrified and very sympathetic, but just on her way out to lunch with Simon and a friend of his.

'She's a lady art dealer from London, absolutely charming, we took her to St Michael's Mount yesterday, well, the thing is, she's very interested in Red's paintings. Isn't that thrilling?'

Rosie is unable to summon up much enthusiasm. 'Very,' she says.

She returns to her knitting. A multicoloured sweater for Red, but it's proving more complicated than she'd expected. After a while she dozes off and dreams of David. They're back at "The

Olive Branch". She's asking him for an explanation of his Will. He carries on stacking up the ale bottles as if she wasn't there. Waking at Crewkerne, she picks up "Hollywood Wives", and Jackie Collins keeps her mind off her troubles for a while.

Michael, meanwhile, still amused at his chance meeting with Ioan's half-sister, is entering The Nylwen Art Gallery to keep his appointment with Joyce. Perfectly groomed as ever, she is chatting to Simon Barclay, who Michael remembers dimly from their Courtauld days.

Although Simon appears charming, there is a wariness about him. 'Good to see you, Michael,' he says. 'We're honoured. We don't get you big fish down here often.'

'You're very kind. But this lovely Gallery enjoys a much higher reputation than our commercial little cellar.'

'Now, you boys,' says Joyce, firmly tucking her arm through Michael's, 'stop this one-down-manship and let us enjoy ourselves.' Tactfully, she steers Michael away to the exhibition in the next room.

They stroll around, occasionally referring to the brochure and commenting. Approaching Julie's work, Joyce nudges him. He needs no such signal. Here is a picture that roots him to the spot. It's Ioan. Unbelievably. Unmistakably. The artist has caught his look, a certain expression. Gold blond, as he'd seen him on the beach, the only white on the canvas is the whites of his eyes, the iris, cornflower blue, looking out cartoon-like from a brush-stoked purple green canvas. Giving the picture a dimension, a depth, is a small flame-haired girl standing in the background. Michael checks the brochure. "Family Secret. Julie Red Williams."

He is impressed, no question. 'Original style.'

'Instinctive,' says Joyce. 'See the other two. Completely different. Variety, yes, but needs guidance.'

'Yours?'

She squeezes his arm, 'Or yours.'

'Mmn. Shamelessly pretty. Excellent colour sense.'

The "Family Secret" was un-priced. Michael offers to buy it for a hundred and fifty pounds.

Simon shakes his head, mouthing, 'Two.'

'Done,' says Michael.

Simon inclines his head in mute acknowledgement and sticks a red dot on the frame. Ioan and his dots, thinks Michael. Simon explains the picture will have to stay in the Gallery until the exhibition closes next month.

'Of course,' says Michael, 'I wouldn't dream of displacing your splendid presentation.' As he's writing out the cheque, a jolly buxom woman arrives. Simon introduces her as Liz Thomas. She appears to be a friend of Joyce's, interested and enthusiastic about the sale.

'If you'd like to meet the artist,' she says, 'I happen to know she's working just down the road in "Rosie's Tea Room".'

'I had coffee there this morning!' says Michael. 'Not the girl with red hair?'

'Yes,' says Liz. 'She's my niece.'

Immediately comprehending the significance of the title, he says, 'And that's her in the painting.'

'Right!' says Liz, grinning.

This must be Ioan's Aunt, thinks Michael, searching her face for a resemblance.

'Joyce, I tell you what,' she's saying. 'Why don't you both come to dinner tonight? Unless,' she turns to Michael, 'you're planning on driving back to London?'

Michael and Joyce exchange looks. Joyce says, 'I thought having come this far we'd have lunch at Land's End. But this afternoon, certainly, I should make tracks.'

'You're more than welcome to stay,' says Liz, 'I have a huge house with lots of room. You could meet Red, and we can have a cosy evening discussing Art and putting the world to rights.'

'That, I'd love,' says Joyce. 'Really. I'm the original philosophic philanthropist. But I'm not so sure about Michael?' She turns to him primly smiling, 'Don't worry, I'll hold the fort tomorrow. Stay over if you want to?'

Michael had learnt since his divorce to go with the flow. The prospect of dining with Red and this jolly aunt of Ioan's intrigues him. 'My partner,' he says, 'likes to pretend I'm the shrewd one. Actually it's quite the reverse. Thank you, I'd like that very much indeed.'

'Grand,' says Liz, handing him her card with a printed map on the back. 'Come early. Get settled in.'

They shake hands and arrange to meet at the Vicarage for dinner at seven thirty.

Joyce drives Michael to Land's End, where, with linked arms they watch the crashing waves of the Atlantic pounding England.

'You're feeling better, aren't you?' she says.

'Mmm. Much.'

'I can tell. You're healing.'

Over a Ploughman's in "The Last Pub in England" he tells her all about Bernard's tiresome 'blue period', and they decide to sign up Julie Red Williams. Joyce takes Michael back to his car, they hug goodbye, and she drives off back to London.

Alone again, Michael can't resist stopping off at "Rosie's Tea Room."

The cafe door bell tinkles again as he enters. He regards it almost with affection.

'Hi!' says Red, from behind the counter. A middle-aged couple sitting by the inglenook fireplace turn to inspect him.

'I'm just writing to Ioan,' she calls. 'Shall I give him y' luv?'

'Um. Well, er...' Michael nods to the couple as he passes them. Reaching the display counter he confides, 'Why not? I'll be writing myself shortly.' Opening his wallet he gives her his business card. 'Here, you'd better have this.'

'Bloody hell!' she says, impressed.

'I just saw some of your work at the Art Gallery. You are 'Red' I take it?'

'That's me. You wanna buy a picture or sommat?'

'I already have. And I'd like to buy some more.'

'You're bullshitting me! Which one d'you buy?'

'Your "Family Secret". The one of you and Ioan.'

Red's voice rises an octave, 'That's not Ioan, that's his mother!' Her grin spreads across her ears.'

'His mother?' Michael is confused.

The couple by the fire are standing and putting on their coats, they indicate they want to settle their bill.

'Hold on a tick,' she goes, leaving his card on top of the display case.

Ioan's mother? He watches Red tot up the couple's bill. Sunlight catches her red curls. That girl's definitely got something.

'See you made good work of me sponge cake?' she says.

'Lovely m'dear,' answers the man in a Cornish accent.

'Rosie unwell?' asks the woman.

'No, she's fine. Up in London. Oh ta!' Accepting the tip, she flicks her eyebrows up at Michael and grins. As the couple leave, she clears their table, calling, 'See yous.'

The tinkling door bell falls silent. The two of them are by themselves.

'So Red... Can I call you Red?'

'Everyone else does. I'll call you...' passing his card on the counter she leans over her tray to read, 'Michael...? No, Mickey's more you.'

'I think,' says Michael, recalling the only person who called him that these days was Joyce, 'I should like that.' Nichola used to call him 'Michael', sometimes 'Mike', but never 'Mickey', which she despised. 'Look, can we share a pot of tea?'

'Sure.' Red trots behind the counter.

'I liked what I saw at the gallery. I think you have talent.'

Putting down the tray, she looks him in the eye. 'Are you for real? Honest?'

'How long did it take you to paint those three pictures?'

''Bout three days each. The bigger one took a week.'

'Interesting. Red, I should like to offer you a contract.'

'A contract? How would that work then?'

'I would pay you a certain amount each month for, say a year. With an option to renew. For that, you would let me have everything you paint. After a year, I'll give you a show in London. With the proviso that you take my advice, and I charge whatever I think I can get.'

'And you,' she says, 'get to keep all the dosh.'

'Exactly. How do you feel about that?'

'How much a week would you pay?'

'I propose, three hundred pounds a month. That's seventy-five a week. How does that sound?'

'Could you make it a hundred?'

'Ah, a business woman! You'd have to let me have everything, mind. No gifts to friends, you understand? That way I keep you exclusive.'

'Exclusive? Me?!' She scoffs in disbelief.

'OK,' says Michael, 'a hundred a week.'

'Do we shake on it?'

'Why not?'

Red, her expression mock serious, walks round to the front of the display case and shakes hands. 'Deal,' she says, then, 'And this is no bullshit? For real?'

Michael holds her hand a little longer than necessary, to emphasise his sincerity. 'For real. I'll send you a contract with all this written down. You do good work, I'll make you famous.'

'Wow!' Red standing on tiptoe gives his cheek a peck. 'You really are that guy from "My Fair Lady", aren't you?'

'Professor Mickey! That's me,' he says, his hands pleasantly resting on her waist. 'Now what about this tea?'

'Pot for two coming up, sir,' and she skips back to the tea urn.

Michael congratulates himself. £5200 a year, at an average of a £1000 picture, could be as much as £36,000 a show. Fine – for a student.

'Tell me about yourself. It didn't say much in the brochure. How much longer have you got at Art College?'

'Nine months on me Foundation Course. Plus another two years if I pass me exams.'

'Oh, you'll pass. By the way,' he sits at one of the tables, 'I met your Aunt, is it? In the Gallery. She's invited us to dinner tonight.'

'Oh no!' she says, 'I've got a date. I'll cancel it.'

Just as he is about to enquire about Ioan's mother, the cafe door bell tinkles and a pretty but worn looking woman in a headscarf comes in. Michael turns to look at her framed in the doorway.

His heart jumps into his mouth.

She's Ioan's double! Yet... Do I know her... is it possible?

As she closes the door she pulls a scarlet and white Hermes scarf off, shaking out a streaked blonde hairdo. Michael's first impression is of a woman looking out of place. Slim snappy ankles in black high heels, but it's a simulated sophistication. Her stocking has a ladder, her make-up is faded. There is a vulnerability, and something else, he can tell she's unhappy... Sad blue eyes... Familiar eyes. Ioan's! Yet... Could it be? He suddenly remembers... Good God! It's little Rosie from the summer show. That pneumatic little Welsh popsy from Bournemouth. Rosie, all grown up. Good God! She is Ioan's mother! What a hoot! His mind reels. I knew there was something about the boy, all that time on the beach, he said he was Welsh, said his Mum had been in show business, I should have realised. Maybe that's what I saw in him. Maybe that's what it was all about. Trying to convince himself of this fact, to explain away his obsession, he marvels how alike they look. Ioan, Rosie's son. Rosie's Tea Shop. Of course!

Rosie sighs, leaning back on the closed door, she smiles a silent greeting to Red. Depressed about Ioan, she is at her lowest ebb. On the train she'd been doubting her worth as a mother, as a woman, even the wisdom of taking on the cafe alone. "Hollywood Wives" hadn't helped much either, her life by comparison seemed useless, bland, and to be going nowhere. She feels alone, unloved and exhausted, all she wants is a hot bath and bed.

A customer, an elegant man in a pale grey suit is looking at her. Examining her. Must be a tourist. What's he staring at? How rude! Good God! A thunderbolt hits her brain! Am I imagining it? It can't be? His hair's almost white!'

Standing up, the man comes forward. He speaks. 'The freckles may have vanished, but I could never forget those eyes!'

Her knees give way, she holds on to the back of a chair and eases herself down, bundling her bags onto a table. 'I never had freckles. Mickey! Mickey Stanhope?!'

'Rosie Thomas! How wonderful to see you!'

'Mickey!' On the verge of crying, she rises into his arms and hugs him. 'Good God! I can hardly believe it!' She holds him tight. So tight. Heavens, he feels good! We fit. Our bodies still fit. Oh God! I never want to move. She checks herself, suddenly aware of appearing foolish. Steady on, steady on, this man is a stranger. 'Sorry. So sorry. It's all too much,' she says, pulling herself away. 'Is it really you?'

'Indeed it is,' he laughs.

'I've had a... rather a strange day. I can't quite take this in.'

'How are you? It must be all of thirty years.'

'Mmm,' she is trembling again. 'Yes, it is... nearly. It must be.'

For a moment neither speak. Grins glowing, they just gaze at each other.

Red, watching, gets the complete picture. She turns away to prepare the tea tray.

'How astonishing. Excellent, really,' murmurs Michael.

Rosie dives into her handbag for a handkerchief. She suspects he's remembering her face as young, chubby and unlined. She's certainly remembering him with bushy black curly hair, and a sinewy firm body.

'So this... is all yours?' he says, looking around. 'Rosie's Cafe.'

'For the time being, yes. What on earth are you doing here?'

'I came to see the young artist here.'

'Oh ta!' says Red, hands on hips. 'Thanks for remembering.'

Rosie detects a resentment in Red, and moving away from Michael, his proximity is unnerving, says, 'How are you, Pet? Did you have a good day?'

'Well, till's full,' she says, placing the tea tray on the table where Michael had been sitting. 'You want to watch 'im. He was all over me, till you walked in.'

'Sorry,' says Michael, 'Rosie is an old friend. The Pavilion, Bournemouth, wasn't it?'

Rosie dabs her nose with a hankie, 'Mm,' and flashes him an edgy smile.

'Long before you were born, young lady,' says Michael.

'Would that have been when you were married to me Dad?'

Rosie, shocked at Red's waspishness, says, 'No! Long before,' but, she thinks, perhaps I confided too much in this girl.

'Thought he might be a friend of family, like. Says he knows Ioan.'

Rosie looks at Michael, anew, astonished. 'You know Ioan?'

Michael swallows. 'Yes. Coincidence isn't it? Obviously, you're his Mother. You're as alike as two peas!'

Rosie stares. 'How? How do you know him?'

'We met on holiday about three months ago. In the Canary Islands.'

'Ah yes!' Very hesitantly she asks, 'Are you aware at all, of what's happened to him?'

'Yes. Yes, I am. I'm so sorry.'

Rosie sits down again, her hands absently pat her bags. 'As a matter of fact, I've just come from his trial. Well, actually it was a sentencing. He pleaded guilty, you see.

'Guilty! What was the... er... the outcome?' says Michael.

She hardly dares to meet his eyes, 'Four and half years.' Putting her hand to her brow to cover her humiliation, she says, 'I still can't take it in. Young years are so precious,' and she pulls her fingers through her hair.

Red is frowning and about to speak. Michael catches her eye and nods to her. Don't. She doesn't take the hint. 'Four and a half years? Bloody hell! What did he do to deserve that?'

Rosie, her head in her hand, struggles. 'I told you... he's gay.'

'So's our milkman,' says Red, 'but he's not in clink for four years!'

Rosie lifts her eyes to search Michael's. 'Do you... know about all of this?'

He nods.

'How? Oh, never mind,' she sighs and looks at Red. 'He was found with an under-aged boy. A friend of mine's son. At least, they used to be friends of mine.'

Red walks over and puts her hand on Rosie's shoulder. 'I'm ever so sorry.' Smiling at Michael over Rosie's head, she says, 'Mickey 'ere's bought our painting.'

'Really?' Rosie is unimpressed, but supposes she should say something. 'You like it?'

'You sound surprised. Of course I do. It is of you.'

There is something wrong in his voice, but his smile and eyes are reassuring.

Rosie looks at Red. 'Mickey? Did you call him Mickey?'

'Yes. He said I could.'

'That's what I used to call you.'

'Rosie,' says Michael. 'You lost your Welsh accent then.'

They gaze, smiling at each other again.

Red taps her foot impatiently. 'Look, it's nearly closing time. Better shut up shop. I'm going upstairs, I've got a letter to finish. There's ye tea, s'pect you'd like to be alone for a bit. Liz is giving a dinner party for 'im tonight.'

Rosie frowns, 'Oh dear! I'm not feeling much like a party.' But I'd like to be with him, she thinks. No, I can't. Not tonight. I'm pooped!

'Whatever,' says Red. At the door she turns, seductively raising her gold-ringed eyebrow. 'See you, Prof!' Pointing an imaginary gun, she shoots him. 'Pow! Deal!'

Alone with Michael, and feeling a distinct thrill about it, Rosie has a niggling curiosity. How odd that he should know Ioan and about his case. How come? Conscious he is looking at her, she adjusts the rings on her finger before asking him. Glancing up at him, she is disappointed to find he is still focused on where Red was standing. He turns and grins. Standing up, she goes to the shop front. 'What did she mean by 'Deal'?' She pushes back the bolts, and turns the sign hanging on the back of the door around to "Closed".

As Michael explains about Red's contract, Rosie sits opposite and pours the tea. Question follows answer – gradually they unfold the story of their lives to each other. Marriages, children, divorce and death – the whole damn thing – almost.

Outside it's becoming dusk. High in the sky, azure blue is turning to grey. Clouds are on the horizon. Street lights flicker along the sea front, their light dances on the forever-ebbing crashing waves. The yellow light from "Rosie's Tea Shop" spills over the pavement. To a passer by, the couple engrossed over the table inside might appear to be lovers, the cosy glow gives the scene such a warm romantic aura.

In truth, romance is certainly, at that moment, creeping up on Rosie.

Not so upon Michael.

Recognising Rosie, has given him an emotional jolt, exhilarating yet distinctly uncomfortable. Ioan's mother? It could, of course, be wild, he thinks, crazy! But it's unthinkable. Anyhow, we're two very different people now. In those days she had been a doll, a beautiful blonde popsy. They'd had some terrific times, marvellous times, but, honestly, hadn't she really been just for sex?

Upstairs, in the window over the cafe, a bright neon bulb flickers on. Its harsh light hits Red's auburn head. She sits by the table at the window to finish her letter to Ioan.

She has so much to tell him.

Chapter Twenty-One

After Dinner Mince

Thrilled to have collared Michael for her dinner party, anticipating a stimulating evening of intellectual and philosophical discussion, Liz sets about organising a menu. She calls Rosie – who's not picking up – so leaves a message inviting her, and to bring along Red. She also asks three bright youngsters over from the chalets – she knows they'll be grateful for a free meal – and with Simon, that will make up an even eight for dinner.

Liz works out the placements at the fully-extended walnut table in the dining room. Simon opposite her, Michael to her right, Rosie next to him. Laid up with silver ware and crystal glasses, a bowl of freshly-picked roses in the centre, it all looks very fine, set under the chandelier, before the grand Victorian fireplace. Leaving her helper, Mrs Spencer from across the way, to finish up in the kitchen, she goes upstairs to dress. Choosing her orange and black kaftan, she selects a string of yellow beads from the multicoloured coil of necklaces that hang over her bedpost. Arranging them over her impressive bosom, she dials her sister's number again.

'Ah, you're back! Did you get my message?'

'No,' says Rosie, 'but Red told me. Forgive me, will you, darling. It's been a dreadful day. I'm really not up to it.'

'The Trial, of course dear, and the journey. But I thought it would save you cooking and cheer you up. The Art dealer who bought your portrait is coming. He's um, quite a handsome fellow. I think you'll like him.'

'Darling, if you're trying to match-make, give up. He's an old friend. We just had tea. He's on his way over to you now.'

'An old friend? Rosie Thomas! How do you know him?'

'Long story. He's someone I knew years ago.'

'Oh. So is that why he bought your portrait?

'How should I know?'

'And you don't want to have dinner with him?'

There is a pause. 'Darling. I'm not looking my best. I'm dead!'

'Yes, I think you must be.'

'Any other evening, but not tonight. Sorry, cariad.'

'I understand.'

'You probably will,' Rosie mutters.

'How do you mean?' Silence. 'Well, if you change your mind, pop in for coffee. Must dash.' Faintly bewildered, Liz goes downstairs to join Mrs Spencer in the kitchen.

Michael arrives in his BMW at the same time as Simon Barclay in his Mazda. 'Jalousie de Courtauld' still hovers round the edges of their greeting. Prickly Simon comments on a framed repo hanging in the hall.

'Ah "The Church at Deuil," Utrillo! A truly instinctive painter.'

'Absolutely,' says Michael. 'As a matter of fact, I have the original.'

Simon chokes. Attempting to disguise it, he affects a coughing fit.

A tragic-looking girl with long black hair enters through the French windows. She is followed by two tall youths, one with heavy bum-fluff on his upper lip, the other with a baby-pink complexion but huge nose. Liz introduces them.

They nod and simultaneously utter three shy 'Hi!'s.

Liz takes the arm of Pink Face, saying, 'This is the young man who's going to make our garden seat. He's a sculptor. Art in use.'

'How interesting!' says Simon. 'Might I have seen something of yours, somewhere?'

'I do seats in forests and community areas,' the young man says, 'trails in inspirational environments.'

'Ah!' Simon nods, trying not to look nonplussed. 'Excellent, excellent.'

Just as Michael is attempting conversation with Miss Tragic, Red turns up cock-a-hoop, like the cat-with-the-cream, with a denim clad fisherman in tow.

'This is Trevor,' she announces, one hand in his, the other holding her crash helmet. 'We picked each other up in the harbour yesterday.'

Liz, not in the least put out, welcomes the boy warmly, she loves a multi-mix of age and background, besides, he evens up the numbers, now Rosie isn't coming.

Over wine, the first topic of conversation is, of course, Red's contract with Michael, which irrationally irritates Simon. Followed by a hearty chat from Red, Michael, Trevor, Bum Fluff, and Pink Face, who all seem to know about motorbikes.

'This conversation is totally incomprehensible to me,' laughs Liz, gathering up Miss Tragic and Simon, and ushering them into the dining room. 'Come and sit down.'

'My first was a Harley Davidson,' she overhears Michael say.

That rings a bell, she thinks. Suspicion dawns. Holding her smile, she indicates the chair next to her saying, 'Guest of honour, next to me.' As they start the hors d'oeuvres – honey dew melon and prawns – she decides to probe. 'I gather you know my sister, Rosie?'

'I think I may have met you before too,' says Michael, 'Years ago in Bournemouth. At a party in the theatre. Early seventies. The opening night of the summer season? At the time, I was a stage hand shifting scenery.'

Liz shuts her eyes for a moment, she dares not remember.

'Sporting an Afro hairdo,' he continues, hands six inches out from his ears, 'this size.'

Amid the smiles, Liz's face falls. Yes, this is the man Rosie had the affair with. No wonder she cried off dinner. Not looking her best indeed! Laughing, she says, 'How could I ever forget. Tell me, is there a Mrs Stanhope?'

'I believe she's changed her name by deed poll. Last year, I was dumped!'

At this, Simon, a fellow dumpee, instantly mellows. He looks, through a large glass of red wine, a little more benignly on his former rival.

Red, trying to be chummy with Miss Tragic, says, 'Heard the one about the cannibal who's on a diet? Only eats midgets!'

Miss Tragic snorts. The three young men hoot. Everyone drinks, relaxes, and laughter and noise fill the air.

Over the trifle, Liz attempts to lift the tone. 'Faced with the banal inevitability of death? Why do you suppose human beings struggle so to emulate the divine Creator, to conjure life from nothing?'

'Ah!' exclaims Simon. 'The mystery of life?'

By the time Mrs Spencer brings in the coffee, the hoped-for 'creative process of art' conversation is under discussion, and Liz is in her element handing round the After Dinner Mints.

Round midnight, under a blue black June sky, the party disperses. The three youngsters, arms round each other, stagger across the lawn back to their chalet. Michael, mildly curious about their sleeping arrangements, climbs the stairs to the guest room, once occupied by Rosie. A slightly drunk Simon flops onto Liz's double bed, and Red blithely mounts her Ninja Turtle and drives back to "Rosie's Tea Room" – where in turn she is blithely mounted by her fisherman friend. In the next door bedroom,

Rosie, confident she made the right decision in declining Liz's dinner invitation, is fast asleep, dreaming – dancing, like Moira Shearer, with a masked prince at the ball.

Waking early, she's not so confident. Regretting she'd not spent longer with Michael, she lies in bed mulling over their meeting. She recalls their brief time so many years ago. Had all that been just a physical thing? We were so happy. Weekend picnics at Sandbanks over Studland Bay. That wonderful trip on the back of his motorbike to Paris when the theatre closed. 'For technical reasons', the public were told, really it was because the Iron had got stuck. That was all so romantic. He never caused me any pain, even when we ended.

I must be mad! What the hell am I doing? She galvanises herself into action, scrambling out of bed and scampering into the bathroom. On with the shower... oh, and the shower cap. As the hot water cascades over her, her mind races. I can't let him slip through my fingers. He's alone, like me. She gives herself a swift but careful make-up, finishing by squeezing two drops of Disc Bleu into her eyes. Just as she's finished dressing in her light beige trouser suit, the front door bell rings. She puts her head out of the window. It's Joe Fudge's van, he's delivering the weekly groceries. Damn it! Tuesday, I forgot. 'Hold on,' she calls to him, 'I'll be down in a sec.' After checking her reflection, she runs downstairs to let him in.

'Mornin!' he says. 'My, but you're looking gorgeous. Where you off to?' He's dressed in his usual cords and rolled-up shirt sleeves. He's holding a bunch of flowers.

'Morning, Joe. Would you mind putting it all in the kitchen. I have to pop out for a breakfast appointment. My stepdaughter's still upstairs asleep.'

'Oh. I cut some African Marigolds. Thought you'd appreciate 'em. Doubles they are. Looked so handsome in the garden this morning. But off you go, m'dear. Leave it all to me'

'Thanks so much, Joe. So kind of you. I'm in a bit of a rush, do you mind?'

Barely breaking step, she nips into her Honda Civic, leaving Joe down in the mouth, knowing he's not going to get his complimentary mug of chocolate this week.

Within eight minutes she turns into The Old Vicarage driveway. As usual, the front door is wide open. 'Morning,' she sings out popping her head round the kitchen door.

Liz is at the sink washing up. Rosie instantly recognises from her body language that something is wrong. Sal barks a single 'yap' welcome, and wagging her tail ambles over. 'You're not much good as a guard dog,' says Rosie, rubbing her back. Hugging Liz from behind she gives her shoulder a kiss. 'How was the dinner party?'

Liz, hands in water, gives her a silent baleful stare.

'Oh dear. As bad as that? Post mortem, then?'

Liz takes out a blue ceramic bowl from the soapy water, and sets it carefully onto the draining board. 'You're too late, you've missed him.'

'You mean, Mickey?'

'Yes, I mean Mickey,' says Liz, widening her eyes mock innocent, sending up Rosie's winsome look. 'He left at the crack of sparrow fart. Didn't even finish his tea. Look, it's still there on the table. Pass it over, will you.'

Rosie picks up the half-empty teacup. She idly strokes the lip with her finger tip. 'Stone cold,' she says, setting it down on the draining board.

Liz has an pursed expression.

'All right,' says Rosie, 'I admit I was hoping to see him. Last night I was so exhausted I couldn't think straight. This morning though, I got to wondering. Oh well,' she shrugs. 'If he's gone.

Que sera sera.'

'Don't you quote your Doris Day Spanish to me, young lady! I know exactly who he is. The question is does he?'

'Whatever can you mean?'

'You know perfectly well what I mean. He was the one wasn't he?'

'Which one?'

The one you had the affair with before you married David? And you let me invite the man to dinner.'

'Liz! Whatever are you talking about?'

'This is me, Rosie Thomas, your sister. I'm the one who put you and David to bed, after you'd missed your period, remember?'

'That was years ago.' Then lightening her tone. 'You're very cross this morning.'

'Did he know? Did this Michael ever know you were pregnant?'

'Of course not. We only knew each other a while.'

Liz sighs deeply. 'Do you plan on seeing him again?'

'I don't know.' Rosie absently picks up a washing-up cloth and starts to dry a saucer. 'We were only teenagers. What have we got in common now?'

Liz gives her another baleful look. 'I'd have thought that was perfectly obvious.'

Rosie draws in a breath, her emotions welling up. 'Liz! How can you say that?'

'Face it,' says Liz, 'it's what you've always suspected.'

'No one can prove anything.'

'Actually with DNA testing, they can these days, but I doubt it will come to that. The boy never had an atom of David in him. "He's no more like me than a lump of coal," I can hear David saying those very words to me now!'

'Here we go again! This is what it's all about, is it? David! Always David! Haven't you played that tune long enough? Now he's dead, I would have thought we'd at least been spared that!' Schoolgirl-fashion, she imitates Liz's Welsh accent, 'He was my boyfriend first.'

Squarely turning to confront her, Liz says, 'Now that he is dead, don't you think it's about time you admitted the truth. At least to me! No, David's not around, poor darling, more's the pity. But it's pretty obvious by that Will of his, what he thought of your carryings-on.'

Rosie is stunned. 'Did you tell him?'

Liz turns to the sink, immersing her hands.

'Did you?'

Taut, Liz puts a wet carving knife onto the draining board.

'You told him, didn't you?' Shouting, she repeats, 'You told him!'

Liz turns on the tap.

Rosie angrily smashes the saucer on the draining board. 'How dare you! How could you, Liz? Why, for God's sake? What gave you the right to judge me?'

'Because I gave you David! That's why. Drove him to Bournemouth that weekend right into your bed. Right after you'd admitted to me you were pregnant by somebody else.'

'I never admitted any such thing.'

'And that was the man, wasn't it? That Mickey Art dealer! The man who bought Red's portrait of you. I should have left you to stew in your own juice, looked after number one. I bloody well would do now.'

'I could never have said that, Liz, because I never knew it. To this day, I still do not honestly know, I swear it. What the hell do you think I've been all these years, some sort of con artist? I have never known, and that is God's truth. I'll swear it on our Mam's grave!' Rosie angrily strides to the other end of the kitchen twisting and flinging down the tea towel. 'How the hell do you think I've felt all these years? The years Ioan was growing up? Waiting to see which one of them he would turn out like. Surely to God, he'll grow up to be like one of them. He'll give some clue, some mannerism, a look, an expression, something. He has to look like bloody one of them! But no, not our Ioan. From the moment he was born he looks like me... like a pretty little girl... and every day more so. "Oh, isn't he like you," they all used to say.' Sitting at the table, she shakily lights up a cigarette. 'And look where that's got him?'

Liz, stands over the broken saucer, arms akimbo. 'Actually it got him a very successful career as a male model. Now calm down, for heaven's sake.' She opens the cupboard under the sink and takes out a dustpan and brush. 'I'm sorry if I got aerated. I've been up all night with Simon blubbing about his ex-girlfriend. The man infuriates me! This saucer belonged to my best coffee set.'

'I'm sorry,' says Rosie, 'but you'd provoke a saint.'

'And you're no saint!' Liz bends and sweeps the broken china into the pan. Standing up, and with a new note in her voice says, 'Well, neither am I.'

Rosie looks up. From her sister's expression she knows something is coming. She inhales her cigarette. 'No confessions, cariad. Not now. Not after all these years.'

Liz halts. A thousand questions in her eyes.

A small smile hovers around Rosie's mouth. 'Oh Liz. What did you expect?'

Liz, rooted to the spot, dustpan and brush forgotten, whispers, 'You knew?'

'Of course. I wasn't that daft.'

In a tiny crumpled voice, Liz says, 'How?'

After a moment, Rosie looks up again. 'One Christmas. You

were always around for me. Then one day you weren't. Neither was Dave. I knew you were together. I just knew it.' She shrugs, very calm. 'What could I have done? Screamed and made a scene? Oh, I thought about it. A million times. I thought you'd ruined my life. Then, maybe, that I'd ruined yours,' and she curls the ash from her cigarettte into a saucer.

'Oh Rosie,' Liz crumples into a chair, 'you make me feel so terribly ashamed.'

'Don't be. If I'd said anything, I would have lost you. Dave too. I tried to be wise for all of us. So I buttoned my lip. Anyhow, it's all over and forgotten years ago. David's gone.' They look into each other's eyes, acknowledging years of anguish. 'Now there's only us.'

'And Red,' says Liz.

'And Red,' repeats Rosie. 'And Ioan.'

Liz, still nursing the dustpan on her lap, looks at the table. With a finger she presses down a crumb of bread. Quite still, she says, 'Can I say something?'

Rosie, with a small smile, says, 'Cariad, we can say anything to each other now.'

'Be wise about Ioan.'

It's Rosie's turn to frown. 'How do you mean?'

'Forgive him. He needs so much understanding right now. I know it's hard for you to see him, but write. Write lots. Admit who he is. It's not the end of the world to have a gay son.'

'Isn't it?' Extinguishing her cigarette, she murmurs from somewhere deep, 'Whose fault is it then?'

'Oh, what's this?' Liz raises an eyebrow, 'A little guilt?'

Rosie's eyes are on vacancy. 'Psychiatrists all agree it's the mother's fault.'

'Where on earth did you get that from? Those trashy magazines of yours?'

'Ioan never had a role model. You of all people knew that. Dave and he were never close. They could hardly talk to one another. I had to compensate. Mollycoddle him, as you used to call it. Probably, it is all my fault. And him being so damn pretty.'

'I have heard you say some stupid things in my life, but that just about takes the biscuit. What utter tripe!' Liz rises to empty the dustpan into the garbage bin. Leaning on the sink, she looks at Rosie. 'That is a fallacious argument. So, you made him a Mumma's boy, that's not why he's gay. There is no blame. It's his nature, not your nurturing that's made him that way. Don't you blame yourself for who he sleeps with, for God's sake. Guilt can be deadening, paralysing.'

'You,' says Rosie, aware Liz is talking from experience, 'are the least paralysed person I know.'

Liz blinks, and to avoid the reference, turns to wipe the sink down. 'Keeping busy, keeps the blues away. Now, are you, or are you not, planning on seeing this Michael again?'

'How can I? He's in London and I'm down here. Anyhow, I hardly know the man. Over tea, he told me, he's divorced and has two daughters. Oh, I won't deny he's nice, very nice. And rich. I'd be a fool not to be interested. A gent, too.'

Preoccupied, Liz resumes her seat. 'It would make for complications if you did.'

'How do you mean?'

'For a start, what would you tell Ioan?'

'He's not exactly around to tell, is he? That's one thing we don't have to worry about.'

'We?' says Liz.

'You and I.' Rosie recognises a dangerous look in her sister's eye.

'Oh. I thought for a moment you meant Michael and you. No, I only ask, because Simon, who knows Michael and his partner,

Joyce, very well from their Courtauld days, told me last night, that they are a couple. They have a very special relationship. Apparently, always did have. Simon says, they now combine their business relationship with a romantic one. I've met her, she's charming. I liked her enormously. I'm hoping she might become a friend. So hands off him, sister dear! He's taken. I'd hate for you to break up a relationship for the sake of some sentimental memory. I think it important you should know, dear. In case you were thinking of, well, I know how inclined you are to dramatise.'

Rosie is suddenly hot with fury again, 'You mean, you think I stand a chance of breaking up their special relationship?'

'Well,' says Liz, 'you have done so before. As you have just reminded me. Twice in fact!'

Chapter Twenty-Two

Correspondents and Conspirators

Ioan has undergone a change in his attitude to prison since being sentenced. Surprisingly, it had been brought about by his cell mate, Terry Boyce, aka 'The Butcher of Beckenham'.

Most people know that when a heterosexual man is denied female companionship he makes do with the next best thing, his hand. Sometimes, another man. In extremis, a goat. Ioan was much prettier than a goat!

Love had never been a part of Terry Boyce's experience. His mother had been a whore, his father, one of her customers. He had been brought up, literally, on the streets of Peckham. Befriended by football fanatics, violence and theft were a way of life. His first job had been as a butcher's boy in a local street market. The lank-haired skinny girl that hung around him in his teens, looking to him for protection from her drunken father, bloomed into the reluctant mother and shrewish wife of his murderous thirties. Now aged forty-two, shunned by his two sons, he had no one in the world. After three months of sharing a cell with a clean and sweet-smelling youth, Terry came to regard Ioan as a kind of domestic pet, a caged lissom Labrador. A barely-conscious urge arose in him to protect, to care and caress him. It never occurred to him such feelings were sexual, but when those caresses were reciprocated, as they were on the night of Ioan's sentence, and by a professional, Terry's natural libido, all those untapped emotions and years of abstinence were unleashed. Like manna in the wilderness, Terry quenched his appetite on Ioan and lay back tumescent.

The following morning, Terry had looked a little hangdog. They were escorted to the exercise yard. Apart, they walked in circles, avoiding each other. Ioan was as astonished at the night's events as Terry had been, but he wore a secret smile. The night had been, in his terms, a kickin' mad, definite result! And cuddly? Terry had been a forest of warmth and fur to hide and snuggle into afterwards. Who ever would have thought! Considering the barren, non-productive misery of his existence at the moment, and looking around at the unprepossessing looks of his cohabitants, Ioan decided, he could have done worse. He'd at least got the biggest and most fearsome of the bunch. Anyway, there wasn't much he could do about it. Complain? No way. He'd get fucked either way if he did. So have fun, enjoy it. Desperate situations call for desperate measures. So an interesting and very sexy development. Glancing over at Terry, he saw him anew, as some yielding protective giant. Talk about looking at the world through cock-coloured glasses! He strolled over to join him. 'Mind if I walk with you?' The big man didn't answer, but he didn't object either.

Returning to their cell, escorted through the recreation area, Ioan spotted Lennie and Rat Face eyeing him. Rat Face scowled, mouthing, 'I'll get you.'

Ioan remembered what the S.O. had told him about sending them to The Block, the segregation unit. If he'd carried out that threat, they might be out for revenge. Ioan's survival technique kicked in. On Rule 43, he was denied weight training or recreational activities, so he initiated his own. He organised a regime of exercises for Terry and himself in the cell. Body pump, athletic aerobics, even pilates, the system of movements which relies on core stability and dynamic flexibility, he'd learnt at his gym in Notting Hill. Terry, proud of his body, joined in eagerly. They worked out together for two hours a morning, one instructing the other for an hour, then swapping over. Only allowed one bath a week, they finished their sessions washing each other down with cold water from the tiny sink. Ioan was determined to be as ferociously fit and strong as Terry. If Rat Face and Lennie were to find an opportunity to carry out their threat, he intended to be ready for them.

One day Ioan asked, 'Terry, can I ask about your wife? Why you're here?'

'Bloody hell, boy! You're a one! Why?'

'I want to know about you. What made you kill her? Did you plan it?'

'Course I didn't bloody plan it. Went beserk, didn't I? Just 'ad enough. She was a nagger, see, boy. Never liked her much. Nagged me to death, she did.'

'So, you could say, she nagged herself to death!'

'Yeah, her own bloody fault! And you? What you in fer?'

'Having sex with an under-aged boy. He was giving me a blow job and his Dad walked in.'

A deep croaking sound exploded from Terry's throat. 'That's bloody funny!'

'The real joke is, the boy seduced me.'

'Beats me why people get so uptight,' said Terry, 'My lads used to sleep together, well, they 'ad to, see, we only 'ad the one room. They was always wanking each other off. Used to worry me at first, but they grew out of it. It was just the circumstance, see. Look at us, outside, you wouldn't look at me, would you? But in here!' he grinned happily, 'here, I'm just what you want.'

Ioan grinned back. 'Funny, I heard they put something in the tea to stop us getting randy, if they do, it don't bloody stop us none, do it?' and he laughed, a warm growling body-shaking laugh. 'You know, boy? That's the first time I done that in seven years.'

'What's that, Terry?'

'Laugh, mate, laugh!'

Today, ten days after his sentence, Ioan is handed two letters, both with "Censored" stamped across them. The first one he reads has blue round handwriting.

"Dear Big Bro, A big up!.

Bet you never thought you'd be hearing from me! Yes, it's your long lost half-sister, the jammy bitch that's inherited our Dad's bread. Strange situ, eh?

Sorry to hear you're locked up, must be real shanky. I'd love to come and visit and cheer you up. Would they let me? Dad showed me your pics when I was a kid, ever since I always looked out for you posing real buff in those swish ads.

I'm staying with your Mum for a bit, we get on real well. I painted her, easy to see who you inherited your looks from. I look like Dad, I'm afraid! Your Mum said I was never talked about, so I'm enclosing a photo of me that was taken last week outside Leeds Art College, where I am at present having a fab time (as you can see from my mad expression!). The other guys are so cool. Hope you can say the same of your cell mates, but from the movies I've seen, they're probably manky and doing your head in. I guess you're learning how to be a proper crook by now, if so, remember the tips, so you can teach me when you get out. Which is when, by the way?.

Your Auntie Liz, well, mine too I suppose, has fixed up for three of my paintings to be shown at an Art Gallery in Nylwen, where she's knocking off the guy in charge. An Art dealer from London came and offered to pay me a monthly salary if I give him all my stuff. He's promised me a show in London next year. And guess what? He turns out to be a mate of yours, Michael

Stanhope. (He's the one who gave me your address.) He knows your Mum too, they seem to have quite a thing going.

Drop me a line and say if I can come and flirt with you. Your affectionate, but crazy half-sister, or half-crazy sister, Julie. (Known by one and all as 'Red' because of my hair.)

Ioan stares at the photo, but is barely able to focus, so blinded is he by words that almost light up the paper, *"have quite a thing going"*. All he can see is a sickening vision of Michael making love to his Mother.

'Anything good?' asks Terry.

Ioan passes over the photo, 'It's m' half-sister. The one I was telling you about.'

'Little cracker!' says Terry, holding the picture up to the light. 'My eldest had a ring stuck through his eyebrow, just like that. Will she come and visit?'

'I've never met her. She wants to.'

'Fix her up, mate. Ask the screw with the book for a V.O. Good-looking bird like her coming to visit us. Laced! Art student... might get 'er to bring us in some dope. That would be a bit of alright, eh? Something to look forward to, eh?'

Ioan nods as he opens the second letter, postmarked S.W.1. The first and last lines are hand-written, the rest is typed. Bloody hell! It's from the man himself.

My dear Ioan,

I hope you are keeping healthy and optimistic. I was so concerned after our last telephone conversation back in April, that I called at your home in Notting Hill hoping to see you. Your flat mates, Polly and James asked me in, and told me of your bad luck. I am so very sorry, Ioan. But as a result, I quite understood your outburst. The whole thing must have been most upsetting for you. Your friends were worried about your possessions as they had plans to redecorate your room for their expected new baby. I advised them to put everything into storage, and I am settling that account monthly for you. Don't worry about this. If there is anything else I can possibly do, please don't hesitate to ask.

A warning. It is possible you have some dangerous enemies inside, no doubt you are aware who they are, so be on your guard, I will say no more.

You'll be surprised to learn that while I was on business in Cornwall, I bumped into your family, your Mother, to whom I explained we had met on holiday, also your Auntie Liz, and your half-sister Red, the girl you told me about on the beach. I spent a delightful evening in their company. They were charming.

Do try and keep in good spirits, Ioan, I think of you often and the good times we had together.

I should very much like to come and visit you. It would be grand to see you again and of course, if possible, receive a letter from you. My very best wishes,

Sincerely, Mike.

A brooding resentment settles on Ioan. What the hell is the man after? Visiting the flat, Polly and James telling him everything. Fucking hell! And what does he know about my "dangerous enemies" and how? Met my family! Ioan looks at Red's letter again... "*quite a thing going*". What the hell is that? What is all this? What's he trying to say? Okay, so he's paying for the storage, so let him, so bloody what! The randy sod's still trying to get into my pants. He angrily rips apart Michael's letter, but it doesn't stop his thoughts. The more he thinks, the more furious he becomes, interpreting Michael's meeting with his Ma, as some weird plan to get at him, to muscle in, get back into his life. The bugger's trying to get at me through her. I'll kill the sod when I get out.

Later that day, he asks the screw with the book for his weekly issue letter and a V.O.

He makes the visitor's order out to "Julie Williams. Sister", and on the letter he is given, he writes to her, saying "Pay us a call".

A fortnight later, the day of her visit, his interest peaks. Walking into the visitor's room with her photograph, he looks around wondering if he'll recognise her. A girl with a mass of red curls, wearing black leathers waves to him. He ambles over cooly, and sits.

Red grins fit to bust. 'Hi!' she says, as if she's known him all her life.

'Hi! You look like a biker in that gear.'

'I am. Just drove down from Leeds.'

'Thanks for the letter. Said you'd flirt.'

'I'll try not to,' she says, flirting. 'Big bro.'

'Wouldn't mind if you did. Sis.'

'Your Mum says you're gay.'

'First time she's admitted that. Guess she has no option now.'

'Z'at why you're here?'

'Didn't she tell you?'

Red shakes her head. 'You don't have to say if you don't want to.'

'My boyfriend's Dad caught us in bed.'

Red screws up her face laughing.

'Yeah, yeah, I know!' says Ioan. 'He was under age, a minor.

'What's happened to him?'

'No one's told me. He's not written. I'm not allowed to write to him.'

'Probably doesn't know where you are. I wouldn't have, if I'd not met your mate Mickey. Michael Stanhope.'

'He's not my mate. Didn't Ma tell you where I was?'

'No. She doesn't know I'm here. Well, with the shit going on about me inheriting our Dad's loot – seems funny saying 'our Dad' – anyway, I thought, best keep anything between us quiet, know what I mean?'

Ioan nods, 'Right.'

'I brought you a Walkman, but they confiscated it. What kinda music d'you like?'

On they chat, mostly about pop music. Toward the end of the session, Ioan decides he likes her. A lot. She's pretty, smart, and a bit like a glass of champagne.

'Ever taken "E"?' he says.

'Course. Why? Want me to bring you in some?'

Ioan grins and nods. They're affinity is sealed.

On her next visit, two weeks later, she smuggles in some 'joey', a small plastic egg of drugs which she deftly drops into Ioan's tea cup. He drinks the tea and swallows the egg. Rescuing it later in the cell while defecating – thank God for the sink – he shares the contents out with Terry. They spend the next two days out of it! High as larks on a summer's day.

Red manages to visit once a month. She is Ioan's only visitor.

Rosie only writes, explaining she loves him, but has staff problems. Making the round trip, would mean a stopover in a hotel and the expense would be too great, she'll try to see him soon. Ioan is philosophical, if anything, relieved, on her last visit she'd barely disguised her embarrassment. Anyway, he gets all the gossip on what she's doing from Red.

As the months go by, visiting days become the most important of his life. Apart from the opportunity Red provides of leaving the cell, she becomes his supplier. In her leather motorcycle gear, he quite fancies her. With the other prisoners in the visitor's room, who cannot fail to notice her, he earns much-needed street cred. She sketches him as they chat, and more importantly, promises to help him with money and accommodation when he's released.

Red herself, finds the whole prison experience thrilling. Completely captivated by Ioan, he comes entirely up to her expectations. His pale blue eyes make her feel gooey, wet with sexual desire. As for his physique and smooth skin, well, he's a Michelangelo work of art. She wants nothing more than to rip his clothes off and romp in a double bed. Fascinated by their forbidden relationship, his decadence and unavailability, she is consumed by frustration.

Their only point of dissension is Michael, who, in Ioan's mind has become an ogre, a lecherous old man chasing his mother with an ulterior motive.

'What's wrong with him?' asks Red. 'I think he's dishy. Made a hell of a difference to my life, I can tell you. Makes me feel great. Confident that I can really paint, know what I mean? Anyway, he gives out you two are great mates.'

'Well, we're not!'

'He's rich as hell too! Your Ma thinks he's fab, I can tell. They gaze, all soppy, into each other's eyes. 'E might be your step-dad one day, what would you say to that? Wouldn't surprise me none if that's what your Ma's thinking.'

'Don't fuckin' joke about it. The man's only after one thing. Me! He fancies me! The man's gay! He tried to seduce me in Gran Canaria. I told him to sod off. Told him I had A.I.D.s.'

'You haven't, have you?'

'Course not. I tell you, he's trying to get at me through her. It's like I'm bloody "Lolita" in that movie. It's me he's got the hots for, not her. I'll kill the sod! The man is gay.'

This does not tally with Red's perception. Ioan, she thinks, obviously has a 'thing' about Mickey. Best keep off the subject.

Each time she's met Michael, she's been left in no doubt whatever, there's always been a distinct whiff of sex in the air. It's only a matter of time, she reckoned, before they eventually did it. She'd grown more possessive of him with every monthly cheque. She'd also grown peevishly jealous of his interest in Rosie.

'You gotta pass all this on to my Mum,' says Ioan. 'You warn her.'

'Piss off! I'm not gonna tell her that! Tell her yourself.'

Unknown to Ioan, and much closer to home, he was in a more real danger.

'Rat Face', Den, Oz and Lennie are sitting, apparently playing cards and drinking tea in the central well area of C Block, in reality they are plotting. Lennie has just successfully bribed a cook in the kitchen with dope in exchange for a knife. The weapon is secured with tape on the inside of his left forearm. It has a four-inch handle and a pointed five-inch steel blade.

Eight months ago, punished for the rape and attack on Ioan, they had emerged after three days in The Block, swearing revenge. The Senior Officer had not been able to give them a lengthy sentence without the authority of the Board of Visitors, and a full enquiry, which he was anxious to avoid, so he had merely given them the minimum three day lock-up. But to Rat Face, it was the principle, Ioan had won. When you do not have much to think about, and not much to think with, eight months is a long time for revenge to ferment.

'There's three of us,' whispers Lennie scratching the tattooed butterfly on his cheek, 'and three of them, think of it that way.'

'How you make that out?' Ossie is picking his molars. He is out of the game, his cards discarded.

'When nonces go to the barves,' explains Lennie, 'they 'ave a screw there to guard 'em, dun they? That's number one.'

'They might 'ave a couple.'

'Shut up and listen.' Lennie doesn't react well to interruptions. Ossie mutters, and wipes something on his stomach.

'Number two. His cell mate, the bloody Butcher. He's always there too, ain't he? Probably up his arse every night an all!'

'I'm not fuckin' with him, mate,' says Rat Face leaning forward. ' 'E's bloody massive. I only want the little fucker that grassed us up.'

'You will, you will. I'll deal with the Butcher,' says Lennie. 'I'll chat friendly with 'im, like, while you plug the poofta with wot I got here.' Surreptitiously he lifts his sleeve. The steel tip of the knife glints.

'So what,' asks Ossie, 'do I 'ave to do?'

'Chat up the screw.'

'Are you crazy, man? No screw's gonna believe me chatting him up!'

'Not as a poofta, you daft nigger. Just ask 'im some crap about rules or sommat as they're going into the barf 'ouse.'

'Such as wot?'

'I don't know, man,' says Lennie impatient. 'Ask 'im about the weather, say you're ill, any-fucking-thing. Just distract 'im so he don't see Den stick the nonce.'

'I knows just where I can lose the knife after,' says Rat Face. 'There's a fan light winda' round the back there.' He takes a card and reorganises his hand. 'Anyway who's gonna care?'

'His Mum?' Ossie looks up from his tea mug, grinning.

'If he's got one,' says Rat Face.

'We all got Mums.' Ossie drains his mug.

'I ain't!' says Lennie. 'We go for it, Friday, OK?'

'Can't wait,' says Rat Face, spitting into the mug and laying down his hand. 'There. Rummy. Gotcha!'

Chapter Twenty-Three

The Defective Intention

Along with his letter to Ioan, Michael sent off three bouquets on his return from Cornwall.

"Many thanks" he wrote on the accompanying card of chrysanthemums and delphiniums to Liz, "for your delightful dinner and generous hospitality. Best wishes, Michael Stanhope."

To Red, with dahlias and magnolias, his card read "Anticipating many happy and profitable years ahead. Professor Mickey."

Pinned onto the third bouquet of red and yellow roses was "Dear Rosie. Grand to meet up after all these years. Love Mickey."

Only Red had answered, turning up at the Stanhope Gallery in bike leathers to sign her contract. Joyce and Michael took her out to lunch to celebrate at Cecconi's, the power restaurant of the Bond Street art world. There, Red's eccentricity of dress was accepted as de rigueur.

Michael's daughters, Susan and Kate had only been to his new flat twice. Even though he had taken them out to the theatre and to dinner afterwards, he'd not been able to persuade either of them to stay overnight in the bedroom he'd had specially decorated. It was becoming increasingly obvious they were getting into their own lives, and managing very well, thank you, without him. As he was managing very well, thank you, without the witch of Maida Vale.

Or so he kidded himself.

A year has passed since Nichola stepped out of his life, and no-one had yet replaced her. With his Malaysian girlfriend Kiany away working on a cruise ship, and with Joyce happily running The Stanhope, he was determined to utilise his singleton status. He had a friend in Spain he particularly wanted to talk to. So, taking three days off, on the anniversary of Nicola's departure, he boarded a plane for Madrid. There, he visited the three great museums, The Thyssen Bornemisza, The Reina Sofia, and The Prado, one glorious museum a day. The evenings, he spent with his old friend.

Rafael Augustin is a retired language professor, who now offers himself as a personal guide to tourists visiting the Prado – at 4000 pesetas an hour. The old Spaniard has a huge black moustache, which Michael suspects is dyed, wears a woolly waistcoat, and has an arthritic leg which he fights to disguise. His lined face, and the crow's feet round his darkly-shining eyes are testimony to a happy but hard life. Thirty years ago, when Michael was an eighteen year old student, Rafael had seduced him. Every year, ever since, Raf had sent Michael a Christmas card.

In a noisy bar near the Teatro Espanol, over tapas and drinks, their first together for two years, Michael brings Rafael up to date on his life. Under the shrill inanities of a television soap opera on the wall, the slurp of the expresso machine, camereros shouting orders, the electronic squawk of a one-armed bandit and the cacophony of motor scooters outside, he tells it all. Covering the break-up of his marriage swiftly, for he's used to telling that story now – at greater length, and with the help of two glasses of anisado, he confesses his feelings for Ioan. 'What the hell's wrong with me, Raf? No amount of travelling, meeting interesting people or viewing beautiful objects, mends whatever it is I'm trying to mend, or find whatever it is I'm looking for. Everything serves to remind me, I'm alone. There is no sharing. Which, all my life, as you know, I've done. Raf, you're the wisest person I know. Help. Give me words of wisdom.'

The old boy looks affectionately at him. A mournful lottery ticket seller wanders up to their table. Rafael dismisses him. 'Miguel,' he says, 'we are all alone in this world, surely you've learned that? All art is love. Which, of course, is why it helps. You're too sensitive. Being bisexual may be awkward, but at least we have a wider choice!' The wrinkled skin round his eyes crinkles up like waxy sweet-wrapping.

'Bisexual?' says Michael, 'I think maybe I'm more gay now. To my generation, being gay was criminal. Oh, I know it's not such a big deal in the Arts. Artists are not in the closet, like so many in other professions. Yet in the inadequate part of myself, there seems to be that fear, that prejudice. I suppose I'm scarred by my upbringing.'

'Of course. For me too. But you're a modern young man. Adapt.'

Michael smiles as he lights up his third cigarette. 'How have you managed to keep so bright, so sane?'

'I tell you. When you're my age, which is seventy-three, you need warmth and someone to look after you. Madrid is high altitude and cold, I have to be here to be with my Tintoretto and Velazquez, but I have a little villa in Granada where it is warm. Best of all, I have my mujer. For forty years.'

'But I thought you...'

'Miguel! You of all people should understand. Believe me, it is possible. I have a woman who loves me – whom I love, who brought up my family. I have, as you have obviously forgotten, two grown-up sons, a daughter, and now five grandchildren. I also have friendly boys I meet in the sauna for pleasure. It happens the world over,' he shrugs elegantly. 'It's not talked about, of course, but it's a fact of life. There are many like us. I suppose it helps that I'm a lapsed Catholic. Try not to love your boy too much. Boys only want other boys. The secret is, find a good mujer, one who understands you, one who knows, and isn't bothered by your adventures. Someone who'll look after you. They exist, believe me. And it's not being selfish, they need love just as much as we do. Let us have some more anisado,' and he turns to wave to a camerero.

On the plane going home, Michael gazes out over the clouds wondering about his friend, and the wisdom of his advice.

Back in the Gallery, a package awaits. The "Family Secret".

He had vaguely thought he might sell it, but after unwrapping it, he becomes possessive, covetous. Indifferent to other people's comments on its quality, he takes it home, where it serves as a constant reminder of the possibilities. Ultimately, it spurs him to action. He decides to contact Rosie. She is, after all, heart-free, and, he persuades himself, was once very close, we share a past, she's attractive, and if I get to know her again, properly, could well turn out to be a kindred spirit, a possible Right Person. First, sound out her stepdaughter, Red. They're close, apparently. She might be able to throw some light on Rosie's state of mind. And I have a cast iron alibi for calling on her. He telephones Red in Leeds to arrange a visit, to appraise her new canvases.

His relationship with Red has settled into a merry flirtatious one, something he achieved with most of the women in his life, but soon after his arrival, he realises she is not above pushing it further.

Since coming into her inheritance, Red has bought herself a warehouse apartment overlooking the River Aire in Leeds' new waterfront cafe-bar-culture area. Standing on tiptoe she greets Michael with a moist lingering kiss. Dressed in skin-tight jeans, a skimpy yellow top shows off her soft young midriff where a gold stud flashes in her tummy button. After making coffee, she coquettishly displays five of her new canvases.

Clocking the bed in the corner, at present stacked with ethnic glitter cushions, it occurs to Michael, that there, he may well be bound, if Red is permitted to pounce, and if he were so inclined. She produces two pencil sketches of Ioan.

'Ah! So you saw him?' Michael has a pang jealousy. 'How was he?'

'Tough. Much tougher than I expected.'

'You've certainly made him look beefier than I remember him. You told him, of course, that we knew each other?'

' 'Course.'

'What did he say?'

'Nowt really!' Red moves in closer. 'I only said we'd met up professionally, like.'

'Well, that's true. Does Rosie... does his mother visit him often? It must be difficult for her, living so far away.'

'It's a schlap, but she's written to the prison governor asking if he can be moved nearer.' Red suits her action to her words. 'Professor Mickey. You're so sweet, coming all this way. I loved those flowers you sent. No one ever sent me flowers before.'

Warily, he raises an eyebrow. 'So you said, when you came to the Gallery.'

Sidling up close, she lifts up her arms and clasps them behind his neck. 'It's not just professional, though, is it? There's more than that bin going on between us. I fancied you ever since you came into the cafe that morning. And later, at that dinner, when you knew all about motorbikes. It really surprised me you were a biker.' She closes her eyes, pouting up her lips to be kissed.

Looking into her deliciously young and pretty naughty face, Michael is tempted. 'I seem to remember,' he says, 'on that occasion you had a young fisherman in tow.'

'Trev. Yes, he was sweet.' She seductively plays with Michael's right ear lobe. 'He was only there to make you jealous.'

'I must have mistaken your body language.'

'No mistaking it now.'

'Red,' he says flatly, 'I'm here to check up on my investment.'

'Professor Mickey!' She kisses him softly on the mouth.

Motionless, allowing her lips to leave his, he deadpans, 'You're working well.' Better not, he thinks. If I do, she'll only boast of her conquest to Rosie, and that would scotch my chances. Taking Red's wrists, he holds them level with her shoulders. 'Listen to me, Red. I'd like nothing better than to roll on that bed over there with you. But we have a contract. A professional arrangement. If we allow ourselves to have an emotional entanglement, it would spoil everything. Your career, for one. Sorry, but it's a no no. Besides, I have a daughter your age. So cool it, eh? Let us keep our relationship business-like.' Kissing both wrists, he drops them. 'I'm going to leave now. Your work is looking good. Don't be afraid of using a broader colour palette, you're colour sense is excellent. And thanks for the coffee.' With that he goes.

Red has not heard one single word. All she knows is her femininity has been affronted. She's been snubbed. Ioan's right, she thinks. He's gay.

Dear Rosie, writes Michael, when he gets back home, he writes on the back of a postcard reproduction of his Utrillo, "The Church at Deuil".

> I have been abroad and unable to follow up our fortuitous meeting – now I'm back, is there a chance we could organise a get together? I saw Red the other day, who told me what a schlap (her word) it was for you travelling up to see Ioan. If you won't think me too forward, may I suggest you combine a visit to him, with one to me?

Hoping you are well and in good spirits.   Mickey.

P.S. I have a rattling great apartment, where you would be most welcome to stay overnight.

Rosie turns the postcard over and places it on the mantelpiece above her fireplace. She sits back on the sofa sipping tea, gazing at "The Church at Deuil".

She decides to call Red on her mobile. 'Hallo Lovely!' she says. 'Convenient for a chat?'

'Sure. I'm having a coffee in the college canteen. How's life?'

'Fine. Any chance of you paying me a visit? I need someone to hold the fort again.'

'Sorry, I'm busting my gut working. Where are you off to?'

'I have to go up to London for a couple of days.'

'Visiting Ioan?'

'Mmn.'

'Great! Give him my love. Can't Liz help you out?'

'I don't like to ask. She's always so busy giving her classes or doing something worthy. I'll ask, though. She might know of someone.'

'Where do you stay when you're in London?'

'Actually, I've just had an invitation from your sponsor, Michael Stanhope.'

'Mickey! An invitation to stay? Bloody hell, get you! It's more than I've had. Well, you'll be quite safe.'

'How do you mean?'

'Well, he's a poof, isn't he?'

'Of course he's not!' Rosie is shocked. 'Don't be so awful. Not at all.'

'Oh come off it, you're not that old fashioned. Of course he is. Gay as fuck! All those arty guys are.'

'Red, you are dreadful. He's an old friend. I don't believe that.

Besides, Liz told me he has a girlfriend, a partner, a Joyce someone.'

'Joyce Howard, yeah, I met her. Fag Hag!'

'Red!'

'She is. Anyways, he won't make a pass at you, if that's what you're worried about.'

'I'm hardly worried.' Rosie straightens her spine.

'Get you! Well, he won't. He's gay.'

Rosie purses her lips. 'Sometimes, Red, you should allow your elders the benefit of their experience of life. Tat ta for now. Byeee.'

She reaches for her favourite biro and writes in her best handwriting...

Dear Mickey,

The significance of the Utrillo postcard was not lost on me. Deuil was one of the places we visited on our trip to Versailles all those years ago on your motorbike. I remember we stopped off at the church at the bottom of a hill, I think it was 11th century and it had a beautiful choir. I can still see it clearly. Do you remember I bought a reproduction of the painting that day? Years ago, I gave it to my sister, who admired it too, she now has it hanging in her hall at the Old Vicarage.

Anyway, glad to hear you're back from your travels. I too have been busy, not alas with glamorous foreign trips. I've been facing the challenge of trying to make a go of my little cafe. Every night and morning, with rolled-up sleeves I'm baking cakes, scones and now even attempting Cornish pasties! I am lucky in that I have a local farmer friend who delivers really top quality organic produce, eggs, cheese, and pork preserves etc. to the door, otherwise I don't know how I'd get time to do all the shopping that would have to be done. The Virginia Creeper in my little garden is turning gold and it's starting to get quite nippy in this part of the world, so not so many tourists about.

As to your invitation, what a kind thought. I confess I'm tempted. The trouble is I have to organise a replacement whenever I leave. May I telephone you when, and if, I can make some arrangements?

Meanwhile, my best wishes. Liz, I know would send her regards too, also to your partner Joyce, to whom I know she took a great shine.

Love Rosie.

Chapter Twenty-Four

Leaving the cell

All night long the tough guys shout to one another from their cells. What with the thudding beat of reggae music and wail of Islamic prayers, sleep is impossible. Dipping in and out of consciousness Ioan finally drifts off. On waking, he forgets – for two blissful fleeting seconds where he is. Then the head-crunching reality thuds in, jeez, if only I could leave my body. Collect it later... where would I go? That fab beach in Gran Canaria? No, that bloody Mike man might be there. Miami, South Beach, yeah, skating, tanning, with all the cute muscle guys. Terry's snores from the underneath bunk float up. Ioan leans over to take a look. Talk about a soft centre in a terrifying exterior, still, lucky day when they put me with him.

'Forget the years,' Terry had said. 'Take it day at a time.' So today, we're cooped up for another twenty-two hours. No, less today, bath day. A chance to leave this bloody cell. Other reasons were exercise – walking in circles round the same boring highwalled yard, but at least there was fresh air and sky – for meals, chapel, a special visit to the library, or a visitor. Red. I wonder, could I ever make it with her?

Ioan had only ever had sex with two women in his life. Once with Maisie, his agent, who he had allowed to wank him off when he was pissed after a party, and with a pretty model girl called Veronica, when they'd both been high. Neither times had it been enjoyable. But incest? Well, with Red, half incest! I've tried most things, who knows?

With three strides Ioan is at the window, standing on the chair he sticks his lips to the metal bars to suck in the fresh morning air. He hears the silver song of a bird. The sound is so rare, it's as if he'd never heard a bird singing before. He can just see the branches of a tree, but not the bird, the tree is losing its leaves. Autumn. A pale glow of sunrise is low in the sky. Looks as if it's going to be a nice day. Pink skeins of cotton wool cloud drift high above. 'Red sky in the morning, shepherd's warning.' He checks himself. Get your mind off outside life. What's the point? Terry's snores are lighter but he's still asleep. Ioan urinates quietly against the side of the bowl, and doesn't flush. The automatic light comes on, it's 6.30am. He combs his hair. Combs are at a premium but Terry presented him with one last week, 'No use to me mate!'

Ioan is shaving at the tiny sink when Terry wakes. 'Wotcha, Terry. Sleep well?'

'Sleep of the fucking innocent, boy!' he stretches, scratches his hairy chest and settles down to watch Ioan shave. 'You've got a bloody cute arse, boy.'

Ioan grins at his own reflection.

'Get it over here. I got a morning woody.'

Ioan dries his face and turns, their eyes meet in mutual understanding. Ioan takes off his underpants and stands before him. Terry flings back his blanket, his body takes up most of the lower bunk, but he leans to one side invitingly.

In a while, apres-cum, lying still, they hear prisoners not on Rule 43 slopping out.

Lost in Terry's arms, Ioan says, 'At Christmas, anything different happen?'

'Might get a bit of telly. Bit more chapel.'

'By ourselves?'

'Bugger me no, with the twisters. Supposed to be escorted, but that don't always happen, see. Have to watch yourself.'

Cuddled up, legs entwined, Ioan feels like a kid. 'Don't suppose we get a tree.'

'Yeah, they send one over from Prisoner's Aid.'

'They don't!'

'Course they bloody don't. Where the fuck you think you are?

'Y'might get a Christmas package though, if y'lucky.'

'What d'y mean?'

'Surprise.'

'I hate that. Tell me.'

'Only 'cause I might need some joey from your sister. I'm working on a Walkman.'

'How you gonna get that?'

'One of the screws...' His body stiffens. 'Hey! Careful, they're on their way. Out. Spy hole.'

Ioan scrambles for his pants, getting them on just in time. A warder unlocks the cell door, pushing it wide open. 'Morning, beauties!' It was the guard with the sense of humour.

It's time to collect breakfast and bring it back to the cell. The routine was, when they finished, they'd put out their metal trays, wait, and later be escorted to the bathhouse.

Carrying soap and a towel, Ioan walks with the usual group, down the corridor through to the general well area. The boos and catcalls begin. He tries to be immune. To the louts, it's their sport. Down another corridor, toward the bathhouse, their guard halts. He's talking to a black guy – Ioan recognises him. It's Ossie from his first cell. Ioan turns to Terry to point him out, but Terry has lagged behind, chatting to the screw at the end of the crocodile of prisoners. Maybe it's the one, Ioan thinks, who he's negotiating with over the Walkman. What an amazing guy! Suddenly a man is in his face, it's Rat Face grabbing him. A stabbing pain stings his side. A biting fucking pain! Rat Face, breathing foully, is stabbing again and again, then vanishes. In agony, arching his back, Ioan gasps, hovering, suspended, about to fall. His hand flies to the pain in his side, something is sticking out. A knife handle! Blade sunk deep into his intestines. He screeches out, 'HELP!'

The other prisoners retreat to the walls, gawping in silence.

Terry turns at the cry, glimpsing a man running down the corridor. He doesn't realise what's happened, but runs to Ioan, reaching him just in time to break his fall. He lays him carefully to the floor.

'Pull it out!' cries Ioan, writhing. 'Get it out of me! For Christ's sake. Oh God!'

'Hold still. Hold still.' Terry grasps the hilt and slowly pulls five inches of steel steadily, smoothly, out of Ioan's body. Blood gushes forth. 'Towel! A towel! Quick,' he shouts.

Towels are thrown down. A warder grabs one and staunches the flow, pressing down hard on the wound. The towel seeps red.

'You'll be OK, boy.' Terry is kneeling, nursing Ioan's head. 'You'll be OK.'

Ioan is unconvinced, terrified.

The knife, dripping hot blood, lies by Terry's knee.

A boot stands on it. 'I'll take that,' says a screw.

Terry hands it up without a word.

The screw blows a whistle, shouting, 'Stand back you lot, stand back. Back to your cells everyone. You too, Boyce.'

'What'll happen to him?' Terry says. 'Where you gonna take him?'

'Infirmary. Back to your cells.'

Ioan, pale and gasping, says, 'Terry, don't leave me.'

More screws arrive, someone calls for a stretcher. Gawping prisoners are moved away. 'Back to your cells. Back, I said, Boyce,' repeats the guard.

The warders seem to know the drill. There is nothing Terry

can do, but obey.

Ioan clings onto Terry's shirt. 'Don't go!'

The warder loosens Ioan's grip. Terry reluctantly stands back, leaving his mate bleeding on the floor. The warder pushes him off. Walking a bit, he turns just as a stretcher arrives and watches as Ioan is carried away. He can't help wondering if he'll ever see his friend again.

In the prison Infirmary, the first thing they do is to set up a drip, and try to stop the bleeding. They can't. Ioan is getting cold. Scared and fearful, his eyes flick nervously from face to face as they work round him. 'Am I going to die?' he asks an orderly.

'No, but you need a hospital PDQ.'

He is rushed into an ambulance. Ioan doesn't take his eyes off the guard sitting by his side. 'You done this before?'

'Lots of times. Save your energy, mate. Don't talk. Quiet now.'

'Where are they taking me?'

'St Thomas's Hospital. Sssh!'

In the A&E, he is aware of lots of people, a baby is shrieking. An Intern examines him. 'This man should be made ready for immediate surgery,' the Intern says, 'otherwise he'll haemorrhage to death. And I want a C.T. scan,' he calls as the stretcher is moving away.

An exhausted looking girl with a clipboard runs alongside Ioan's trolley. 'Can I have the name of your next of kin and their contact number, please?'

'Cool. That makes me feel so great,' says Ioan trying to smile, 'Mrs Williams. Um. Can't remember the number. Ask the guard guy.'

'Are you allergic to any drugs, penicillin? Are you H.I.V.?'

'No, no. God, hope not!'

"Radiography" is written above a door. Under they go.

His wound padded, he's passed through a C.T. tunnel.

'Keep still,' says someone.

It's like going into space in some futuristic time warp... being sent off... to another planet to... die... Ahhh! the pain. Is this it, then? Can't breathe. Is this really it? Get to know what all the fuss is about, anyway. That'll be something. Get to know what happens. Am I really dying? Come on then God, show us, take me. Haven't you done enough already? Four and a half bloody years in prison for a fuck! Come on then, take me! What do you want to do with me, eh? You think I'm wicked?... huh!... you should see some of the other buggers. It's your call, mate! It's you or the other place. I'll have more fun there, I bet. Fuck me then, come on then, fuck me, God! Oh God... the pain. Take me. Take me. Please!!

A hand is on his shoulder. Ioan opens his eyes. He's out of the scan, back in the room. A black nurse is looking down. 'All right, luv?' With the help of a male orderly, she transfers him expertly back onto the trolley. 'Don't you go away now!' she says smiling.

Within moments the Intern and the surgeon are studying the resulting scan.

'What's happening here, sir?' says the Intern, pointing to a monochrome shadow. 'Or rather, what's not happening? Is this at all possible?'

The surgeon peers closer.

'Yes. Ah yes,' he mutters under his breath. 'Rare, but I have had one before. If we can't repair this one, we'll have to tie off the renal artery and go for it... Tricky. Orderly! Into theatre immediately. Just my luck!'

Chapter Twenty Five

The Lost Summer Season

The telephone rings in Michael's apartment.

'Hallo?'

'Mickey? Is that you?'

'I recognise that voice. That Welsh lilt hasn't quite vanished, I'm happy to say. How are you, Rosie? I got your letter.' He moves to the sofa with the hand set and puts his feet up. 'Are you in London?'

'No, Nylwen. I loved your card. Um, I was going to ask... Look, I've found someone to look after the shop. So I'm ready to take you up on your kind offer.'

'Great! When would you want to come?'

'That depends on you. But I was hoping next Tuesday, if that's alright?'

'Sounds just fine.'

'I'm feeling guilty, I haven't seen Ioan in months. It's such a dreadful journey, but if I could stay with you, well, I could see him the next day. But only if it's no trouble, mind.'

'Rosie, it would be a great pleasure and no trouble at all. Really.'

'I'd be arriving about tea time.'

'I'll get in a cake.'

'Mickey! It'll be so strange, after all this time.'

'Won't it just? I look forward to seeing you then.'

'Me too. Bye.'

'Bye Rosie.' Michael lies still a moment thinking. He reaches for his address book and proceeds to book seats for a musical and a table for two at 'The Ivy'.

Both are in demand, so it takes time and clout. Fortunately he has both.

'Sixty-two, Pall Mall, please Driver.'

Just asking to be taken to such a grand address makes Rosie feel fraudulent. She feels she's still just that little girl from Pontypridd. As the taxi drives up the incline out of Paddington Station, she sits clutching her handbag – country mouse in town, anxious all should go well. She is thrilled at the idea of seeing Mickey again, but has silly juvenile feelings of inferiority at being his house guest. Stupid, she tells herself. As a publican's wife I've mixed with all sorts, paupers and, well, if not with Kings exactly, with the County set – Charles and Margaret Court Smyth for instance – and no more hoity-toity lot could you find than them.

Back in her chorus girl days, during the summer season, she'd thought Mickey a bit of a toff. Though he'd only been a scene shifter, his good looks and obvious breeding singled him out from the rest of the stage crew. The first time she'd noticed him was at the technical rehearsal, standing in the wings – in a sleeveless vest, tall, with his mass of black curly hair. He grinned at her as she'd taken up her position at the side of the stage.

'Excuse me,' he said. 'We just polished the floor. You take care. Don't want to snap those pretty ankles of yours.'

Get the BBC tones, she thought.

At the dress rehearsal, when she appeared for the first time in her toothpaste tube costume, he'd openly laughed at her. 'Those plastic pants are three much, luv'. But you can brush my teeth any day!'

'You wash y' mouth out first!' she uttered.

Upstairs in the dressing room all the girls were talking about him.

'M' ovaries are in a complete turmoil!' said one.
'Wish I was in the oven when his buns were baked.'
'First one to score,' said the dance captain, 'reports to moi!'
'Careful, you'll shock Miss Pontypridd here,' one teased.
'He looks like Jim Morrison.'
'Too young!'
'In your dreams!'

After the show, he was hanging around the stage door just as she was coming down the stairs. He'd changed and looked nice, smelt of Cologne too.

'Fancy a bite, Rose?'

'How d'you know my name?'

'I looked it up in the programme. Mine's Mickey,' he said, extending a hand.

It felt nice. 'Hi, Mickey! Actually the programme's got it wrong. It's Rosie.'

'Rosie,' he said, 'do you like Italian?'

'Never had it.'

She'd never dined alone with a man other than David before either, but she wasn't going to admit that. 'Have to eat somewhere,' she shrugged. 'Don't mind if I do.'

Astride the back of his motorbike, she'd held him round his waist to stay on, that felt even nicer than shaking his hand.

In "Mamma Amalfi's", he ordered spaghetti vongale for her, and penne alla carbonara for himself, then, grinning and looking straight into her eyes, he asked, 'What made you want to be dancer?'

'That's what Anton Walbrook asks Moira Shearer in "The Red Shoes".'

'What does she answer?'

'"Why do you want to live?"' Rosie had seen the film twelve times.

'Is that how you feel?'

'Well, not quite, but I'd love to be famous. Dance in films. Wear lovely dresses.'

'You should be in "Hair." They don't wear anything.'

'Oh no! How awful. I couldn't do that!'

There's a show coming on soon about auditions, "A Chorus Line," you should try for it.'

'I don't have an agent.'

'How did you get this job then?'

'My dance teacher, Mrs Wells in Cardiff, is an old friend of the choreographer. Do you live in Bournemouth?'

'God, no! My parent's home is Cheltenham. I'm here studying at the University, at Poole, reading French history.'

'Golly! Is that interesting?'

'Riveting.' He started explaining how riveting. It was the first time in her life she'd heard anyone talk of a world of culture. By the time the first course was over, he'd almost infected her with his enthusiasm for art and history. When the bill came, she offered to go 'Dutch', but he wouldn't hear of it. Afterwards, walking along the moonlit sea front, she told him she'd once seen a film about Marie Antoinette with Tyrone Power. Mickey told her about all Versailles, the affair of the necklace, and the French Revolution. How brave the Queen had been, led to the guillotine in a cart, with her head high and her hands tied behind her back. All thrilling stuff. On the way back to her digs, on the back of his motorbike again, he took hold of her hand and placed it firmly on the flat of his stomach, saying, 'Hang on.' When they reached her doorstep, he took her in his arms and gave her a smoochy French goodnight kiss.

After the opening night of the season, there was a party in the theatre bar. Michael showed up in a black velvet suit looking like he'd stepped straight out of a seventies fashion mag, just gorgeous.

Liz had driven down from Pontypridd too. Rosie introduced them. Walking Liz back to the Bed and Breakfast place she'd booked, she nearly told her about him, but even then the shadow of David was between them, so she said nothing, and just kissed her goodnight. As she walked away, Mickey was waiting at the bottom of the road on his motorbike. 'Hop on,' he said. And they joined the others back at the digs and partied to the wee hours.

He stayed with her all night.

Rosie sits back in the taxi smiling. He was only the second boy she'd ever been to bed with, and she can still remember how much she enjoyed it. We had so much fun in those days, why did we ever stop? Ah yes. He took the dance captain out after we came back from France, and I got jealous. What a fool! It was after that I missed my period for the second time, and Liz drove Dave down in her old banger to see the show.

She looks out at Hyde Park, a couple are smooching on a bench. No, she reflects, maybe my marriage wasn't made in heaven. Oh, from David's side maybe, he was certainly fond of the old nookie. I did grow to love him though, later, after habit and warmth had grown up between us. Of course, right at the very start, in schooldays, I had a crush, he was gorgeous. But when we married, he just became a kind of teddy bear. 'Love' was never mentioned. Not even on the day he popped the question. That Sunday morning on Bournemouth pier.

After breakfast in the digs, they'd walked along the sea front. On the pier, "See How They Run" was showing, she remembered because a girl in the dressing room was having an affair with a boy in the cast. David had taken her hand and they'd sat on a bench facing the sea, under a sign, "All Cash Jackpot, £5 Win". It was the same bench she'd sat on last week with Mickey. She'd felt a bit funny about that at the time.

'Rosie,' said David, in his deep Welsh voice, 'I've something to say. It's grand in the show, you are, but, well... Now I don't want to give you the wrong impression, like, but... it makes you look cheap, luv'. I don't like to see you like that. All the fellows ogling you. Makes me feel bad. I don't like it. I know it's jealous I am. I admit it. So, I want to bring you home. You want to forget all about this show business nonsense. It's not real, it's artificial, Rosie. I missed you something terrible since you been away doing this dancing lark. I, well, I... My Mam says she thinks we should make a go of it. Make it legal, like. Settle down. Your Mam likes me too, don't she, and Liz? Both families get on, so it would be a good thing, like, from that point of view. And we're both so good together, aren't we. So why not? I just don't think I can manage without you, Rosie. What do you say?'

Part of her had wanted to hit him, but she needed him. If she wanted to have this baby, to be secure and be looked after, she had to be married. David was solid, well off, she knew she couldn't manage on her own, couldn't be a single parent in Pontypridd. So with an enormous sense of relief she'd said, 'Oh Dave!' her baby blue eyes moist, 'of course I will.'

Afterwards, Sunday lunch with Liz was a celebration. Rosie hugged her sister with glee, delighted her plan had succeeded. David bought a bottle of champagne and they talked about an Autumn wedding. In the late afternoon, David and Liz drove back home to Ponty. Alone, Rosie wanted to see Mickey, but he was off somewhere on his motorbike. She had to wait till the next performance on Monday night before she saw him. There he was in the wings, wearing his vest, as usual. She went up to him.

'Can't see you no more. I'm getting married.'

He just stared at her. 'What on earth are you doing that for?'

'I was asked.'

'But you're a kid. You've not seen anything of life. Why?'

She shrugged.

'Cat got your tongue?'

She couldn't possibly tell him why. 'David's me childhood sweetheart,' she said.

'Well. Congratulations! And to lucky old David. I think you're mad, mind, but I wish you luck. So, I was your last fling?'

'Suppose so.'

And he was too... until that supply schoolteacher arrived at Liz's school. But that was only a wee affair. Not at the time, of course, but... Liz got so cross.

The taxi drives up Piccadilly and passes the Ritz Hotel. On receiving Michael's letter ten days ago, Rosie had realised that, wherever their new, more adult, relationship might hopefully lead, it was vital she looked her best. So she'd her hair done and invested in a new outfit. The new camel hair overcoat with a tie waist, she's wearing. The shop assistant in Penzance, where she'd bought it, had told her it made her look like a film star. Rosie knew the girl was flattering her to achieve a sale, nevertheless it encouraged her to try on a glamorous cream wool dress, like one she'd seen on Marilyn Monroe. She'd put on more weight recently, and it suited her. Rosie thought the dress very nearly did for her, what it did for Marilyn. At the moment, it is neatly folded in her overnight case.

As the cab pulls up opposite Clarence House, her excitement increases. She pays the driver. The front door of 62, Pall Mall is made of wrought iron and frosted glass. She presses the top bell marked "Penthouse" and waits.

A woman's voice answers, 'Hallo?'

'Oh! Mr Stanhope? I mean, this is Rosie.'

'Take the lift to the top floor,' says the voice.

The door clicks open. The vestibule is in white marble. Rosie is impressed. She checks her reflection in the lift mirror. At the top, as the lift doors part, a sophisticated woman, perfectly groomed and dressed in a scarlet suit and pearls greets her.

'You must be Lizabeth's sister,' says Joyce, 'I've heard so much about you. Do come in. Michael is on the phone.'

The hallway is elegant and cool, a spot-lit statuette, an Elisabeth Frink, stands on a glass refectory table. Joyce introduces herself, explaining she's on her way out, but hopes to see Rosie tomorrow.

Heavens! thinks Rosie, she knows I'm staying the night, what must she think?

Michael welcomes her warmly with a kiss on both cheeks. He wears a pale blue and grey cashmere sweater over jeans, it brings out the white in his hair. He dresses like a young man, she thinks, and recalling what Red told her recently, makes him look a bit like a gay, too.

The first thing she notices on entering the living room is the Utrillo over the fireplace. Suddenly overcome with warmth and affection, she gasps, 'Mickey! "The Church at Deuil!" You got it!'

'Of course. Here, let me take your coat.'

'Mickey! I am impressed. When? When?'

'About twenty years after we'd been there.'

'How fantastic! Doesn't it look sweet? And we were there. It seems a lifetime ago.'

'It was. But with this to remind me, I don't forget.'

How romantic, she thinks. Very promising.

Michael hangs up her coat, and carries her overnight case into the spare room – the one he'd earmarked for Ioan eight months ago – 'Bathroom ensuite. All yours. I'm just next door.'

Rosie walks to the window, looking out over the untidy jostle of chimneys and fire escapes north of Pall Mall. 'It's all so grand round here.'

'Posh chimney tops, you mean? You are funny.'

'How far away is your Gallery?'

'Just up the road. Joyce takes care of it most of the time.'

'She seems nice. Is she your partner?' That was the word they used nowadays.

'Business partner, yes.'

'Oh, yes, Liz sent her love, I should have said. Where does she stay? Live, I mean?'

'At her home in Hampstead.'

Rosie, feeling foolish, looks out of the window again.

'We're not lovers,' Michael says, 'if that's what you're speculating.'

She turns, hoping she's not blushing. She laughs and shrugs, 'Well, how am I to know?' She slips into a Welsh accent, 'Well, this is all very lovely, as my Mam used to say.'

'Tea?'

'Ta.'

As Michael goes into the kitchen to switch on the electric kettle, she trails after him, taking in the opulent living room, the coloured ceramic bowls artfully lit from beneath, deep sofas and armchairs. It's the home of a rich man. If I'd not married David, she muses, this is the sort of lifestyle I might have had. 'Looks like I made a big mistake,' she calls out.

'How's that?'

'Letting you get away.'

The serving hatch slides open, Michael's head pops out. 'You were the one who got away. You were always going on about some boring Welsh rugger player. Real passion killer!'

'Was I? How dreadful of me.'

She leans over the serving hatch counter and watches him lay out a blue tea set on a tray, rather too meticulously. Yes, she thinks, Red could be right, he might be a gay. I wonder if Ioan's drunk out of those cups? 'Those are very pretty,' she says.

'They're Malvern. They used to be my Mother's.'

Maybe he's a mother's boy too... like Ioan. 'Back in those Bournemouth days,' she says, turning into the room, 'you were a penniless student. I wanted security.' She sings out the word 'Wrong!' like a gong and laughs. Sitting on the arm of the sofa she wonders at herself for being so honest. It's being with Mickey, I suppose. I feel so good with him. He knows me so well, or used to, why should I be anything but myself? 'Of course, I was in love a bit too,' she calls, 'but, well...' Shut up, she thinks, just stop talking.

Michael appears in the kitchen doorway. Quietly he says, 'Ioan told me about his father's Will. It must have been devastating for you.'

Not sure how she feels about Michael knowing this, she realises she's been cheated of telling her story. This, she thinks, is her cue to ask exactly how well he knows Ioan. Just as she's about to frame the question, Michael speaks.

'For Ioan too. I hope he has access to some architectural books in Wandsworth. He'll want to study, utilise his time.'

She'd never thought of that. Watching Mickey move books away from the coffee table to make room for the tea tray, she says, 'Were you the man who was going to sponsor him?'

'We did discuss the possibility.'

'He told me about you.' Her instinct, or maybe her wisdom bids her say no more. Possibly, she doesn't really want to know. She looks up at "The Church at Deuil". 'Do you remember when we went to Versailles?'

'Of course. Deuil,' he says indicating the painting, 'is only a few kilometres away.'

'I think we were in The Queen's Antechamber or The Abundance drawing room, one of those fabulous rooms covered in ormolu with fantastic ceilings, I've never forgotten. There we were in our jeans with all the other tourists, looking for an

English speaking guide, do you remember? The others were all jabbering away in foreign languages. Then we spotted a French woman talking English, and we surreptitiously attached ourselves, but she spotted us. "You're not with me!" she shrieked. "You're not with my Paris group. Go away, go away." The whole room turned on us and stared. We felt dreadful, do you remember?'

'Indeed, I do. You cringed.'

'I can still feel that humiliation, isn't that silly?'

Rosie stands and shivers. Wrapping her arms around her body she drifts toward the window. 'We said, that's what it must have felt like when you were out of favour with the King and the Court ostracised you.' She gazes across the street. 'I wonder if anything like that goes on over there at The Court of St James?'

'Probably,' Michael joins her at the window, close. She looks melancholy. 'Don't worry about it,' he says, 'it wasn't a metaphor for life!'

'We had a meal with some Spanish tutor of yours, do you remember?'

'Mm um. Rafael Augustin.'

'He was sweet. He told us we'd make handsome sons.'

'Very embarrassing.'

She doesn't smile.

'Rosie. Why so sad suddenly?'

She pauses. 'I think it's seeing you again.'

'Why? Seeing you again makes me feel very happy.'

'Just a pang. You remind me,' her head inclines towards his, 'of the me that might have been.' She half smiles. 'My life has been a bit of a flop, I'm afraid.'

'Come now, don't be so hard on yourself. Don't we all think that about ourselves at some time or another.'

Rosie shrugs. 'Do you?'

'Nearly all the time. I wanted to be a painter, oh so badly. But

I never had the talent. Instead I'm a shopkeeper. We both are. It's not such a bad thing.'

'But what about fulfilling one's potential?'

'Ah! Well...'

'As a Mother I've not been exactly...'

'Now, if you're worrying about Ioan...'

'No, no, it's not just him. It's me. My life! You know sometimes I used to live vicariously through him, my own life was so dull, without achievement. His life always seemed to be so much more interesting, poor darling, up till now. Even my marriage was...'

'Now, look here,' interrupts Michael, 'stop this. We're not put on this earth to make good marriages. Anyway, what about that sexy little tea shop of yours? That's an achievement.'

'Mmmn,' she can feel the warmth of his breath on her cheek. She moves away, embarrassed at her confession and from the unnerving closeness of his body. 'Sorry,' she says, 'it's not only seeing you again and the way you live. I've felt like this for some time. Even before Dave died and Ioan went to prison. It's the helplessness, the frustration, I suppose. If I had my time over, I would never have married. I should have been independent, like these girls today. Like Red. Stuck to being a dancer. Though I suppose if I had, I'd be rather an ancient one by now. Maybe I might have become a famous actress,' she turns round suddenly smiling, 'who knows?'

'My ex-wife is an actress.'

'How exciting! Do you keep in touch?'

'No,' he says firmly. 'Not if I can help it.'

Rosie senses 'hands off' and changes the subject. The kettle is starting to sing in the kitchen, she moves towards it. 'Is there anything I can do?'

'No, no. It's all prepared,' he says, overtaking her. 'Cake, biscuits or both?'

'What sort of cake?' she calls.

'Fortnum's special. Jam sponge.'

'Gorgeous! My husband used to love sponges.' I mustn't keep talking about Dave.

Michael's head appears in the hatch. 'Red tells me you're a terrific cook.'

'Not bad. I make everything for my cafe, I have to. Housewife and Mum, that's me. When I look at Ioan now though, I can't help wondering, if I somehow...?'

'I think,' says Michael disappearing, before reappearing at the kitchen door carrying the tray of tea, 'this conversation is getting a little too heavy! Let's not go down that road yet awhile. Do you mind? Not on our first date in twenty-nine years.'

Rosie looks up into his eyes. 'Sorry. Yes, I agree.'

Keeping the mood light, Michael says, 'Maybe you should have remained a mistress. My mistress, a la de Pompadour or du Barry!'

'Never du Barry,' says Rosie, 'most awful tart, wasn't she? I think you told me once she died very badly. No, Pompadour was the one, wasn't she? I wouldn't have minded being her. Might have been a bit of a strain though, all that good taste and tact. Not sure I'd have been very good at that. Shall I be Mum?'

'Please.'

Michael watches her pouring tea, a smile hovering.

After a moment she laughs, 'It's no good, I can't remember if you take sugar.'

'Two please. Just as well we don't remember everything. We won't have any surprises.'

Grinning behind their teacups, they sip.

'I do recall one thing about you,' says Michael.

'What's that?'

'You used to like musicals.'

'I still do.'

'Me too. Love 'em. Tonight I'm taking you to see "My Fair Lady".'

Rosie gives a scream, 'Oh you lovely man. How fantastic!'

Michael dips his chin, flicking up his eyebrows in amusement.

For a momentary flash, Rosie thinks she recognises Ioan in his movement. Did I imagine that?

Chapter Twenty-Six

Going For It

Rosie is floating on a euphoric pink cloud of music and delight in the Royal Circle at Drury Lane. Radiant with excitement and glowing from the reflected lights on stage, she looks, to use her favorite word, gorgeous. Savouring every scene and song, she's enthralled and empathises totally with Eliza Doolittle who, she considers, is not a million miles away from herself. After all, she too lost her accent and became a lady.

Quite by chance, Michael's ex-wife, Nichola, happens to be at the same performance. Fortunately, she has seats on the Prince's side of the theatre, fortunately, because had she been on the King's side, alongside Michael, he may have been more than a little put-out. George III had named the two staircases on either side of the foyer, so he that wouldn't have to talk to his son if they chanced to attend the theatre on the same night, yet in the foyer one is obliged to mingle.

After the performance, as Michael and Nichola arrive at the bottom of their appropriate staircases with their partners, they spot each other. Nichola inclines her head in a decorous Regency greeting. For an instant Michael mistakes her for an acquaintance, but then recognises the gold embroidered jacket she is wearing, he had bought it for her. Her face, he is shocked but maliciously gratified to observe, is less attractive than in their married days. Plastic surgery had done something odd to her expression. Over-made-up and plumper, she approaches.

'Darling,' she says, smiling so fiercely she might be advertising toothpaste. 'How thrilling to see you. Wasn't it just divine?'

'Nichola! My dear,' his voice sounds natural enough, leastwise to himself. He kisses her cheek. 'Let me introduce Rosie Williams. Rosie, this is my ex-wife, Nichola.'

Jolted off her cloud by this perfumed woman scrutinising her with undisguised curiosity, Rosie returns her gaze, grateful for her cream Monroe frock. 'How do you do?'

'A situation jagged with sophistication!' laughs Nichola gaily. However she does not extend her bejewelled hand. Walking on, she says to Michael, 'You know Derek of course.'

'Of course,' Michael nods to the short, shaven-headed git his daughters live with. There is nothing to say, except what should not be said, however they manage to keep a semblance of conviviality going until they reach the steps in the street. Once there Nichola moos Michael a farewell kiss.

'My love to Joyce.'

They part, civilised, polite, and painlessly.

Michael could cheerfully have shot them both.

'She used to be so beautiful,' says Michael as they walk away. 'Still, who has the lovelier woman on his arm tonight?'

Rosie snuggles up, feeling privileged that Mickey should prefer her to a woman of such cut glass sophistication. Arm in arm they step through the night air over the cobbled stones of Covent Garden to the famous "Ivy" restaurant.

The maitre D greets Michael by name, and they are shown to a table by the wall.

'Mario,' says Michael. 'Could we have a bottle of Chateau Larnande, the '96, I hear is rather good.'

The restaurant is full and lively, the air electrically charged with status and money. Seated at their table gleaming with silver and glass, Rosie looks around the airy, subtly-lit room. All the ghosts of the famous she's read about in show business biographies and autobiographies, seem to be hovering around the walls. Among the celebrated diners, she recognises a TV presenter she saw featured in "Hallo". At the time she'd studied her picture minutely, her hair was a shade Rosie rather fancied, a fact she had pointed it out to the hairdresser in South Kensington months ago. The colour of the girl's hair tonight, though, was nothing like it. Rosie thought it looked very ordinary. Michael appears not to have noticed the presenter, or to care. Aware she should try to match his insouciance, she looks away. But at another table, she recognises someone else. She can't resist whispering, 'That's Sian Phillips over there – don't look – she's Welsh too.'

Michael grins, for an instant the chorus girl is back. His smile fades and becomes steel, though, when he notices Wilfred Abery entering. Rosie would hardly be a suitable audience to his homo-erotic references to prison life. Wilf, still clad in leather and sun-glasses walks in the wake of two expensively dressed predatory matrons, a Prada-suited delinquent is by his side. As Michael looks away, Wilf spots him, he table hops over, except in Wilf's case, lurches.

'Mike! Hail! Don't see you often at this watering hole.' He turns to Rosie, and with glib chivalry takes up her hand and kisses it. 'How do you do?'

'Rosie,' Michael says, 'meet Wilf Abery. Wilf, this is Rosie Williams.'

Ignoring his loitering delinquent, Wilf ploughs in, 'Did you succeed in contacting your miscreant?'

Michael inwardly squirms but flashes him a smile. 'Thanks, yes.' He taps the back of his fingernail on a Turner Prize programme Wilf is carrying. ' How was this? Who won?'

'A Time Switch! Madonna said 'motherfucker' and everyone apologised – not, alas, for the time switch – for the 'motherfucker!''

They laugh, and with a wave of his fingertips Wilf heads back to his predatory matrons, the Prada delinquent casts a wan smile at Michael before following.

The young man reminds him of Ioan, and he wonders how long Rosie and he can continue without talking of him. He had previously determined not to mention his name, but as they are finishing their entree, he opts for an oblique reference. 'What time do you plan on seeing Ioan tomorrow?'

'I'll have to ring up, I've forgotten the visiting times.'

'If it's in the afternoon, you could come along to the Gallery in the morning, see Joyce, and I could drive you over there.'

'Perhaps you could visit him too?'

'Well, I'd like that very much. But I believe there's some ruling that the prisoner has to make a request himself.'

'You're right. Yes, a "V.O." I'll ask him. I'm sure he'd love to see you though.' Rosie fiddles with her wine glass. 'It's rather a relief talking about him. I don't seem to be able to these days, even to Liz. People in Cornwall are... well, slow to let you in.'

'You can talk to me about him anytime.' Michael waits, but no further chat seems forthcoming.

'Sometimes I wonder,' says Rosie after a moment, 'how it will affect him. He's mixing with such awful types in there.'

'That will depend on his strength of character.' Struck by the duplicity of his own character, Michael asks, 'Now, what would you like for dessert? They have some amazing puddings.'

'What's "ile flottante creme vanille?"' asks Rosie, reading.

'Meringues in custard!' says Michael.

They order one each. 'Would you like some coffee, liqueur?'

'Not for me.'

'When we get home, perhaps.' Waving to a passing waiter for the bill, he says absently, 'Red has done some amazing sketches of Ioan lately.'

'You mean sketches of him in prison?'

Reacting to her frown, he says, 'Have I spoken out of turn?'

'No, no, it's just that I wasn't aware she'd visited him.' What Rosie doesn't like to admit is, she'd no idea Red had even met Ioan. Red kept that quiet, she thinks. Tonight, though, she doesn't care. The wine is like liquid gold. Suspended in this sophisticated romantic restaurant – in twenty-eight years of marriage, David never treated her to anything like this – she wants to forget, to push reality away. Tonight, for the first time, her pipe dreams are reality, she is mixing with the "Hallo" crowd, the "OK" set, meeting celebrities, and Michael, her lover of years ago, has returned to claim her. Giggling slightly, she says, 'This is all like something out of "Dynasty" to me. What a magical evening it's been.'

'And it's not over yet!'

In the back of the taxi, sitting by Michael, her heartbeats quicken. Will he kiss me? Will anything happen?

Returning to the plush penthouse, in the entrance hall, Michael helps her off with her new camel overcoat and leads her into his bedroom.

He flicks on a light. The "Family Secret," spot-lit, hangs opposite his bed.

Rosie gasps at her portrait.

'The last thing I see before I fall asleep.'

'You may not believe this,' says Rosie, 'but for much of the time that was being painted, I was thinking about you.'

'How fitting then, that it should hang here.'

Michael takes her in his arms. 'Do you think?' he whispers in her ear, 'we'll remember how to do this?'

'I'm a little out of practice,' she murmurs.

'See if this reminds you,' Michael bends to kiss her softly, tenderly, lovingly.

To Rosie's immense relief and rapture, she remembers. It's like coming home after years of roaming, her spine relaxes, her body goes weak. Falling beautifully into the fulfilment of her fantasies, she allows herself to be ravished.

Michael doesn't usually smoke in bed, but right now he needs to. Conscience and her mumsy smell is torturing him. She's not nearly as good as Kiany in bed. Not as good as her son, either.

Rosie watches him light up. 'You shouldn't smoke in bed,' she says.

'Can't sleep,' says Michael.

'Me neither. I'm too happy.' She kisses his chest and snuggles in to him closer. 'Isn't it wonderful? Extraordinary. After all these years. I always used to think David and I would grow old together. Be "the folks who live on the hill." I never dared dream this could happen. It feels so completely right.'

Michael feels like dying... still, who is to blame? Who went for it?

'When you first met Ioan,' Rosie is saying, 'you said you were on holiday.'

'In Gran Canaria. Mmnn.'

'What did you make of him?'

Michael inhales slowly to give himself time to think. 'How do you mean?'

'I mean, did you think he was a gay, at all?'

Here we go, thinks Michael. 'Of course not,' he says. 'Why?'

'How did you find out about him?'

Michael inhales again, his mind racing.

'I mean,' says Rosie, 'that he was in prison?'

'His flat mates told me.'

'Ah!'

Through a chink in the curtains, a street light from below falls across the "Family Secret."

'When you first met him? Did he remind you of anyone?'

Michael knocks some ash from his cigarette into the glass ashtray on his bedside table. 'Mmn?' he says trying to sound sleepy.

'Remind you of me?' She nudges him. 'That picture could almost be of him too.'

'Nooo! Red got you to a T.'

'Did it never occur to you?'

'What? How do you mean?'

'Mickey. How many years ago did we last make love?'

'What are you getting at?'

'Ioan will be twenty-eight in January.'

'So ?'

The word hangs in the darkness.

'Darling,' says Rosie, 'for an intelligent man, you're awfully slow. Did it never occur to you that Ioan could be yours?'

Michael's brain, like eggs in lemon juice frying in a pan, curdles and sizzles.

Chapter Twenty-Seven

Put to the Test

Mr Blakeley pulls off his skin-tight rubber gloves as he enters the surgeon's wash room. Discarding them into the incinerator bin, he pulls down his face mask, it hangs like a lop-sided bib under his chin as he scrubs his hands.

'Damn shame,' he says. 'Let's hope he won't have a long wait.'

Ioan meanwhile, still anaesthetised, is wheeled out of Surgery. He is hooked up to an I.V. drip, a gasto-nasal tube in his nose. Thirty seconds or so after his pre-med, or it may have been as Mr Blakeley was cutting into his flesh on the operating table, as skilled hands and sterilised instruments were invading his abdomen to remove the damaged organ, Ioan's imagination took him on a disconcerting trip through his subconscious.

Even now, as he is transferred onto a bed in a small private room, linked men, like dangling silhouette cut outs, dance frenziedly before him on his retina. Ioan is transforming into a golden statue, a gleaming Michelangelo David, standing high above the city. Frenzied creatures swarm below, seemingly a living blanket of dark shapes. They approach. A molten throng of greedy mammals seeping ever nearer, unstoppable. They become men, hungry, clamouring. He tries to run, but the treacle of their earthy masculinity sticks, cements his feet. He is crippled, paralysed. His golden skin melts, sliding down his body like golden syrup, dripping from his arms, his chest, down his stomach, flanks, calves. Men below gorge off his juice, exult in the pool of his liquid flesh, jeering, crouching to suck up his mulched carrion. As their mouths slaver, their faces metamorphose into recognisable acquaintances, boys from school, lost friends, sex partners, hundreds of them, Jonathan, Michael, Lennie, Rat Face, Ossie, Terry. They leap up at him, clawing, biting, fighting for chunks of his body, tearing away lumps of his flesh, leaving him bare, cold, skeletal, till there is nothing left. Nothing, nothing...

On the other side of his pitiless subconscious is a sea of cotton wool. Someone is calling, patting his arm. Shouts of 'Ioan! Ioan!' His eyes flicker, coming to he sees something, two nurses. One fat, the other, Chinese. His mind clears immediately. He asks for water, they don't understand, his voice doesn't work, his speech is slurred. A sort of pain starts to register.

There's a heavy bandage on his stomach. Hours and faces float by, in and out. Something is in his arm... a drip in a vein. Bleak room. Dead white paint, walls, a television, cupboard, bedclothes. Is that Ma? Flowers! It's Ma. Talking. A woman in white, a nurse. 'There he is. Hallo there! Back from the land of Oz, are we? Your Mum's here waiting to see you.'

Ma's smiling head floats into view. 'Cariad! Darling. How are you?'

He feels her warm hand.

The nurse says, 'There's a smile. He's fine. I'll see if I can find Mr Blakeley for you,' she goes to the door. A man is standing there. Who's that?

Ioan parts his lips, his voice croaks, 'Terry?'

'Who's Terry?' says Ma, 'I don't know any Terry. Here's someone else come to see you. An old friend,' she turns. 'See.'

The man approaches. He's grinning. 'Hi there!' he says. 'How goes it?'

God! It's that singing guy from Maspalomas beach.

'How are you feeling, Ioan?'

Oh yeah. The sponsor, ha! The guy I had.

'Hardly recognise you with your hair black,' says Michael.

What's he talking about?

'I went to Cornwall. Met your Mother. Turns out we're old friends.'

Ma and you... Friends? With a jolt the anaesthetic fog clears. Yeah. Red said he was fucking Ma. Oh no! 'No,' he stammers, 'no!'

Ma, soothing says, 'Don't worry. You haven't quite come around yet, have you?'

'Where's Terry?'

'I don't know who you mean, darling. Look, this is your friend, Michael, see.'

'Remember?' says Michael. 'In Gran Canaria? On holiday?'

Ioan focuses. All connections are made. Oh yes, I remember, I bloody remember, mate. Fury unites his body to consciousness. He feels wide awake. 'Why are you here?'

Ma and Mike smile at each other across the bed. Ma says, 'Mickey is a friend from my show business days. I was staying with him last night in London. When I called Wandsworth, this morning, and they told me you'd had an operation, we thought it would be nice if we both came to cheer you up.'

'...Water.'

'It says "Nil By Mouth",' says Rosie. 'The nurse told me to do this.' She pours water from a flask, dips her fingertip into the glass, and moistens his dry lips. 'There. Is that better?

Glowering at his mother, Ioan says, 'Did you sleep with him?'

Rosie stares at him for a moment, then puts the glass back on the bedside.

'Did you?'

Rosie flicks Michael a look.

'Red says he's your lover.'

'Red had no business saying that.'

Ioan persists, 'Is it true?'

Michael rests his hand on the bed. 'Ioan, old chap, don't let it worry you. Don't worry about it, old chap.'

'Old Chap! Old chap? What is that? Did you? Just tell me. Did you and Ma f..?'

'Ioan!' Michael stops him. 'Please. You need rest. It's nothing to get anxious about. Your Mother and I are old chums. We've known each other for years.'

'He's using you, Ma.' He grips her hand. 'He's using you to get at me.'

Rosie blinks. 'Whatever do you mean?'

'I know him. He's gay!'

She stares back.

'He's fucking homosexual, Ma!'

'Ioan!'

'He's phoney. Pretending to like you to get to me.'

Bewildered, she looks across at Michael. Their eyes meet and his hand reaches out across the bed. 'Rosie,' he whispers, 'he's delirious.'

Ioan feels Michael's hand resting on his thigh. 'Look, Ma. Look where his hand is.'

'Sorry,' says Michael, snatching it away.

'See. It's me he wants really. They all do. Get him away from me. Get him away!'

Shakily Michael rises. 'He still has the anaesthetic in him.'

The vehemence and passion in Ioan's eyes give him a mad look. 'You leave my Ma alone. Get away. I know what you're doing. You don't fool me, man. Don't you bloody dare.'

Michael swallows hard. 'I'd better leave.'

'No, please,' says Rosie, withdrawing her hand from Ioan's. 'Ioan. Apologise.'

Ioan lies silent, sullen.

'Apologise to Michael at once,' repeats Rosie.

'I think we should both leave,' says Michael. 'Come.'

Ioan, hatred in his eyes, seethes, 'I know what you're up to. You're not getting away with it. You're not getting at me through my Ma.' Glaring, he turns to her. 'I know him. Pleaded with me, he did. Gonna pay me, he was. Pay me to live with him. "Sponsor" was his word for it. All the time I been in stir, he's been paying for my stuff to be stored. Ask him. You ask him.'

'Nonsense,' says Rosie. Frowning she turns to Michael. 'You're not, are you?'

'I thought he might appreciate the help.'

'How?' leers Ioan. 'By having sex with you?'

'Ioan!' snaps Rosie. 'I'm sure it was very generous of Michael.'

'Don't you get it, Ma? He fancies me. He's just like the rest of them.'

Rosie all but shouts, 'Stop! Just stop this will you.'

Ioan mutters, sulking, 'Just like the rest of them. He's bloody playing you, sucking up to get to me.' He looks daggers at Michael. 'You're not bloody winning, mate.'

'I'll wait outside,' says Michael leaving.

Rosie shoots out a hand to stop him. 'Mickey.' She is trembling as she pulls him closer, burying her face in his jacket. 'I'm so sorry!' Taking his hand to her cheek, she kisses it. 'So very sorry.'

'Oh Pleeease!' says Ioan. 'What the hell is this?'

Rosie looks up at Michael. 'Just give me a minute.'

Without a word, Michael leaves.

Once the door has closed, Rosie looks back at her son. Her nostrils dilate and her mouth hardens, speaking low and controlled, she says, 'If you spoil this for me, Ioan, I swear I will never forgive you as long as I live.'

Ioan moans. 'Oh Christ! What is this? Answer the bloody

phone, woman! Spoil what? You think this is some great romance? I'm telling you, I had to tell him I was H.I.V. to stop him fucking me!'

Rosie stares at him horrified.

'To stop him seducing me, Ma! Oh, don't look like that, it's okay, I'm not. I just said that to get him off me. I had to. So stop fooling yourself he's in love with you. He's not. You're not to be with him. Understand? You just can't.'

'Am I not allowed to have any feelings?' says Rosie. 'Is that so impossible? '

'Oh, piss off!'

'Don't speak to me like that.' Rosie is almost crying with fury. 'How can you? I won't have it! Don't I deserve some respect? Some happiness? Has it always got to be about you? You just can't bear to see me happy, can you? If you weren't like this, so bloody ill, heaven help me, I'd slap your face so damn hard. You perverted little queer. I'm ashamed of you.'

Ioan reaches for her hand. 'Ma. I'm telling you this for your own good.'

She pulls away, she wants none of him. 'Your filthy life! You're jealous. That's it, isn't it? Jealous of me, because you want the man yourself? You make me sick!'

'I've already had him. Jealous, no way!'

'You disgust me. You are in exactly the right place in that prison. That is just where you belong. And the quicker you get back in there, the better.' She turns to go.

'I'm telling you we had sex! He wanted to fuck me!' Ioan shouts.

Rosie freezes. Her mind reels. She shuts her eyes in horror. It's not true.

Again Ioan shouts to her back, 'We were lovers! You want to make love to him now? Michael and I had sex. We made love.'

Rosie cannot allow such thoughts. It doesn't bear thinking about. I'll go mad! I'll lose him. I'll lose them both. I can't. She turns back to her son. His pupils are enlarged, he cannot know what he's saying. He's delirious, yes, Mickey's right. Yet... if... If it were true? What of the future? Just as things were coming right. The life glimpsed last night. There could be no future. Not if... We could never be with each other again, ever. Crossing to the bottom of his bed, she says quietly, 'Ioan, you have to stop this. This is so wicked of you. Michael is a very old and dear friend. I knew him long before you were born. There was a time when... he might very easily have been your father. So you just have to stop saying this.'

'What I'm saying is the truth, Ma. I know him.'

'So do I, and far better than you. You're confused after your operation, you're still delirious. Now calm down, you should be resting. Here,' she sits beside him and picks up the glass of water, 'let me moisten your lips again, they're all dry.'

Outside in the corridor, the instant Michael closed the door, he shut his eyes in shame and self-loathing. As his forehead had hit the door jamb, he kicked himself for coming with Rosie, but the desire to see Ioan again had proved too strong. Opening his eyes he met the curious gaze of a uniformed Wandsworth prison guard. The man was sitting in an alcove opposite, holding a lurid-looking paperback, he nodded.

Michael nodded back brusquely, wondering if he'd heard any of the conversation inside. When the nurse had shown them into Ioan's room, the guard had challenged them with, 'Relatives only'. The nurse had answered, 'Parents', and Rosie had squeezed Michael's hand.

Michael needed privacy. He walked over to the window. Looking out, he barely takes in the magnificence of the view. The gleaming Houses of Parliament opposite, the noonday sun shining on their spires and the sparkling flowing Thames beneath. With eyes glazed and thoughts frenzied, he tries to make sense of what's just been said. The bad night he'd spent had fogged his orderly mind. Now it lurches, groping its way from the explosion that had taken place in his head last night, to Ioan's accusation just now. Why had the boy reacted that way? Those mad eyes. He saw right through me, into my very soul. Read me like some metaphysical mind-reader. Every word he'd said was true. Yes, I do want to be with him. And Rosie? Last night... hinting I'm his father! For God's sake! After all these years. Impossible! Yet was it? It could actually be. But, oh God, if so, then I've had sex with my own son! As horrified as Michael had expected to feel, wished he could feel, his emotional feelings for Ioan, inexplicably, had remained undiminished, in fact, as he'd deliberated about it last night, it explained so much, increasing, rather than devaluing his obsession. He recalled Ioan talking about his father on the beach, "a sawdust man... I always hated him... we never talked about anything serious, not like us".

This morning, when Rosie had come off the phone to the prison authorities and told him Ioan was in hospital after having had an operation, Michael became as anxious about him as her. Longing to see him, even to tell him of the possibility of their new relationship. Driving Rosie here, to the very hospital he had driven Nichola to when their daughter had an appendectomy, he experienced the same anxious feeling, exactly the same. Parenthood and worry go hand in hand. But, oh Lord! Ioan's words just now. And Rosie's reaction. Hugging me. Kissing my hand, as if we were already engaged. Last night's lovemaking had obviously been deeply important to her. What the hell have I done?

Whichever way Michael tries to reason with himself, to exonerate himself from his seduction of Rosie, he cannot but admit the truth. It had been an act. He is disgusted at himself. His self-deception. His ulterior motive. The 'Gay Lolita' notion had popped into his head after meeting Rosie in the cafe. Amused at first at conceiving such an audacious idea, he dismissed it as a joke. But by the time Red's painting arrived, and Ioan had still not replied to his letters, something had to be done. The fantasies he experienced in front of the "Family Secret" in his bedroom, intermingling Ioan and Rosie in a concoction of sexual unification, convinced him that Rafael's advice, "Find a good woman", could apply to Rosie. It was possible. She could well be that woman. Why not? Her romantic susceptibility was obvious. But going to bed with her had been suffocating. Her body, perfumed, soft, white and sticky, like Turkish delight, without the delight. She was still the simple, endearing, silly little girl she always had been. I doubt she even knows the word bisexual. No way, as Ioan would say, could such a relationship work. The most fun thing about her was the fact that she was Ioan's mother. Lust finds a way, and the way had worked. He had at least seen Ioan again, but not like that. As he'd watched Ioan propped up on the pillows with pipes and drips sticking into him, Michael's heart had surged. Yes, he'd wanted to hold him, hug him, but not as a lover. A filial love, it had to be. No longer lust, surely? Or am I still deluding myself? No, no... A filial love. It has to be, it must, if we're to have any future. But how to put the mess right? I'm supposed to be civilised, for Christ's sake. How could I have used Rosie like that? My erect bisexual cock has no bloody conscience whatever. Appalled by his cruelty, his deviousness, he gives up. Leave right now.

'How is he?' asks the guard.

'Still a bit dopey,' says Michael. 'The anaesthetic. Do you know what happened?'

The guard starts to tell him the story.

'Stop,' says Rosie to Ioan. 'Please. No more talk. Just rest.'

'But I have to make you see, Ma. He knew about you. I'd told him all about you.'

As she sits by Ioan's bedside, Rosie's insides are in turmoil, with body tense, fists clenched, her nails sticking into her palms, she is at breaking point. She shuts her eyes desperately trying to keep calm, trying to let his perverted misconceived prattle float past her. Prison, she reasons, has changed him, coarsened him beyond recognition.

After her night of bliss with Michael, waking in his bed this morning, breakfasting with him, seeing what a dear and caring man he was, Rosie had been very nearly in heaven. His concern for her following the phone call to the prison. Insisting on driving her here to the hospital himself. They had become anxious parents visiting their son. Now this! Ioan has to stop. The man he's talking about, this man he's telling these wicked lies about is his own Father. He has to know it. I have to tell him.

'I told him all about Dad dying,' Ioan is saying, 'how lost you were. I even told him you were in Cornwall staying with Auntie Liz. When all that with Jonathan happened, I dumped him, I didn't want to know him. I told him to bugger off and he couldn't take it. He deliberately tracked you down to try and get to me, don't you see that?'

Rosie smoothes the bedsheet and absently strokes it. 'You're exhausting yourself with all this nonsense. You must be quiet. Relax.'

'It's not nonsense, Ma.' He's running short of breath, on the point of hyperventilating. 'He can't love you... He wrote me in prison... He wanted to come and see me.'

'Stop! You must be quiet.' Rosie stands up. 'I'll get the nurse.'

With a sudden energetic frenzy, Ioan rasps, 'Get with it, Ma! You have to understand. It's not you he wants. It's me! He'll make you unhappy.'

'You are making me unhappy now, Ioan.' Rosie's eyes sharpen as she leans over him. 'Now listen to me and be quiet. Michael is normal, straight, as you would say. And yes, I can prove it. We are lovers. He is also a gentleman, a distinguished Art dealer who came to visit Liz's art gallery. We met again quite by accident. So calm down and be happy for me that I've found someone. Someone I'm very fond of. Someone you should be glad to know too. Someone that...' but Rosie is unable to say the words. 'I'm going now. I have to talk to your surgeon.' As she turns to the door, she wonders if she'll ever have the courage to tell him.

'Is it his money you're after, or are you just sex starved?'

Suppressing an urge to spin round and hit him hard, she clasps her hands. 'One day, I hope you'll be very sorry you said that,' and she goes.

'Stupid bitch!' mutters Ioan. 'I won't ever see her again, that's all. Never. Not if she's going with him. Bastard! I'll get Terry to beat him up.'

In the hall, Rosie, grim and emotional, closes the door behind her. She looks at Michael, who is sitting talking to the prison guard. He stands up, looking anxious.

'Where's the nurse?' she says.

'I don't know. This gentleman here,' Michael indicates the guard, 'says there was a fight. Ioan was stabbed.'

Rosie looks at the man. He is holding a gaudy paperback, his index finger is stuck between the pages keeping his place. He looks a pleasant enough sort, I suppose they think Ioan might escape, she thinks. The nurse who had shown them into Ioan's room comes bustling along the corridor. 'Mrs Williams,' she says, 'Mr Blakeley is free now. He'd like to see you.'

Rosie looks at Michael. She holds out her hand. 'Come with me,' she says.

After a moment, Michael takes her hand, and together they follow the nurse.

Mr Blakeley is well-polished, well-fed, and well into his fifties. Smelling of antiseptic and Penhaligon's eau de toilette, he gleams from his Brillianteened hair via a sumptuous silk tie, a superbly tailored suit to his shiny black shoes. Sitting with ankles crossed beside a white laminate utility desk reading a file, he is spending one of his two days a week on National Health duty. He glows with self-righteousness, even in this box-sized cell of an office, so very different from his carpeted acreage in Harley Street. As the nurse announces 'Mr and Mrs Williams', his ample bottom rises a few inches above his chair.

'Come in. Please sit down.'

'Actually,' says Rosie, 'this is a friend of mine, Mr Stanhope.'

'Of course. How do you do? Do please sit down, won't you. Well now, Mrs Williams. How did you find your son...' he glances down at the file in his hand, 'Ioan, isn't it?'

'Yes,' Rosie sits, barely able to hold her emotions in check. She appears reasonably collected, but her hands grip her handbag too tightly. 'Actually he was, rather... aggressive.'

'Ah! Anger. Yes. Hardly surprising after what he's been through. That would be the result of his prison stay, I expect. He's suffered a severe blood loss. But he's strong. Did you know your son was born with only one kidney?'

'Good heavens no,' says Rosie.

'Rather lucky to spot it, actually – the wound was in the right side and had severely damaged the kidney, but on the scan, no left kidney showed. Astonishing!' Mr Blakeley hands a an X Ray across the desk. Rosie ignores it but Michael holds it up to the light. 'Of course it's not unknown,' he continues, 'I have come across it before. About one in seven hundred and fifty are born without, and it is more common in males. However I'm afraid to tell you that with such a traumatic injury it was impossible to save the kidney. A normal single kidney grows faster, and is larger than a normally paired kidney, you see. For this reason it is more vulnerable to injury. Has... er Ioan, never had any problem before... sport wise for instance? Football, boxing, field hockey?'

Rosie shakes her head, 'Never.'

'Interesting,' he nods. 'So in fact he follows the pattern. In general people with one kidney have few problems, lead perfectly normal lives. There's a greater chance of developing high blood pressure, but life span is normal. So I'm afraid he's going to be on dialysis until we can find him a suitable donor. But the good news is, I don't think we'll be sending him back to prison, for awhile.' He grins broadly. 'Now, questions?'

Rosie's head is reeling, yet she is absorbing everything. She looks across at Michael. Enigmatic, he is steadily regarding Mr Blakeley. 'How,' she asks, 'do you go about finding a donor?'

'We look for a cross tissue match. Either cadaver or a living donor. Which is where family members can be extremely helpful.'

'In what way?' asks Rosie.

'Well, I fear the UK has an acute shortage of organ donors. There's a waiting list of some five and a half thousand, many of them doomed to die before an organ becomes available. So the possibility of a family organ donor should be fully explored if at all possible. Does Ioan have siblings?'

Rosie swallows, 'He has a half-sister. She's er... about seventeen.'

'Possible, possible,' says Mr Blakeley scribbling in the folder, 'We should try a biopsy, if that is, she'd be at all willing? Would she be?'

Numb, Rosie says, 'I have no idea.'

'Anyone else?'

'Myself, of course. If I'm not too old.'

Chivalry was one of Mr Blakeley's most practised attributes. 'Mrs Williams,' he says, 'I should have no doubts on that score. A little while ago I transplanted the kidney from a fifty-eight year old man into his eleven year old grandson. Both are doing excellently well. In that case neither of the boy's parents had the same blood type as their son, but if it turns out you do have the same blood type, and you would be willing to offer one of your kidneys, I should have no hesitation in operating.'

'Then please,' says Rosie, 'do the test at once.'

Michael clears his throat. 'How long,' he asks, 'can Ioan survive on dialysis?'

Mr Blakeley reaches for some papers. 'I happen to have some figures here somewhere. Ah yes.' Reading from a sheet, he says, "Seventy-seven per cent, survive a year. Twenty-eight per cent, survive five years. Ten per cent, ten years." He lowers the paper. 'If he were to have a transplant, survival rates are, of course, much higher. Seventy-seven per cent survive ten years after a living relative donor.'

So Rosie was cornered. Ioan's life was at stake. What was it Liz had said? "Now they can prove it with DNA testing". Her theory could finally be put to the test. Proof! Was Ioan really David's son or Michael's? She looks across at him. Would he offer to have a biopsy? Could she even ask him, especially after what she'd just heard from Ioan? But he might be able to save Ioan's life. 'I have an older sister,' she says, 'Ioan's aunt. Might she be a suitable donor? I'm sure she'd be willing to take the test.'

'Three blood relatives. A good start. But, of course, nothing is certain. Is the boy's father alive, Mr Williams?'

Rosie looks across at Michael again.

Michael turns to look at her.

'I'm not sure,' says Rosie.

'If there is any chance,' says Mr Blakeley, 'that you can contact him, I suggest you try. I appreciate in some instances this can be difficult, but for the sake of your son's life, it is imperative. There is always a stronger possibility of a parental match than any other.' He takes up a pen and looks at her. 'If I may have the names and contact numbers of his half-sister and aunt?'

Rosie still holds Michael's eyes, desperately trying to transfer her thoughts.

'...Mrs Williams?' repeats Mr Blakeley.

Michael turns to the surgeon. 'Mr Blakeley. May I ask, what exactly is involved, from a donor's point of view? How long, for instance, would one be immobilised? I mean, what do you actually do, cut the donor's stomach open?'

'Good heavens no. Not nearly so invasive. Using laparoscopic nephrectomy, I make a small incision near the navel, as well as four small holes in which I can insert instruments. The laparoscope has a miniature camera which enables me to watch what we are doing on a video screen. When the kidney is disconnected, the instruments are used to wrap it in a plastic bag and slide it out through the two and a half inch incision. The donor is able to leave the hospital in a couple of days. Provided, of course, they're well and fit in the first place.'

Michael turns to meet Rosie's eyes again.

Mr Blakeley's eyes flick, shrewdly, from one to the other, and back again. 'I should stress,' he says, 'that the results from a living donor are excellent, and the risk is small. Far less than an appendectomy, a hernia or gall bladder operation. Of course the decision to donate a kidney is a very personal one. For many, the chance to give such a priceless present to another human being, is a once in a lifetime opportunity to feel good about oneself.'

Michael grins. 'I am fit, and very well,' he says. 'I should like to take the test.'

Rosie holds out her hand, grasping his, she says, 'Mickey! Bless you. Thank you.'

'For Ioan's sake,' he says, 'For Ioan. There is one thing though, Mr Blakeley. Ioan told me some time ago he was H.I.V. positive. Could that affect his operation in any way?'

Fear and ice cut through Rosie. She lets go Michael's hand, realising his question confirms the unthinkable, is in fact true.

Chapter Twenty-Eight

Redemption

Palm Springs. January 2001

'You have a letter,' says Joyce, dropping it onto the low table beside Michael's sunlounger. Michael is snoozing by the hotel swimming pool. Over the tops of the palm trees, the Californian mountain range of San Jacinto, bask brown and rugged in the baking sun. The mist spraying from the humidifiers under the roofs of the surrounding bungalows is so fine, it looks like smoke. Joyce has just come from Reception, where her son, who is manager of "The Posada Hotel", Palm Springs, has given her a large brown envelope containing mail sent on by her secretary in London. Joyce's Junoesque figure, is sheathed in a fluorescent pink one-piece swimming costume. Her eyes are obscured by large expensive sunglasses, her salt and pepper hair brushed up, revealing fifty-P-sized gold earrings. She unties a floaty pink sarong from around her waist and sits beside Michael. 'Sorry, did I wake you?'

'I always knew you had good ankles, girl,' he says, lightly caressing them before reaching for the letter. 'I never appreciated before what a fine frame they carried.'

Joyce gives him one of her looks as she tears open an envelope. 'Thank you, sir. Oh look, a Christmas card.'

Michael is opening his letter, 'Ah ha! From Ioan.'

'Not before time,' says Joyce. Michael reads.

H.M.PRISON. EXETER
1st January, 2001

I really don't know where to begin. Happy New Year, Dad, I guess, is as good as anything. That probably sounds a bit facetious, but this whole thing is so weird. What the hell do I say? Seriously, the main thing is I suppose, to say thank you. Such a pathetic couple of words for what you have done for me. I owe you my life. What a result! So I have to write to express something of my feelings about all of this. It wasn't till after the operation they told me it was you. Ma sat by my bed and got all tearful telling me about the affair you had in Bournemouth years ago. I couldn't get my head round it to begin with. The whole thing is so way out, but I have to admit, it's kind of sexy too. Not many guys can say they've done it with their own Dad. Maybe that was the reason it didn't really work.

'Thanks a bunch!' mutters Michael.
Joyce looks up. 'Mmn?'
'Says I was no good in bed!'
'Obviously didn't know how to bring out the best in you.'
Michael gives her one of his looks, which is his imitation of one of her looks.

I felt like a real asshole behaving the way I did when you came to see me that day with Ma. I think I must have been crazy, sort of jealous of her, and jealous of you too, just mad. You were always so kind to me, right from the start and behaved like the gent you are. I was so angry, selfish and self-centred I couldn't see straight. Now to discover that you are my true Father, and that you have done such a wonderful thing for me, it's awesome, really. You have made me feel that I know who I am at last. I am filled with a sense of belonging and joy. Does that sound corny? But I mean it. For as long as I can remember (I tried to tell you when we first met). I never felt I belonged or was in sympathy with the guy I knew as my Dad, although, of course he did pay for my education, so I guess I should be grateful to him for that. But because of you, I feel for the first time in my life, I am complete, and when I get out of here, I have such a desire to do well. I mean, by trying to be an architect, I know it takes ages, but I do want to make you proud of me, if at all possible.

Here in Exeter, I was put in the Infirmary when I arrived, now I'm well, they've put me back in a cell. I thought Wandsworth was bad enough, but there at least I shared a cell with a guy who turned out to be a mate. He was actually a murderer, but to me he was a guardian angel, and I miss him a lot. This place is even more bigoted and it's hard to make friends. I don't know how I'm going to survive another three years and seven months, but if I do I'll certainly be a tougher person. Hope you are okay and have not had second thoughts about wanting your kidney back, I've grown to love it. You are indeed part of me, as I am constantly reminded every time I see the scar on my side.

Michael examines his scar. It's healing. Every morning he takes two Vitamin E pills and, on Joyce's recommendation – she is hot on alternative medicine – rubs in emu oil. 'Their bellies are full of fat,' she said, 'speeds up healing dramatically.' Sun helps too, he tells himself.

I am so grateful to you, Mike. It would help me a lot to see you, if you are up for it. I would seriously appreciate a visit. It would be grand to be able to talk together like we did in Gran Canaria, no wonder we got on so bloody well! You have done the most fantastic and lush thing anyone has ever done for me. And I promise to try and make your sacrifice worth it, by making my life better. You are a grand person and I am very proud and happy to be your son.

Things between Ma and me are a bit difficult. I got moved here to be near her, but she's not been to see me yet. I guess I rather buggered things up with her for you both. I wish there was some way of making amends. Please forgive me for the awful things I said. I deeply regret it. I wish you a fab New Year and hope you had a good Christmas. Hoping to see you soon
Sincerely, your son, Ioan.

Michael passes the letter to Joyce and looks around the baking surroundings. The cicadas rasp. They are quite alone. The other hotel guests are either indoors or out. 'Only mad dogs and Englishmen,' Michael mutters. The dazzling sun on the pool is blinding. Last time I was in this heat, he thinks, I was with Ioan, on that beach. Not quite a year ago.

'Mmm,' says Joyce, passing back the letter. 'Glad he appreciates you.' Swapping her reading glasses for sunglasses she puts them away in their case. 'How do you feel about that?'

'Delivered from damnation. Redeemed.'

'Good. That's good.'

The sun beats down. They are both silent. But inside their heads, mountains move.

'You do realise,' says Michael, 'I'd make you miserable if we were married?'

Joyce's sunglasses hide any emotion she may feel at the mention of the word. Her features remain composed. 'What is perfect in marriage? Ain't no such thing! I was married to an old man for thirty years. He was everything to me. But some would say, I missed out on my youth. Everyone compromises.'

'You're very wise aren't you? With all my grey hairs, I feel I know nothing. Have learnt so little from life. Except, maybe, knowing myself better.' He puts his head on one side to look at her. 'I love you too much to make you unhappy.'

'So. Not half empty then, but half full. The glass, I mean.'

'Oh, I know what you mean. I promise you this, I'll never let anyone rock our boat.'

'So why don't we just leave things as they are then?'

Michael takes off his sunglasses, gives her a slow sexy wink, and dives into the pool.

Chapter Twenty-Nine

Heart To Heart

Her Majesty's Prison Exeter is situated conveniently for visitors, but, frustratingly for its inmates, slap bang next door to Exeter Central railway station. All day long in his cell, Ioan could hear the trains pulling in and out, going to the West Country and leaving for London, where his thoughts followed and lingered, reliving the good times, the nights out clubbing, cruising with the gay guys.

Not as crowded as Wandsworth, he at least has a cell to himself – albeit five paces by three – and is able to have a shower three times a week, but the abusive catcalls and hatred that men on rule 43 are accorded is far more vicious. After the kidney transplant and his eventual rehabilitation on leaving the Prison Health Centre, a new fury had replaced his former acceptance, but sitting incarcerated for eighteen, sometimes twenty hours a day in his cell, as oceans of boredom flooded his mind, his resentment seeped away slowly with the weary routine of daily existence. Eating catcalls, exercise yard catcalls, chapel catcalls, library catcalls, the constant noise of rap music blasting from the opposite cell at night, all this could have driven him crazy. He learnt to numb his ears to be able to sleep, to control his anger so he would not be put 'on report,' to conquer his bitterness, and to still his emotions in order to keep calm, to do this, he affected a cool equability. But it is a short step from being placid, to becoming listless, shorter still the drop into the pit of depression. With the bromide they put into his tea, his libido was at zero. Not even the cutest looking crook excited a glance. His lost sex drive was altering his personality. Unable to make friends, missing Terry's blunt wisdom, he had to force himself to resume his exercise routine to keep fit. Taking his Aunt Liz's advice and for something to do, he started reading up on yoga and Buddhism.

On arrival he had requested three Visitor's Orders, for 'Mother', 'Girlfriend', and 'Father'. The appropriate papers had been sent off, but so far only Red had visited. Seeing her once every six weeks was the one thing that kept him sane. He didn't care that she didn't bring him in any dope, or 'joey' as Terry had called it. It was the joy of seeing her. His new interest in her had dated from receiving her joky get well card after the transplant operation. It had read, "So shit happens! We'll not be committing incest after all. Shame. Heal quickly and we'll think of some other sins. See you soon. Love Red."

On her first visit, he had told her about the scene he'd made with his mother and Michael in hospital. Now that everyone's true relationship was clear, he was anxious to mend bridges. Red had promised to try and bring Rosie around.

He received a letter from Michael saying he would visit on his return to England at the end of February. In his solitary hours, Ioan's thoughts kept returning to him and the revelation that he was his Dad. It clarified and explained so much. Why he'd always felt an alien around David, why he'd never had the slightest interest in that boring man. His own artistic outlook on life, which David had always belittled, was clearly his inherited genes working. With Michael's actual kidney inside of him, giving him life, he was constantly reminded, and couldn't wait to talk with him again, wickedly curious to know where their new relationship might lead.

When Michael did eventually arrive, by train, in March –

almost a year to the day that they had met on the beach – he had to undergo a rigid security check. Walking through a metal detector, like in an airport, a second portable metal detector was passed around his body, over his crutch and down his legs. He was hand-frisked, his shoes removed, even the inside of his mouth examined.

He now sits waiting in the long Visitors' Hall, watching the door from which the prisoners will emerge. His chair is actually a stool with a low back, he'd retrieved from underneath a picnic-style table which is clamped to the floor. The centrally placed red prisoner's chair is also bolted to the ground. Around him are similar numbered tables in rows. The walls are painted regulation green up to the dado rail, where a kind of nicotine beige colour takes over to the ceiling. It is 15:15 on a damp Thursday, March afternoon. All visitors must be out by 16.45, so after all the searches are complete they might have an hour together. Michael, too, has had thoughts about how their relationship might continue, to which end he has prepared a little speech. Beady eyed officers trained not to miss a trick watch over the crowd. They walk up and down with headsets and microphones. Two officers are sat watching the TV monitor screens at the far end of the room.

Ioan walks in and scans the room. He looks almost hunted, thinks Michael, noting the dark rings round his eyes, his sallow complexion and scruffy hair. When Ioan spots him, beyond his immediate and still devastating smile, his eyes seem to search Michael's face for a reaction, examining him hard as if wanting to know something important. Dropping down into the red chair opposite, he says in a low almost embarrassed voice, 'Mike. Fab, you're here. Thanks for coming.'

'How are you?' asks Michael, holding out his hand.

Ioan takes it, glaring defiantly at the guard overseeing their greeting. 'Great. You?'

'The better for seeing you.'

Ioan swallows self-consciously, dipping his chin. 'You look brown.'

'Glad you noticed. It's expensive Californian tan. But you, now? Tell me, how are you holding up?'

Ioan shrugs, 'So so. Been reading a bit.' Then with a spark of his old enthusiasm, 'Your kidney feels great, man. Just like mine. Few problems at the start, but now it's okay. Quite a mind fuck, eh? You okay? Here, I mean?' He indicates his side.

'Can't tell it's gone. Remarkable, isn't it?' As the guard watches them before moving on, Michael nods pleasantly. He gets no reaction. When the guard is out of earshot, he leans forward and with a provocative twinkle in his eye asks, 'So, what do we call each other?'

'I answer to most things,' says Ioan. Then with smirk, 'How about if I call you Sugar Daddy?'

Michael compresses his lips to disguise the stab he feels. 'Your half-sisters call me "Dadda".'

'Oh shit! Jees! I hadn't thought about them.'

'I brought their picture to show you.' He removes his wallet from his breast pocket. 'I've told them all about you.'

Ioan's eyebrows shoot up. 'Everything?'

Michael does not answer. Instead he produces the photograph, 'They're dying to meet you.'

Ioan smirks at Michael's attempt to ignore the hurdle they have to overcome. 'No way I'm calling you Dadda, man! That'd be too way out. Perverted, man.'

Michael shoots him a look. 'Okay then, "Mike" and "Ioan" it stays. But you have to let me call you "son" sometimes. I'd like to.' They hold eyes, silent. Michael grins, Ioan does not.

Nodding at the photo, Ioan says, 'These half sisters? What are their names?'

'This one's Kate.' Michael points to the youngest of the two figures, a girl with a mass of curly fair hair. 'She's still at College. Wants to work on a Game Reserve looking after wild animals. She's lovely, a free spirit.'

'Free spirit,' echoes Ioan softly.

Michael bites his lip. 'Sorry, that was tactless.' Sensing that showing the photograph of his daughters is too much, too soon, he seeks to somehow dissolve Ioan's obvious discomfort. He decides to launch into the speech he has prepared. 'Ioan, I should like to...' Simultaneously Ioan starts to say something. 'I beg your pardon,' says Michael. 'You go first.'

Ioan hesitates. 'It's just that... I have to say something. To clear the air. It's about what I said when you came to the hospital with Ma. About you chasing her to get to me. I was wrong, I know that now. Crazy...'

'Forget it. You explained it very well in your letter. I understand.'

'Red told me you went to Cornwall to see her paintings. Not to see Ma at all.'

'Perfectly true. Although I remember you telling me she was staying there. It's amazing. Makes you suspect the presence of some mystical Intention.' Michael raises his eyebrows in mock wonder at the mysteries of life.

'Like there was some plan in the Universe, you mean. That's exactly what I've been thinking. Cause if you hadn't have rated Red's painting and signed her up, you wouldn't have met up with Ma, and Ma would never have known where you were, and I wouldn't be alive.'

'Makes you wonder, doesn't it?' says Michael, trying not to feel fraudulent, trying to forget he'd only returned to the cafe that day because he had mistaken Red's portrait of Rosie for Ioan. 'But you were right in a way,' he admits, 'I wanted to see you very much when I came to the hospital.'

'Life's strange.' Ioan's mouth twitches. 'Weird. That time, when I told Ma you and I had had it off...'

'Ioan, we have to forget all about that.'

'She won't. How can she? I know her, she never forgets anything. I know that's why she's not come to see me. Have you seen her at all?'

'She visited me after the operation, she was staying in my flat. I saw her briefly when I came out. But no, I've not seen her since.'

'There you are then. It's my fault. I've buggered up your relationship. How can you be together again without her worrying about what I told her?'

'To be totally honest with you, Ioan, I don't think your Ma and I are destined to be together, as you say. She's great but... you have to understand that all those years ago when we had our fling, we were just kids, younger than you are now. It was just a fun affair, nothing serious. We were never in love or anything like that. Now we're two quite different people. We were pretty different even then. The only thing is, well... You are the wonderful and very remarkable result of that friendship.'

'Wonderful? Huh!' Ioan sneers. 'I don't feel very wonderful.'

'The negative things that happen in life are not important, Ioan, believe you me. Life is all ups and downs. It's maybe a truism to say it, but the downs are sometimes more character-forming, more beneficial in the long run than the ups.'

'Oh Mike, stop. Do stop, man.'

'What is it?'

'You really are an old royal blue Conservative, aren't you? You think I'm benefiting from being locked up with these murderers? You really think I'm learning how to be a nice clean-living lad here? You think living with scum, drug addicts, thieves and rapists is character-forming? Do me a favour, man. I'm more likely to pick up their habits and turn to a life of crime myself when I get out. Prison does not improve people, man. If you think I'm coming out of here with some new respect for authority, no fucking way. Two-thirds of these guys come back inside of a year, they tell me. They don't get better, they get worse. They're scum. Screws included. And I'm learning to be one too. I have to, to survive.'

Michael, cut short by what he perceives is going on in Ioan's head, backs off, he has no wish for any confrontation. 'I'm sorry,' he says, 'that was glib of me. What I was trying to say was, you'll be out of here soon. Try to think of what's good ahead, what's positive in your life. All things come to an end, Ioan.'

Ioan sneers, his mouth contorted but silent.

'Ioan. Son. Look at me.' Ioan's fiery eyes flick to his. 'Of course you're not going to turn to a life of crime. You're not the type. But you will be stronger. More resilient. Remember what you said to me that day on the beach about your shallow existence? Well, no one can accuse you of that now, eh?'

Ioan seems to control his anger or, at least, to disguise it. Smouldering, he stares at the photo of Michael's two daughters. 'No, I suppose not.' Without looking back at Michael, he says, 'Anyway... Go on telling me about your daughters.'

'Yes. Um... Actually, I wanted to say something myself. Get it out of the way. Er... It's funny, but before my first daughter was born... this one here, Susan... this, by the way, is by way of being a confession, I was dead worried that if I had a son, I'd love him too much. Kiss and cuddle him to bits, and maybe that wouldn't be healthy, be very unhealthy in fact. I was so relieved when she was born a girl, when they both were. I knew I'd be able to love them with impunity.' Michael has come to the part of his speech he'd rehearsed. In preparation he tidily returns his daughter's photograph to his wallet. 'Now that I do have a son, and it's you, and we've done... what we have, let's get that out of the way. Acknowledge it, laugh at it, if needs be. But forget it. Let's not let it paralyse any future we may have. If we're ever going to have a decent relationship, a friendship, which is what I would very much like, we have to move on. Right? I think, in fact, I know, I can love you with a filial love. You understand me?'

'Sure. Are you telling me you were scared of seducing your own kids?'

Michael's eyes fall away. 'Well, I suppose. Before they were born.'

'So you must have been gay even then?'

'That's a difficult question. I was afraid.'

'Shit! Well. How right you were. 'Cause you did eventually seduce one of your kids, didn't you?'

Michael blanks out the horror. 'Ioan,' he says. 'Don't'.

'Just kidding!' sings out Ioan.

Michael is not at all happy at the turn of the conversation.

'Oh, come on now, Mike,' says Ioan, 'you said, we should laugh at it. Anyway, I seduced you, if you remember. I had to do something, you were so bloody hung up about us. No way you were going to make the first move. I knew you wanted to. Anyway, we didn't know our true relationship then, right?' He shrugs. 'And we had fun, admit it.'

Michael is finding it hard to look Ioan in the eye. Under his breath he whispers, 'Well.' Suddenly his voice is firm. 'But we don't feel that way now. Right?'

Ioan smirks. 'What if I say, I do.'

Panic hits Michael.

Ioan giggles. 'Your face! Don't worry, you're quite safe. I've got your kidney to keep me warm.'

'Can't you be serious, for Christ's sake.' Michael is aware he sounds pompous.

'We only had a shag, Mike. Your problem is you're still scared of being gay.'

'I'm not gay. I'm bisexual.'

'Ops! Sorry. Whatever. But you just admitted you were uptight about it even when you were married. With all your sophistication, Mike, you're guilt-ridden. Admit it, man. You're gay. Oh, the gay gene at the butch end of the spectrum. But you're gay alright. Just stop worrying about it.'

Michael looks at him with embarrassed amusement and not a little admiration. 'Has it never been a problem to you?'

'Never. Homosexuality, bisexuality, they mean nothing. Either you're sexual or you're not.'

Michael nods slowly, 'Well, I'm certainly sexual.'

'But you think you can love me without any of that? Love me with impunity, eh?'

Suspecting Ioan is laughing at him, Michael is undeflected, he has to prove his sincerity. 'Sure of it. It's why I'm here. To assure you of that.'

'Pity! So you don't fancy me anymore?'

Again Michael looks aghast.

Ioan laughs. 'Joking! I'm really going to enjoy our new relationship.'

Very slowly Michael's face reluctantly melts into a grin.

Ioan says, 'You're going to be so bloody easy to send up. Don't worry, man, one day, when I get out of here, I'm going to make you so fucking proud of me.'

Having his leg pulled is a new experience for Michael, he's relieved to be on safer ground. 'Do we know when that is likely to be?'

Ioan hunches forward, elbows on the table, fingertips touching. 'My original sentence was fifty-three months. But if there are no black marks against me, if I don't get put on report, I only have to do two-thirds, that's thirty-five months. I've done eleven. So I've only got twenty-four to go. As long as I don't fuck up.'

'You won't. Two years, well. I'll be right outside those gates waiting for you.'

'Red's promised to be there too. On her motorbike.'

'Ah well! I bow to youth. Good, good. What are your feelings about her? You know she's one of my top contract artists? I have a lot of faith in her.'

'She's great! When we thought we were related, the brother and sister thing, we had this kinda kinky thing going on. Attraction of the forbidden. Now it turns out we're just, well, ordinary, the feeling is, well, it's still there. And it's mutual. It's fab! I'm mad about her. Never thought I'd say it, but maybe I've got a bit of bisexuality in me too. How about that?' He leans forward, whispering, 'Something in the blood, eh?'

'Try it,' grins Michael. 'You might get to like it. Move on. That's what life's about.' He remembers Ioan's expression "Grit in the blood" that he'd used on the beach to describe what he then thought was his Welsh mining ancestry.

'Right,' Ioan grins mischievously. 'So now you know about my non-existent love life. How's yours, Daddy O?'

'Oh! You've perked up.'

'Must be seeing you.'

'It is quite healthy, thank you,' says Michael, nodding his head in a comic fashion, 'Son.'

'If the lady is not my Mum, am I allowed to know who she, or he is?'

Michael scratches his eyebrow, grinning. 'It is not a he! It's a lady,' he nods, repeating his comic bow, expecting Ioan to send up again. 'Actually, it's taken me rather by surprise. It's someone I've known, respected, and loved too, in a way, for years. When I was in St Thomas's just after the operation...'

'After you saved my life,' says Ioan.

'After we discovered we were related,' says Michael, 'she visited me. I was on my bed dozing. She kissed me on the lips. I never wanted her to stop. I held her, even got an erection. And I was on medication at the time! So that was something.'

'Great! So what are you doing about it? Going to get married again?'

'Just holding it steady. She knows all about my life. All about you. I've been totally honest with her.'

'You could never be anything else, Mike.'

Michael looks at him suspiciously, but Ioan's expression is one of genuine affection.

'So tell me,' says Ioan, 'about these half-sisters of mine? What are their names again?'

'Susan and Kate. Where's that picture?' He takes out his wallet again. 'Here.' Immediately a guard is beside him. 'Just showing a photo,' says Michael. The guard looks at it and strolls away nonchalantly. 'This one, Sue here, has just got herself engaged to a lawyer. He seems a pleasant enough fellow. So, we'll be having a family wedding in the summer.'

'I'll be unable to attend, sorry. Prior engagement.'

Michael grins. 'I'm quite looking forward to it. Except of course I'll be obliged to make a speech on the joys of married life in front of my divorced wife and her toy boy, plus, have the privilege of picking up the bill afterwards.'

'Could be fun. Let me know how it goes. Particularly with your ex. My wicked step-Ma, which I suppose is what she is... or was.'

'Mmn, I suppose so,' says Michael with sigh.

'Does it still hurt? Her, I mean. From what you told me before, on the beach, you were pretty cut up about all of that.'

'I loved her. A lot. For twenty-three years. She's woven into the tapestry of my life. But... well. Have you never been in love?'

'Jeez, no one's ever asked me that before. I don't know. Not properly. Not painfully anyway. Of course, if you're talking about sex '

'Which I'm not.'

'Which I am. Then tons of times. Hundreds. Thousands. If all the men I've had were laid across the Atlantic Ocean, head to toe, I could walk to America!'

'What a picture that conjures!' chuckles Michael. 'And I thought I was promiscuous!'

'There you are, you see. It's in the blood.'

'I've certainly had plenty of relationships in my life,' says Michael. 'With beautiful women before I was married, with my wife, with men, even. But then life is about what you were and what you become.'

Michael had quoted that very line to Joyce the other night. They had discussed it at length. Both had confessed that, though they'd always been fond of each other, it was only at this moment in time, after the journey they'd both made with other people, that they felt right for each other. Any earlier, they decided, and their romance would have floundered.

'Tell me, Ioan,' continues Michael, 'this boy you're accused of seducing? Did you really do that?'

'Hell no, I did not! I'm no paedophile, Mike. I swear. He was the only chicken I've ever had... and he made all the running. How did you find out about that?'

'Your Mother told me. The day I met her again, she'd just come back from your trial.'

'Jonathan.' Ioan's eyes glaze. 'Well, my whole life changed because of him and how I felt. So I guess I must have loved him, in a way. That's why I pleaded guilty. As it turned out, I didn't have much option, but I knew I had to protect him from going into Court, that would have scarred him for life. I knew had to do that.'

'And what about you? Is all this going to scar you for life?'

Firmly shaking his head Ioan says, 'No. I'm not going to allow it. This last eleven months something's happened inside of me. I shared a cell in Wandsworth with this murderer. He taught me about survival, in here,' he taps his chest with his fist. 'How to make myself strong. I suppose I loved him too, in a way.'

Michael frowns.

'Maybe it was just the circumstance, least that's what he said. But he made life kind of bearable. I write to him now. Occasionally he writes back, he's not very good at it. When I get out, I've told him I'm going to visit him. He's never received a letter or had a visitor in seven years, how about that? Everyone there, well, the whole world really, thinks he's a brute, an evil monster. He's not. He's funny, warm, sexy.'

'Oh really?' says an interested Michael.

'Oh really, yes,' but Ioan is not to be drawn. 'A kind man. An all round super sensible bloke. When I first saw him I thought, "Shit! God help me." Strange isn't it? He epitomises something in all of us, in a way.'

'How do you make that out?'

'Well, we all of us have everything in us. The best and the worst. I don't just mean good and bad. It's human nature, the way it is. I think if you recognise this about people and about yourself, you get to a better understanding, you reach a kind of stability.'

'Ioan, I think maybe you're growing up.'

'It's just the more time I spend here, the more I realise, like you said just now, that everything I am, is the result of what I was. All my life's experience. Like meeting you, and learning about myself, and Jonathan. If I hadn't loved him, I wouldn't even be here having to deal with all this shit.'

'And even more fascinating,' says Michael, 'is how this experience will affect what you will become.'

A whistle blows. 'Time's up,' an officer bawls at the far end of the room.

'We have to stay put, till the vistors have gone,' says Ioan. 'When can you come again?'

'Soon. I promise.'

They clasp hands warmly and Michael leaves with the other visitors, turning to wave at the last moment. Walking to the station he thinks of Ioan in his cell, and wonders how he himself would endure such a place. It is not until he is settled in his first class compartment reviewing their conversation, that he realises how uncomfortable Ioan had made him. For moments back there, his son had actually been flirting with him.

Nothing hurt Rosie more than not getting on with Ioan. As she sat by his hospital bed having to explain how he came to be Michael's son, she had had to dig deep into herself. It was the hardest thing she'd ever had to do. But a relief. Yet her explanation, that she'd never known she was pregnant until after she married, only airbrushed the truth. With her romantic notions about Michael smashed, almost turned to disgust, then having to become intensely grateful to him, her week's stay in his apartment – for that's what it turned out to be – had been like living in an emotional tumble dryer. With Mr Blakeley's assurances that Ioan's operation had been a success, she'd been relieved to return to the clean Spring landscape of Cornwall and her busy life in the cafe. By the time Ioan was moved to Exeter jail, her life had become more structured, her business had improved, tourists were arriving, extra staff taken on, but most distracting of all, a romance was in the air.

When she heard from Red that Michael had visited Ioan, ungenerous resentment arose, and she thought she better shift. So allowing Red to persuade her, they arranged to visit Ioan six weeks after Michael had done so.

To her relief there was no tension. Ioan seemed genuinely pleased to see her. Never having seen him in Red's company before, she detected, or thought she detected, a change in him, and wondered at their obvious rapport. Red was clearly taken with him, telling her usual silly jokes, and Ioan, to her surprise, reminded her of something she'd done when he was a baby. 'I must have been about four or five,' he said, 'I was sitting at the table and Ma gave me a leg show. For every mouthful of food I ate, she did a high kick and a pirouette!'

Rosie clapped her hands in delight. 'It's true,' she said. 'It was the only way I could get anything down him. Oh, but you were gorgeous!'

So the horrors of the hospital accusation were forgotten, and like so many mother and son relationships, became family baggage never referred to, but always remembered.

It was not till May that Michael was able to get around to making his second visit. Once again Ioan flirted. Two months later, on a blazing hot summer's afternoon, Michael made the trip again. This time, to negate the worrying sexual frisson, he brought along Joyce.

Joyce imagined she'd dressed down for the prison visit, wearing a simple red polka dot sleeveless dress and pearls, but to the guards and the prisoners, she looked the grandest person they have ever seen in Visitors' Hall.

'Thank you for my V. O.,' she says, extending her hand to Ioan as if acknowledging a compliment at a cocktail party. 'I'm really honoured to be allowed to visit you.'

'Curiosity,' says Ioan, 'I wanted to meet the lady who'd captured my Dad's heart. After all, you might be my new Mum one day.'

'Don't put me in competition with your dear Mother, please, she's far too pretty. Anyway I was dying to meet the boy who used to be in all those glamorous ads.'

Flattery from a cultured sophisticated woman being rare, Ioan responds warmly. Gleefully leaning forward in his prisoner's chair he says, 'So Mike, how was your daughter's wedding?'

'Fun,' says Michael. 'I loved it.'

'It was perfect,' says Joyce, chattily. 'We had a gloriously sunny day. The ceremony was at Gray's Inn Chapel in the city, the groom has some legal connections. The Reception was in the Palm Court Room at The Waldorf. Do you know it? Divine! There was an orchestra...'

'How many guests?'

'Over two hundred,' answers Michael. 'More than in the chapel.'

'Did you walk your daughter up the aisle and make your dreaded speech about happy marriages in front of your ex?'

'I did indeed.'

'Susan looked fabulous,' says Joyce. 'So, I might add, did Mickey here.'

Michael and Ioan grin at each other, enjoying her bias. 'You should have seen this one's hat,' say Michael nodding to Joyce, 'upstaged everyone. But I have to tell you Ioan, in the chapel, after I'd delivered Sue to the groom, something rather touching happened. I stepped back into the pew and stood next to Nichola. Her boyfriend was standing on her other side. Those words "Till death do you part" are pretty devastating, you know, very moving. As we waited for Susan to say "I do," I felt Nichola's hand creep into mine and give a squeeze. When I looked at her, I saw a tear.'

Joyce looks at Ioan and raises her eyebrows, as if to say 'What about that, then?'

'So what do you take that to mean?' says Ioan.

'Well,' says Michael, 'shall we say, it made me feel warmer towards her than I had previously.'

'What, because she cried?' says Joyce. 'Any mother would have done the same. I did at my son's wedding.'

'So what about the speech then?' asks Ioan.

'Hilarious!' says Joyce. 'All about how he wished their path to happiness could be strewn with rose petals, but life being what it is, it was more likely to be tin tacks!'

'We all danced,' says Michael. 'Eventually I even asked Nichola. It was strange. Being so close after so long. I never thought we'd be able to talk again, let alone be friends. Now I feel it's possible. So,' he smiles at them, 'one door closed and another one opened.'

For a moment Ioan and Joyce look at him, both understanding and appreciating the healing journey he had made.

'Probably,' says Ioan, 'it's easier for you now you have a partner.'

'You're absolutely right, Ioan,' says Joyce, putting her hand in Michael's. 'Absolutely.' Then turning to him, she asks merrily, 'Now tell me, how long do we have to wait till that cell door of yours opens for good?'

'Nineteen months,' says Ioan.

After a beat, while her eyes flick to Michael then back to Ioan, she says, 'And what a celebration we'll all have then.'

Chapter Thirty

Going Straight

On the misty May morning that Ioan's door did open, Red was waiting outside the prison gates on her Ninja Turtle. Grinning fit to bust, she held out her spare crash helmet.

Ioan couldn't keep his hands off her. Swinging his leg over the back of her motorbike, he clamped his body and thighs tight to hers. With the exhilaration of freedom, the rushing cold air, the zooming flashing scenery, he became intoxicated almost beyond self-control. Red burned up the roads across Dartmoor and Bodmin moors to Penzance, she'd been waiting over half her lifetime for what was going to happen next.

Rosie, thrilled at his early release and in happy anticipation of what she had perceived as encouraging signs of heterosexuality, had insisted they spend their first night together under her roof. Knowing more was at stake than a good night's sleep, she had lovingly made up the spare bed with fresh sheets and filled the room with daffodils. The following morning she couldn't resist tapping on the bedroom door and taking in a tray of tea. She was not disappointed. The lovers were glowing. Red, ecstatic with the fulfilment of her fantasy, Ioan lying back machismo, his masculinity proven at last. Rosie laid on the full honeymoon breakfast, after which they sped off back to Red's studio in Leeds, where they spent the next two days glued to each other in bed.

But Red's studio was an unsuitable love nest.

During the years that Ioan was completing his sentence, Red, with success and money had become more grounded. With typical generosity she had upgraded her Gran's semi in Leeds, buying her a new sofa, carpets and washing machine. The Banker's Order to Rosie had been stopped eighteen months ago, at Rosie's request. Since leaving Art School she'd visited Paris, spending her time studying the Masters in the Musee D'Orsay and acquiring a more determined search for internal truth in her work. Under Michael's tutelage she had developed a strict self-discipline. Every day from nine-thirty until five, she painted. This time was sacrosanct. Not even phone calls were permitted to break her concentration. Only a break for lunch was allowed.

So Ioan had to find himself an occupation.

He had not forsaken his promise to Michael to work at becoming an architect. His reading in Exeter jail had convinced him that, as there was no recognisable 21st Century style, in the way the 1800s or 1900s are recognisable by their buildings, there had to be room for an early modernist approach. He reasoned that only as an art form could architecture survive. But looking at his own meagre designs and drawings, he became less convinced that he could improve its chances. However, with assurances from Red, he was prepared to make a stab at gaining some qualifications. But the more immediate need for cash in his pocket, combined with his inherent conviviality, obliged him to take a job as a barman in a nearby waterfront pub.

Sex offenders are required to notify the police of their address within fourteen days of their release. Ioan had considered changing his name to avoid this and any future aggravation stemming from being a 'jail bird'. After a discussion with Red, who reasoned, 'You're hardly a paedophile who's going to re-offend,' he took 'the butch pills', which was Red's phrase for stiffening the sinews, and called in at the local police station, performing the duty on auto pilot, without chagrin. The last three years had strengthened his psyche as well as his muscles.

The following day, the morning post delivered a letter addressed to them both from Michael. They read it sitting up in bed, drinking cups of tea, like an old married couple.

Dear Red and Ioan,

Grand talking to you on the phone the other day. Delighted to hear you have become an item, consequently making you, Red, an even closer member of the family. We think you'll suit each other admirably. Joyce says that you should both be shrunk, cast in porcelain and put on the mantlepiece, you'll look so cute together.

I enclose some Private View invitations to give to your chums. As you know from previous viewings, it is principally for buyers who have already purchased, so they can pat themselves on the back. However this year we thought it would be appropriate to combine the occasion with a party for our new family. I have sent invitations to your mother, Ioan, and to Simon Barclay and Liz, taking the view that as they were your original champions, Stanhope Galleries should acknowledge that.

Joyce has been in talks with the B.B.C.'s Late Night Review, who have asked if they can have a televised interview with you. There will be other press people around too. I'm sorry about this, but I think in this business, it's wise not to deny them when they are interested, there are all too many times when they are not!

The renewed interest in your work and the way it is selling would seem to confirm everything we discussed about the new look of your canvases. You've managed to capture a spiritual quality into the vistas of your beloved Yorkshire moors with which people seem to empathise. The jokey semi-surreal pictures I'm personally not so keen on, but there is no doubting their 'sensational' appeal. It'll be interesting to see how they sell.

Ioan, I wonder if you remember my talking about Daniel

Schlesinger, the architect who turned the basement here into our gallery. I ran into him the other day, it seems he has a branch office in Leeds! I asked him about the possibility of taking you on. When I told him you were my son, all hesitations and objections dissolved. Hurrah for nepotism. You may have to start on the bottom rung, but at least you'd be with a reputable company and learning. There would be a salary. I'm aware you are reluctant to sign for the alternative seven year degree course. Anyway, it's there if you want it. Give him a ring for an appointment. His number is: Leeds (code 01131) 2459308.

If anything occurs to you or you have any worries, don't hesitate to call, otherwise see you on the day. Remember the drill, arrive early to greet the punters. Joyce joins me in sending love. Professor M.

'Christ,' says Ioan, 'I'd be a bloody tea boy!'

'Don't be so ungrateful. He's only trying to help. No bad-mouthing now.'

'Sorry. I owe him my life too. My life!' He points to the scar on his side. 'Hi Mike!'

'Better a tea boy with a future, than some big-bellied beer lout in that stinking pub you're working in. Now, who am I going to give these invitations to? Gran has got to come this year, she didn't come to either of the others. Do you think your Mum will mind meeting her?'

Ioan slips his bare muscular arm around her. 'Now she's got this new man, why should she care? That stuff with your Mum was all years ago.'

'Anyone you want to ask? Pity we can't get your mate Terry. I'd love to meet him.'

'Doubt you would, he's pretty way out. When we're in London I should try to see him. I'll call up Wandsworth nick.'

'What about that boyfriend of yours?'

A wry look crosses Ioan's face. 'Which one?'

'The one that put you away. The kid, what was his name? How old will he be now?'

'Jonathan Court Smyth.' The name had not passed Ioan's lips for over two years, though its owner had appeared in his dreams. After a moment he pulls her towards him. 'Not a good idea.'

'Why not? Would you be embarrassed?' she asks, nibbling his shoulder.

'Babe! I'm beyond that.'

'Aren't you curious about him? You might still fancy him.'

'What are you like?' He looks deeply into her eyes. 'That's over. You've turned me straight. Can't you tell? I love you, you daft bint. Give us a shnog.'

She does and there the conversation ends... but the idea lingers in Red's mind. She has unexpected feelings lurking, like needing a little emotional security.

Two days later, while Ioan is having his interview with Daniel Schlesinger, she visits the Reader's Room in the local library. Finding the phone book for the Canterbury area, she searches for the name Court Smyth. She finds it and copies down the address. Posting one of her Private View invitations, she writes on top of the envelope, *"If away, please forward"*. On the invitation itself she writes: *"Jonathan. Please come. Ioan will be there"*.

Chapter Thirty-One

A Private View

Jonathan is still a good looking boy, or adolescent rather. As he strides up Cork Street in the sunshine he wears orange sneakers, purple trousers, and a black "Lord of the Rings" T-shirt under his pale fawn jacket. His honey-coloured hair is no longer cut in a neat public school way, it is a wiry halo of curls in rebellious teenager mode. At eighteen, he is lanky and prone to spots, his early precociousness become gauche sophistication. At heart though, he is still a dreamcatcher and idealist, which is why, at this very moment, he is overcome with feelings of apprehension and excitement, causing his tummy to turn over.

Church bells sound. Sunday morning in Mayfair is usually deserted, not so this morning. There are a mass of polished parked cars, Rolls, Mercedes, Daimlers, and Volvos gleam in the sunlight, no doubt belonging to the high-roller visitors at the fashionable Private View taking place. In the vast glass frontage of the Art Galleries, Waterhouse and Dodd, Stoppenbach and Delestre, The Mayor Gallery, Jonathan is reflected looking up at the street numbers, in his hand, the invitation. On it, a purple reproduction of one of Red's moor paintings, printed underneath is " 'Heather' by Red Williams. 2005, oil on canvas, 88 × 100 cc." On the reverse side:

RED WILLIAMS
Stanhope Gallery
Summer Show

> You and your friends are invited to the opening party
> of our new exhibition.
> 11am to 1pm Sunday 6 June 2003
>
> rsvp 02078964453
> please bring this invitation with you

In blue felt tip above the address is: *"Jonathan. Please come. Ioan will be there"*.

Jonathan is totally mystified as to how he came by such an intriguing invitation. When he telephoned his acceptance last week, the girl who took his call had been unable to enlighten him. The address of his Camden Town flat share on the envelope was in his mother's handwriting. Since receiving it, eager, delirious with excitement, he'd been imagining meeting Ioan again, wondering how prison had changed him. His dread was that Ioan had become a bitter ex-con, who would deny what they had once been and reject him. The more hoped-for, indeed, longed-for reaction, was that Ioan's arms would open wide, he would run into them, and they would be together for evermore. For since his last sight of Ioan, waving from the back of a police van in the precincts of Canterbury Cathedral, Jonathan has come to realise that, no matter who comes in between, first love never dies.

Arriving underneath window boxes filled with red geraniums, glechome, callistephus and blue felicia plants, Jonathan identifies "The Stanhope". Looking through the window it appears the party is in full swing. He runs his hand through his hair, and heart fluttering, he pushes open the glossy black front door.

Inside, the noisy room is packed. There is an electric thrill, a buzz of excitement, TV camera men with lights are interviewing celebrities. A throng of well-dressed guests stand in groups, even on the staircase down to the basement area, chattering, drinking, and seemingly ignoring the paintings. A waiter, about Jonathan's age, wearing a white monkey jacket and a very tight pair of black pants, offers him drinks on a tray.

'What is it?' Jonathan asks.

'Bucks Fizz,' says the waiter.

Jonathan takes a glass and drinks, searching the faces. No sign of Ioan. He dismisses the crowd as art snobs.

His assumption is quite wrong, for Michael and Joyce have taken great care with the guest list. The 'arrangement' they had made so casually in Palm Springs, was proving emotionally satisfying and mutually beneficial. So much so, they had amended their policy of 'business only' at Private Views, to include their extended families. Both Michael's daughters are present, the eldest, Susan with her new husband, and to confirm their new friendship, Nichola has been invited with her partner. Joyce's son is over from America, and Red has brought along her Gran.

'Red's Gran', as she is introduced to everyone, turns out to be a tough, stout north country woman with tea-cosy white hair. Though out of her milieu, she is quite unfazed by the curious ritual she finds herself part of. At the moment she stands full square by the front desk, firmly holding onto a large gin and orange. She is with Michael and Joyce, and a rich but stingy baroness, politely listening to Liz, who is enjoying herself hugely, holding forth on the art of 'making Art', in this particular instance, on her exciting world of monoprints.

'The fact that they have to be printed before drying dictates all the good things about them. You're on your mettle. There's no time to get fussy'.

'Darling,' whispers Joyce in Michael's ear. 'Is that young man over there anything to do with you?'

'Where?' says Michael, spotting Jonathan. 'Oh, sweet! Unfortunately no. Probably one of Red's lot,' and he resumes his courteous interest in Liz.

'If you'll excuse me,' says Joyce, extracting herself, 'I'd better go and see.' She edges her way elegantly through the mass of guests towards Jonathan. 'Hallo there. You're looking a bit lost. Can I help? I'm Joyce Howard, your hostess.'

'Hi! Jon Court. Actually I'm looking for a friend of mine, Ioan Williams. I was sent this.' He shows her his invitation. 'No idea who sent it. I'm not into all of this stuff, I'm afraid. Feel a bit of a fraud actually. Art's not quite my thing.'

'Oh dear! And what is your thing, Mr Court?' asks Joyce, glancing at her carefully designed publicity.

'Well, history, I suppose. I'm at Goldsmith's.'

'Are you indeed. Congratulations. This is Red's handwriting. You'll find her downstairs, she's being interviewed by some television people. Ioan will probably be with her. By the way,' she gently taps his arm, 'during your studies, you'll soon discover Art becomes history.'

'Yes, I suppose it does,' says Jonathan, not sure whether he's being sent up or not.

'Nice meeting you, Jon. Enjoy.'

'Thanks,' Jonathan buffets his way through more people. 'Excuse me,' he says to a group standing at the top of the stairs. They part.

'Good Heavens! Is that Jonathan?'

He turns. A merry looking woman is smiling at him. It's Ioan's mother. Reddening up, he splutters, 'Oh. Hi! Mrs Williams.'

'Goodness, so it is,' says Rosie, her smile fading. 'What a surprise!'

'Gosh! Yes. Hallo. How are you?'

'I'm well. What brings you here? Are you a painter, an artist now or something?'

Jonathan senses disapproval. 'No, I'm er...'

'Sorry,' says Rosie, turning to an open-faced, sandy-haired fellow standing by her side. 'This is my husband, Joe Fudge. Darling, this is a friend of Ioan's, Jonathan Court Smyth.'

Jonathan shakes his hand. 'How do you do, sir?' Then grinning broadly, 'So, you're Mrs Fudge? Great! When did you get married?'

Rosie and Joe smile at each other. 'Nearly two years ago,' says Rosie.

'I used to deliver groceries to her Tea Shop. One mornin' she made me a Cornish pastie. Well, after that I was a gonna!' says Joe, giving Jonathan a wink.

'I've changed my name too. I'm Jon Court. I dropped the Smyth part.'

'That couldn't have pleased your Dad much,' says Rosie.

'No.' With a lovely shy smile, he adds, 'Had to do something. Assert my independence. Could hardly drop the Court part, I'd sound far too plebeian. I would have been just plain John Smith.'

'Give us a pint of your best bitter, eh!' laughs Joe.

'Right,' says Jonathan, as if hearing the joke for the first time. 'I wrote to you, actually,' he says to Rosie. 'I sent it to "The Olive Branch". I wanted to know how to get in touch with Ioan. The letter came back, "Return to sender."'

'Oh Jonathan! I'm so sorry. I mean, Jon. With all that happened you were rather, well, forgotten, I'm afraid. It was a difficult time for all of us.'

'All that business. You know, it wasn't me. It was my father's doing.'

'I know, I know,' says Rosie, measured. Then smiling brightly, 'But it's all over now.'

'I was never able to thank Ioan for keeping me out of it. For taking the blame.'

'Yes. Well. I daresay you'll be wanting to do that now.'

She looks into the open area below, 'He's down there. But I warn you, he's changed. He went through a dreadful ordeal.'

'Where? I don't see him.'

'Just there.' She nods, indicating the basement.

Jonathan scrutinises the faces. TV lights are shining on a boyish-looking girl standing in front of a painting. She has short carrot-coloured hair, a mass of gold ear piercings round her ears, and wears a red top over black leather pants and boots, but he doesn't see Ioan. 'Who's the redhead?'

'Oh, there's no show without Punch!' says Rosie.

'How do you mean?'

'She's the star of this little shindig.'

Finding his eyes she watches his reaction. 'She's Ioan's new girlfriend, Red.'

Jonathan is grown-up enough not to give her what she wants. Avoiding her gaze, he searches the scene below again. He thinks he recognises someone... but can't be sure. It could be, but the guy has a bald patch and is thick-set. 'Excuse me,' he says moving off.

'Nice to see you,' Rosie calls.

He tries to smile, but is concentrating hard on the figure downstairs. The face is turned away watching the redhead. The man's physique is totally unlike the slim dark prince he remembers, and yet, there is something. 'See you,' he says casually to Rosie, making his way downstairs. With each step, the beating of his heart tells him the balding man must be Ioan.

Rosie gasps for air and looks up to the ceiling. 'Let's get the hell out of here, I can't take much more of this.'

'Thought you were enjoying yourself, Pet,' says Joe.

'Are you mad? Being this nice is killing me! It's so pretentious. These pictures are giving me the willies, a splitting headache too.'

'They're very jolly though,' says Joe, attempting a connoisseur's gaze. But the only paintings on the walls of his farmhouse are a Christmas card snow scene on the pinboard, and his nephew's portrait of "Cows with Uncle Joe and Auntie Rose."

'I told you,' continues Rosie, 'I only came here to see Ioan.' Then remembering her obligation, 'And to be civil to Mickey. It's the least I can do. I owe him that much.'

'And to check up on his new woman.'

'I couldn't care less about his new woman. Not with you beside me, anyhow.'

'If you'd not come, just think how your big sister would have carried on.' He imitates Liz's Welsh accent, 'You lost all sense of reason with that man.'

Rosie smiles and covers Joe's mouth affectionately with the tips of her fingers. 'Ssh!'

'Out of the corner of her hostess eye, Joyce had noticed Jonathan stop to chat with Rosie and Joe at the top of the stairs. Being somewhat of an expert on human nature, she is aware that, considering their new relationship, she should make an extra effort with them. Excusing herself from the stingy baroness, who is talking to Michael about Red's confrontational and impassioned style of painting, she joins them. 'I'm so glad you were able to come. I was beginning to despair of ever having a moment's get-together. Joe, you must be a very brave man, being thrown in among this incestuous lot.'

'She's told me all the family history,' says Joe. 'It's nothing to a Cornish man, like me. My Father married his Auntie!'

Joyce looks a little askance, but laughs, as obviously that is what's required.

Rosie leans forward. 'How's Mickey? Truly?'

'Wonderfully well. He complains he has to put his feet up in the afternoon like most of us, but apart from that, it doesn't seem to have made much of a difference. It's extraordinary.'

'That was such a magnificent thing he did for Ioan.'

'I suspect,' says Joyce, 'that apart from his natural feelings for you and Ioan, it was a much-needed cathartic action.'

Rosie and Joyce share a moment of mutual womanly understanding.

'You know,' says Rosie, 'I was quite in awe of you when we first met.' Behind Joyce, she notices a couple nudge and glance at her. The knowledge that her private life is public knowledge to most of the people in the room would once have horrified her, now she doesn't care. Joe's love, she feels has transformed her, she feels more confident and content than at any time in her life.

'I confess,' says Joyce, 'that I was a teeny bit jealous of you too. But tell me, you must be so pleased with Ioan. Our young Romeo down there. Isn't it the very best thing that could have happened? For both of them?'

'The best.' Rosie tries not to sound possessive. 'This is the first I've seen him for months.'

'That, my dear,' says Joyce, 'is parenthood. My son is around here too somewhere and I haven't seen him in two years! We should get them together.'

As they talk, they step aside to make room for the elderly baroness, whom Michael is ushering downstairs. 'That's the one,' says the baroness, pointing. 'Over there. That large orange one. It's alright, I can manage.' Cautiously, but grandly she proceeds down the staircase.

Michael's departure from the group by the front desk has left Liz alone with Red's Gran. Liz's has been trying to think of a way of asking about Red's mother. The old lady nudges her. 'Your sister over there looks very thin.'

'She's lucky. She's always been slim,' says Liz.

'You should try "Weight Watchers". I lost three pounds my first week.'

'Good heavens!' says a confused, but sociable Liz.

Gran leans in towards her. 'Would you like to see a picture of my daughter?'

Liz is riveted. It's as if the woman had read her thoughts. 'Red's mother, you mean? Yes. Very much indeed.'

The old lady opens up a brown holdall. From a wallet she extracts a small monochrome snapshot. 'There,' she says, handing it over. 'That was Phyllis.'

Liz looks. Stares. Is it someone she knows? No. But she recognises the brassy type.

'Do you recognise her?'

Liz peers again. 'Should I?'

Gran nods towards Rosie. 'She would. Phyllis was her barmaid, when Dave ran that pub in Croydon.'

Liz looks at Gran astonished, then across at Rosie. Liz's relationship with her sister has splintered in recent years. The underlying tension between them had flared again over Rosie's marriage to Joe, whom Liz had known locally as a worthless lady's man. Rosie had ignored all her warnings. Liz was furious with her for sacrificing her independence for the first man that came sniffing around. After all the support she'd given her getting that damn cafe up and running, now "Rosie's Tea Shop" was finished, done, dusted and sold, and all for the sake of Joe Fudge, the travelling grocer. So Liz doesn't go over and show Rosie the snapshot of "Phyllis", to share with her the humiliation she feels, that David betrayed both of them with a cheap trashy tart. She looks at the photo again. I suppose it had to be with someone like this.

'Did you ever meet her?' asks Gran.

'No. I lived in Cornwall in those days.' Liz feels she should say something pleasant. 'She's pretty.'

Gran holds out her hand for the picture. 'Worry, she was. Proper do all that was. Still, he did well by Red, I'll give Dave that. He'd never have handled Phyllis. Nobody could. Loose cannon, she was, even though she was me own.'

'What happened to her?'

'Died. Drugs. Anyways, I had the compensation of bringing up Red, didn't I? She's lovely. Good girl. Temperamental mind, but a good lass, good lass. You a mother?'

'No. I never married.'

Liz feels obliged to add, 'But I was very fond of my brother-in-law. David, I take it you knew him?'

'Oh yes. A grand lad. Chewed the fat over many a jar, we did.'

Liz wonders how much this woman really knows. 'Yes, he was a good man.'

'Who's a good man?' beams Simon Barclay, arriving with two glasses of red wine. 'Me? This one's for you.'

Liz, underneath her optimistic and hearty exterior, doesn't like to admit it, but Simon has metamorphosed into a lame duck. Since giving up the curatorship of the Nylwen Art gallery, he's become a tiny bit of a bore, but having an admirer, or 'Your beard', as the youngsters at the Vicarage call him, is comforting and preferable to going to functions alone. She introduces him to Gran, as she frequently does, as 'My partner, Simon Barclay'.

Simon beams and shakes Gran's hand.

Michael stands at the top of the staircase, a beautifully crisp blue shirt and luxurious tie glow beneath his pale grey suit, he looks every inch the polished entrepreneur. He watches the baroness descend, then surveys the proceedings. Spotting Nichola, his wife of twenty-three years, chatting to Ioan and Red, a wry smile creeps over his face. Amazing how, given time, life's strongest emotions evaporate, just disappear, or in this case, dwindle to a wary conviviality. Which is what he now feels towards her – she who had once been the centre of his world. The physical and emotional turmoil Ioan had once inspired has cooled too. Now a relaxed fondness has replaced his former obsession. Could it be, he asks himself, that at last I'm becoming mature? Or is it merely finding Joyce? He feels her arm slip through his.

'A success, do we think?' she says.

'If we only knew in the beginning,' he answers softly, 'that it would all turn out alright in the end.'

'Ah but that's what makes the effort worthwhile,' says Joyce. Then suddenly looking up into his face, 'You are talking about the party?'

'What else?'

She grins. 'What time did you book the table for?'

'One thirty. So,' he says, looking at his watch, 'time this little lot were leaving.'

'We should be getting on our way,' says Joe, after a gentle prod from Rosie.

'That does not include you, Joe Fudge,' says Michael. 'If my ex-wife is invited to lunch, then so is my ex-girlfriend with her second husband, step-dad to my long lost son. Did I get all that right?'

They all laugh. Simultaneously there is a whoop of laughter from downstairs. Hoots and shrieks! They all turn to look over the banister rail.

Lit by television lights and standing in front of one of Red's giant Technicolor canvases, Ioan is boisterously greeting Jonathan.

Joyce, who is standing next to Rosie, says, 'That's the young man I saw you talking to just now. Who is he?'

'His name is Jon Court,' says Rosie. 'He's the boy Ioan went to prison for.'

Joyce and Michael, Rosie and Joe are suddenly spellbound. Joyce sneaks a look at Michael. He is transfixed. So that was the boy. After a moment he becomes aware of her watching him and turns. He relaxes and shrugs, 'It's just, Ioan's a part of me. Now he always will be.'

She takes his hand. 'Darling. You don't have to explain.'

'And all the time you were sitting at the front desk.' He kisses her fingertips. They both turn to Rosie, but she too is hypnotised by the performance going on below.

Joyce says to no one in particular, 'I wonder what they're saying?'

Ioan is thumping Jonathan on the back. 'You bastard! How fantastic!' He punches him rapidly in the solar plexus. Jonathan is simultaneously laughing and shouting at him to stop. They're like Labradors playfully greeting one another in the park, unselfconscious and apparently unconcerned by their audience. 'Shit!' says Ioan. 'What the fuck are you doing here? Wait a bit, wait a bit,' he looks at Red. 'Did you...?'

'Hi!' says Red, combining sass and cool. 'You're Jonathan I take it? I'm Red.'

'Hi,' says Jonathan. 'How do you do? Congratulations on all of this. It's fab!'

'Thanks. Like your T-shirt."

'You did!' says Ioan. 'You invited this bugger here, didn't you? This is the little fucker I went down for.'

'Where, I have to tell you, Jonathan,' says Red, 'he was at it daily with a brute of a murderer in his cell! He never stops talking about it.'

'You weren't?' says an incredulous Jonathan.

'Tell 'im,' eggs on Red. 'Go on, tell 'im.'

'Piss off. Why d'you have to invite this little sod?'

'Just testing. Thought you'd like to see the love of your life again.'

'You're the fucking love of my life, you crazed groovy chick!' Ioan grabs her, bends her over backwards and gives her a smacking kiss. A press bulb flashes. Together they turn, almost losing their balance. Both laughing, Ioan holds her horizontal, posing for the camera. The photographer obliges with another flash, "Macho cave man with redhead".

Ex-con with meal ticket, thinks Jonathan, unconvinced by the show of slop for the cameras. Superficial show-offs! He sees right through them. They're acting. Pretending to be hip young lovers for the benefit of this piss elegant audience. Nevertheless, his eyes never leave Ioan's face. He's watching his every move, hoping for some secret sign that will show that they're still special. Craving for some clue that this is just some hetero performance he is giving, that now it's possible, the two of them can live together happily ever after.

'Excuse me,' says the rich but stingy baroness, tapping Red on the shoulder. 'Can I have a word with you?'

'Hallo baroness. How are you?' says Red.

Ioan turns to the hovering waiter and helps himself to a glass of Bucks Fizz.

'That orange painting there,' says the baroness. 'That's the very one I wanted, and it's been sold. How much was it?'

'Eighteen thousand,' says Red.

'Well, I would have paid you that,' says the baroness.

'Tell you what,' says Red, 'I'll do another one for you. Identical. What do you say?'

The baroness's face freezes. Unable to speak, she totters away, her lips compressed.

Ioan is still standing by the waiter. Jonathan, with a sickening stomach, has witnessed him drink, wink, slip a piece of paper intimately into the young man's trouser pocket, and simultaneously mouth something into his ear, almost kissing him in the process.

'I saw that!' cries Jonathan.

Ioan makes a shush sign. The waiter walks away.

'What did you say to him? Did you give him your mobile number?'

'What's it to you, Spotty?'

'You faithless slut! Red! Did you see that?'

'What?' says Red.

Jonathan's face is crumpled, he turns to Ioan. 'You've become a frightful yob.'

Ioan punches him hard in the belly. 'You always were a prissy little madam.'

Upstairs, behind the banister rail, Ioan's mother and father, Joyce and Joe have open mouths. They have seen everything. Michael's face particularly is a study in disappointment and ironic amusement. Joyce shakes her head sadly. 'Oh, why do that?'

Michael catches Rosie's eye and raises his eyebrow. 'Something in his kidney?'

'Or something in the blood,' says Rosie, straight-faced.

'Do you think Red noticed?' asks Joyce.

'Come,' says Michael, 'let's all go and have lunch.' And with careless joie de vivre turns away singing the last line of Alan J. Lerner's song from "Gigi".

'*Oh I'm so glad... That I'm... not young... any... more.*'

THE END

Acknowledgements

I'd like to thank Michael Truscott and the John Miller estate for kindly allowing me to use John's beautiful gouache on the front cover. My grateful thanks also to Max Bygraves and Lantern Music Publishers for their permission to quote his lyric to "I'm a Pink Toothbrush".

The lyrics to "I Wanna be Around", words and music by Sadie Vimmerstedt and Johnny Mercer, © 1963 Commander Publications, U.S.A. Warner/Chappell North America Ltd. London WQ6 8BS, are reproduced by permission of IMP Ltd, All Rights Reserved.

Thanks also are due to James and Carmelita Nicholls of "Nicholls and Co, Solicitors" for their invaluable legal expertise surrounding Ioan's story. I also gleaned information about prison life from two moving and painful autobiographies "Marking Time" by Michael Betisworth, published by Macmillan, and "Inside" by John Hoskison, published by John Murray. Among the people who have helped me in various ways are Martyn Goff, Val Ashton in Wales, Max Cooper in Bournemouth, Stewart Mclean in Glasgow. Lou and Nick, Sally Mates, Josie Kidd and Norma Flint for their advice and encouragement, and Richard Wakeley who filled me in on hospital procedure. To "Chips and Bits" in Leyton, my special thanks for rescuing Chapter 16 from my collapsed floppy disc.

I'm especially grateful to everyone at Troubador Publishing for their help, and to the inestimable Jeremy Thompson.

RC
June 2004